get
o... ... time
with his head. I don't care what happens to the rest
of his body.

The rest of my top staff participated, though some
of them wore masks. Masks could not hide their
visages from my awful wrath. I know the name of
everyone who conspired to humiliate me. At night,
when I am strapped to the bed, I use the point of a
loose screw to inscribe their names, one by one, into
the patina. My bed stinks of fresh paint because the
minions here are efficient and desire that everything
remain pristine, so they paint over my list every day.
I don't care that my list disappears. I am really scribing the names in my memory while I try to erase
the things my inferiors said to me.

The things they said to me!

"We caught you being nice to a random dog."

"Your personal assistant used sarcasm on you,
and you didn't have him flogged."

"You smiled in public, and it wasn't the smile
that sends small children screaming into the night."

"You're letting the intervention proceed without
ordering us all killed immediately," said Rusty.
"Boss, you're losing your edge. Trust me. You need
help. You're not our ruthless Master anymore."

—from "Art Therapy" by Nina Kiriki Hoffman

Also Available from DAW Books:

Hags, Harpies, and Other Bad Girls of Fantasy,
edited by Denise Little
From hags and harpies to sorceresses and sirens, this
volume features twenty all-new tales that prove
women are far from the weaker sex—in all their allur-
ing, magical, and monstrous roles. With stories by C.S
Friedman, Rosemary Edghill, Lisa Silverthorne, Jean
Rabe, and Laura Resnick.

Under Cover of Darkness, **edited by Julie E. Czerneda**
and Jana Paniccia
In our modern-day world, where rumors of conspiracies
and covert organizations can spread with the speed of
the Internet, it's often hard to separate truth from fiction. Down through the centuries there have been
groups sworn to protect important artifacts and secrets,
perhaps even exercising their power, both wordly and
mystical, to guide the world's future. In this daring volume, authors such as Larry Niven, Janny Wurtz, Esther
Friesner, Tanya Huff, and Russell Davis offer up fourteen stories of those unseen powers operating for their
own purposes. From an unexpected ally who aids Law-
rence in Arabia, to an assassin hired to target the one
person he'd never want to kill, to a young woman who
stumbles into an elfin war in the heart of London, to a
man who steals time itself . . .

Army of the Fantastic, **edited by John Marco and**
John Helfers
How might the course of WWII have changed if sentient
dragons ran bombing missions for the Gemans? This is
just one of the stories gathered in this all-original volume
that will take you to magical place in our own world
and to fantasy realms where the armies of the fantasic
are on the march, waging wars both vast and personal.
With stories by Rick Hautala, Alan Dean Foster, Tanya
Huff, Tim Waggoner, Bill Fawcett, and Fiona Patton.

IF I WERE AN EVIL OVERLORD

EDITED BY
Martin H. Greenberg
and Russell Davis

DAW BOOKS, INC.

DONALD A. WOLLHEIM, FOUNDER
375 Hudson Street, New York, NY 10014

ELIZABETH R. WOLLHEIM
SHEILA E. GILBERT
PUBLISHERS
http://www.dawbooks.com

First Printing, March 2007
1 2 3 4 5 6 7 8 9

DAW TRADEMARK REGISTERED
U.S. PAT. OFF. AND FOREIGN COUNTRIES
—MARCA REGISTRADA
HECHO EN U.S.A.

PRINTED IN THE U.S.A.

ACKNOWLEDGMENTS

Introduction copyright © 2007 by Russell Davis

"If Looks Could Kill," copyright © 2007 by Esther M. Friesner

"The Man Who Would Be Overlord," copyright © 2007 by David Bischoff

"Ensuring the Succession," copyright © 2007 by Jody Lynn Nye

"The Life & Death of Fortune Cookie Tyrant," copyright © 2007 by Dean Wesley Smith

"Daddy's Little Girl," copyright © 2007 by Jim C. Hines

"Gordie Culligan—vs.—Dr. Longbeach & The HVAC of Doom," copyright © 2007 by J. Steven York

"The Sins of the Sons," copyright © 2007 by Fiona Patton

"Loser Takes All," copyright © 2007 by Donald J. Bingle

"The Next Level," copyright © 2007 by David Niall Wilson

"Advisors at Naptime," copyright © 2007 by Kristine Kathryn Rusch

"A Woman's Work . . . ," copyright © 2007 by Tanya Huff

"To Sit In Darkness Here, Hatching Vain Empires," copyright © 2007 by Steven A. Roman

"Stronger Than Fate," copyright © 2007 by John Helfers

"Art Therapy," copyright © 2007 by Nina Kiriki Hoffman

CONTENTS

THE SINS OF THE SONS
Fiona Patton   140

LOSER TAKES ALL
Donald J. Bingle   165

THE NEXT LEVEL
David Niall Wilson   186

ADVISORS AT NAPTIME
Kristine Kathryn Rusch   205

A WOMAN'S WORK . . .
Tanya Huff   222

TO SIT IN DARKNESS HERE,
HATCHING VAIN EMPIRES
Steven A. Roman   245

STRONGER THAN FATE
John Helfers   269

ART THERAPY
Nina Kiriki Hoffman   285

INTRODUCTION

Russell Davis

In the movie *The Return of the Jedi*, at the climax of the film (WARNING: SPOILER ALERT—IF YOU ARE ONE OF THE TWELVE PEOPLE ON EARTH WHO HASN'T SEEN THIS MOVIE, THE FOLLOWING MAY WRECK IT FOR YOU), with Luke Skywalker is on his back, the Emperor standing over him and shooting cool bolts of Force lightning into his body. Darth Vader stands nearby watching his son die. It's over for the Jedi and the Rebel Alliance. Evil has won. Then Vader allows sentimentality to get the better of him and he picks up the Emperor and throws him down a bottomless pit to his death.

I have to admit that when Vader grabbed the Emperor, one of the first thoughts that ran through my mind was, *Don't do it, you fool!* You see, the sad truth is that I kind of like rooting for the bad guy.

I have a strong background in role-playing games, particularly fantasy role-playing games, and as a player character, I've crossed paths with innumerable bad guys, often in the guise of an Evil Overlord. They're always doing the same kinds of things: crushing the peasant population; ravaging a beautiful, young princess; stealing and taxing and in general making life as miserable as possible. It's hard not to enjoy their antics. (Fortunately, I've also *played* Evil Overlords, so I have some sense of how to face them. And have yet to have been bested by one, though I suspect that they didn't have the advantage of reading this anthology.)

The concept of a list of things one might consider doing should one, in fact, become an Evil Overlord has been around a long time. It's been one of the longest running jokes on the Internet, forwarded via e-mail and found on numerous Web sites. Many of these lists touch on fantasy, science fiction, even mystery and thriller tropes and clichés that speak directly and humorously to those who enjoy role-playing games and novels in these genres.

It's worth noting that the "Evil Overlord List" by Peter Anspach is certainly the most popular and widely known of these lists, though by no means the only one, nor even the first one. In the dim, dark year of 1984, a group of friends and I developed a very similar list called "The Rules of Oblivion," which took to heart such statements as, "Take nothing for granted. That rabbit may be armed."

For this anthology, we challenged fourteen of today's best authors to come up with a story about an Evil Overlord and what he or she (not all Evil Overlords are men) should consider doing to protect themselves and their dark realms. Many writers, such as Esther Friesner and David Bischoff, came through with enjoyable tales featuring familiar characters and offering plenty of laughs. Others, like David Niall Wilson and Steve Roman, took a more serious approach—which has, I admit, left me wondering what they might be plotting next.

But no matter how a writer approached the subject, as the editor (the ultimate Evil Overlord in this anthology, one might say), I got the pleasure of reading and reviewing them all . . . and now I get the added pleasure of sharing them with you. In short, the pleasure is all mine, but I hope it will be yours, too.

Funny how being an Evil Overlord in the publishing field has these little perks, isn't it?

Enjoy!

—Russell Davis
Sierra Vista, Arizona

IF LOOKS COULD KILL

Esther Friesner

"Oh, shut up," said Prince Lorimel, tossing his long, golden hair in a peevish manner. It was a bad idea, under the circumstances. The manacles holding his slender-yet-powerful arms were ancient oxidized relics of the previous owner of Castle Bonecrack. (In fact, up until the moment of Prince Lorimel's incarceration, they had held the last few skeletal remnants of the previous owner of Castle Bonecrack, per orders of the current management of said premises.) They did their job well enough, but the wear and tear of centuries—to say nothing of the corrosive teardrops of a succession of luckless prisoners—had roughened the iron with colonies of thorny rust that snared any soft and silky thing unfortunate enough to brush against them.

Case in soft-and-silky point: A handsome elf prince's glorious, gossamer hair.

Result: "OW! This is all your fault, Gudge."

"Aw, now, Master m'lud Lorimel, don't 'ee be takin' on so, naow." The coarse yet good-natured voice of Prince Lorimel's companion-in-shackles (though not comrade-in-arms) echoed through the foul dungeon. It was this same voice, nattering about how stone walls did not a prison make, that had provoked the prince's outburst, with concomitant hair-tossing, in the first place. "I di'n't do nowt t' yer Worship's purty hair, nay. See, 'tis as I told yer Reverence's noble pa, lo these many turns agone, 'The best thing a wise elf prince can do fer hisself when it so happens as he's misstepped matters and ended up in some evil overlord's dungeon is bide his time all still an' quiet-like, waiting fer what must come.' Yer Eminence'll notice that *still* part, as means yer not to move more'n needful, 'cos squirmin' about'll only—Well, I expect yer Highness has found that out fer yerself already, what with yer purty goldy hair all of a tangle and—"

"Gudge?" Prince Lorimel interrupted.

"Aye, m'lud?"

"Shut *up*."

Sweet silence descended upon the drear and dreadful dungeon once more.

It was not to last, of course. Prince Lorimel was an elf, right enough, and as such, immortal. The long lines of the years spilling into centuries and even eons gave the elves the rare ability to wrap the glowing silence of their own deep thoughts around them like the comforting warmth of a well-loved blanket. Also, most elves ran out of really interesting conversation before they hit their three hundredth birthday.

But the prince's retainer and fellow captive, the being known as Gudge of Willowstone-Thickly, was not an elf at all. What he *was,* was open to some debate among those wizards who found fascination in such blood-and-breeding puzzles. Evidence pointed to the short, fubsy, somewhat swarthy fellow having a mix of troll and brownie ancestry, seasoned lightly with a bit of pixie (on account of his ill-governed tongue), and perhaps a soupçon of goblin. All of this, however, was strictly on his unknown father's side. His mother was a full-blooded human girl who really should have been a *bit* more circumspect in her choice of Midsummer's Eve companions. From a midnight frolic between the rows of barley, Gudge of Willowstone-Thickly took his life's beginning, and from a subsequent amorous alliance of his mother's with a slumming elf lord came his introduction into the court of the Lofty Elves.

The Lofty Elves were, of all the elf tribes ever to skim the surface of Intermediate Earth, the fairest, the oldest, the wisest, and the most jaded. They had seen it all and been it all and after they were through, they complained about it all at some length, in verse, accompanied by the *tinkle-ploing-dingle* that passed for elfin music. (That effete *doodle-oodle-hey-lally-lally-moo* was what came from an orchestrative tradition relying on altogether too many harps and not enough bagpipes.)

And so, when His Awesome and Devastating Unspeakableness, Lord Belg of Castle Bonecrack, decided to stop torturing puppies and start conquering as much of Intermediate Earth's prime real estate as he could get his scaly paws on, it was an occurrence greeted with a loud shout of outrage but also with covert mutterings of delighted anticipation by the bored-out-of-their-pretty-skulls-till-now Lofty Elves.

Prince Lorimel had one such pretty skull, but at the moment the odds did not favor his continued ownership thereof. No sooner had word of Lord Belg's evil schemes reached him in his father's forest palace, than he had sworn a mighty oath to sally forth and defeat the Evil One single-handed. He then promptly conscripted Gudge to accompany him as his squire, valet, dogsbody, and drudge-of-all-work, because *single-handed* was a romantic concept in theory, but in practice it meant *wash your own socks*.

There was a delectable irony behind the fact that Prince Lorimel and Gudge had been captured by one of Lord Belg's troll patrols while the prince was excoriating his servant for doing such a piss-poor job of washing said socks.

Now, socks were the fourth furthest thing from the elf prince's mind. His thoughts had turned to matters of far graver import, matters that well might determine the fate of worlds!

"My hair," he whined. "My beautiful, beautiful hair!"

The dungeon door screeched and groaned on its

hinges as the troll who served as Lord Belg's chief turnkey entered. He chuckled with foul glee when he saw the mare's nest that Prince Lorimel's struggles had made of his gorgeous tresses.

"Awwww, diddums elfy-welfy gettums purty hair all snarly-warlied?" he asked in a voice like treacle and carpet tacks. (His penchant for taunting Lord Belg's prisoners with baby talk was why the Evil One had not needed to employ a full-time torture-master nor, in some cases, an executioner.) "Izzums elfy-poo gonna cwy now his hair's gotta go all snippy-snip bye-bye?"

"Here, now!" Shackled as he was, Gudge lunged at the troll. "Doan' 'ee be sayin' such vicious cruel things t' me Master, nay! We been through worse'n this, him 'n' me, an' let me tell 'ee, just gimme a bucket o' water, a fistful o' soapwort, an' a light cream-rinse afore ye goes talkin' 'bout cuttin' off his Worship's hair, aye!"

The troll guard blinked, taken aback by his first confrontation with someone who had a more annoying speech pattern than himself.

"Hunh!" he snorted. "Save yer breath; 'tain't up t' me if yer precious master gets shorn or not. Lord Belg's daughter's heard tell that there's a pointy-eared princeling locked up in Daddy's dungeon and now 'tis but a matter o' time before she comes down here to . . . *take care* of him. Heh, heh, heh."

Up until this point, Prince Lorimel had been doing his best to ignore the cumbersomely pictur-esque conversation between Gudge and the guard. Now, however, he perked up the aforementioned pointy ears and took a keen and sudden interest it what had just been said.

"A daughter?" He tensed like a well-bred bird dog in an aviary. "Did I hear you say that Lord Belg has a daughter?"

The troll turnkey smirked and gave the elf prince the once-over before replying, "An' what's it to ye if'n he do, Snoogums? Or do the very thought o' His Aweseome an' Appalling Vileness doin' the Goblin Twist-an'-Tickle put ye off yer feed?"

"Doin' the what?" Gudge wanted to know.

Prince Lorimel made an impatient sound. "The carnal act of which yon odious troll speaks is that which we Lofty Elves more delicately refer to as 'making the bogle with two backs.' "

"Nah, thass not what I mean." The troll shook his head. " 'Cos Lord Belg *did* make a bogle wi' two backs once, only the poor thing di'n't know was he comin' or goin' an' so we had to—"

"Ohhhh!" Light dawned on Gudge of Willowstone-Thickly, albeit a foggy, heavily overcast light. "*I* gets it now. You mean Lord Belg was doin' the Haystack Ramble; the Weasel Bounce; the Three Apples in a Gunnysack Shimmy; the Naked Morris Dancers—"

"Gudge, shut *up*!" Prince Lorimel shouted so loudly that pale green veins stood out in high relief from his alabaster skin. "Or do we have to have *another* little talk about oversharing?"

"Scoop me hollow fer a pun'kin pie, *nay*," Gudge replied in haste. "I ain't got th' bruises healed up from th' last 'little talk' we had, bless yer gracious Grace's strong right arm."

"Y'know, if ye two blatherboxes don't care no more 'bout Lord Belg's daughter, why don' I just be on me way?" The troll guard was miffed at being ignored by his prisoners.

"Nay, good lump of loathsomeness, stay!" Prince Lorimel exclaimed. "Speak more to me of Lord Belg's daughter. We of the Lofty Elves had no idea that the Evil One was a father as well as the slaughterer of untold thousands of our kin. It gives him an unexpected air of domesticity."

"Oh, he's a father, right enough," the troll replied, licking his lips in a lascivious manner. "An' no wonder, as many times as he's taken purty young wenches as captives t' slake his unnatural appetites. I'm only s'prised as His Direness don't have more kids'n what he's got."

"I ain't," Gudge piped up. "A feller spends as much time as that'n does in th' saddle, ridin' all over th' land on evil conquest bent, that'll be causin' a certain amount o' damage to his—"

"*Gudge!*" This time the elf lord yelled at his attendant so loudly that the sound waves rived the rust from the manacles securing them both. Prince Lorimel's entangled hair was freed and immediately fell back into place in a gleaming flaxen flood.

Gudge gave his master a sidelong, sulky look. "I'm only sayin' what yer thinkin';" he grumped.

"Trust me, Gudge, the day I spend one wink of time thinking about Lord Belg's, er, connubial apparatus will be the day I eat a badger sandwich. A *live* badger sandwich," Prince Lorimel clarified.

"Ahuh," said the guard. He took a grimy pad of paper and a pencil stub out of his belt pouch and made a note. "So I takes it ye'll be wantin' the vegetarian option fer yer dinner t'night instead?"

The elf prince rolled his eyes expressively. "Are you sure you two aren't related?" he asked Gudge.

Gudge declined to comment.

"Listen, my good troll," Prince Lorimel said to the turnkey. "Forget about my dinner—"

"Oh, I intend to." The troll grinned affably.

"—and tell me more about Lord Belg's daughter. You said that she knows I'm here and wishes to, as you put it, *take care* of me herself, is that right?"

The troll's ugly head bobbed like a cabbage in a boiling stewpot. "Aye, that's true. She's allus the one as *takes care* o' our prisoners. She'd've been here sooner, 'cept she just heard 'bout you bein' here over breakfas'. That'd be 'cos Himself's a selfish ol' bastard as likes t' keep his playthings fer his own use, exclusive. But now that the lass knows . . ." The troll's voice trailed off suggestively.

"Oh, me poor master!" Gudge wailed. "An' him so young! A mere slip o' a lad what ain't seen more'n two thousand eight hunnert an' fifteen summers, aye. An' what's t' become o' poor loyal ol' Gudge after that evil hussy's gone an' killed 'im deader'n dog droppin's? Oh, woe's me an' alack the day, wurra-wurra, lawks an'—"

"Shut up, Gudge!" This time the troll joined sentiment with the elf prince. It was a pretty impressive display of interspecies cooperation. Clearly Gudge had missed his calling in the Diplomatic Corps.

"Aye, shut yer toad-pie-hole, ye big baby," the troll continued. "Izzums scared t' be left all alone after Lord Belg's daughter sees t' yer fluffy-haired elfikin master? No worries: She'll be sure t' *take care* o' ye, too!"

Somewhere in Castle Bonecrack, a great iron-tongued bell cleaved the air with a doleful knell. The troll snapped his pad shut and stuffed it back into his pouch. "Noseweed break time! See you folks later, an' by 'later' I mean 'dead.' Mwahaha!" With that, he swaggered off up the dungeon stairs and slammed the heavy door behind him. His exit was immediately followed by a litany of locks, bolts, and chains securing said portal, then by the sound of his flabby feet retreating in the distance, and last of all a deep and funereal silence.

It did not last. In less time than it would take a man to draw two breaths, the tomb-worthy stillness was shattered by the sound of loud, exultant laughter.

"M'lud?" Gudge cocked his shaggy head in Prince Lorimel's direction. The maniacal hilarity was tumbling from the elf prince's rosy lips. "M'lud, are ye feelin' quite, y'know, that thing what's th' opposite o' slap-assed crazy?"

Prince Lorimel shook his head and regained his self-control, gasping for air between slowly abating gusts of chortles. "I am *not* insane, Gudge. I am merely mad with joy. Did you not hear what that troll said? A daughter! Lord Belg of Castle Bonecrack, scourge of a thousand kingdoms, menace of a thousand more, and evil overlord for all seasons, *has got a daughter*. And she is coming here, to this very dungeon, to *take care* of me. Do you realize what that means?"

Gudge thought about this long and hard. At last his brows unknit and he replied, "No."

The elf prince uttered a heartfelt cry of utter exasperation, then drew himself up to as full a height as his manacles permitted and looked down his nose at his companion with supreme scorn.

The tales men tell by firelight of the elves recount how some tribes possess certain powers that mortals cannot hope to master. Some cause plants to thrive and fruits to mature out of season. Some can make such lovely music that fish of the sea and birds of the air are ensorcelled by the sound and whole deer leap into the waiting frying pan if the song so bids them. Still others have the gift of healing wounds at a touch, which is a talent frequently called for after one of those ill-thought-out whole-deer-in-the-frying-pan incidents.

As for the Lofty Elves, their talent was neither song nor growth nor healing. Their talent was contempt. Indeed, in all the realms that might claim elf infestation, the Lofty Elves' powers of condescension were famed in song and story. They could break treaties between nations with a simple lift of the lip. A raised eyebrow had toppled empires. It was even claimed that once upon a time, one of their kings rode forth alone to face an army, gave it a cool glance, clicked his tongue in derision and remarked, "Bitch, *please*." And while his faithful hunting bitch, Lady Liza, looked on, the entire army went into spasms and died of mortification.

This was all very well and good, but either the talent had grown wobbly with the ages, or else Prince Lorimel's condescending gaze didn't have quite enough oomph, or—most likely—it just didn't work on Gudge.

"Beggin' yer Gracious Glory's pardon, but why 'ee be starin' at me like a cat what's got bowel troubles?" he asked.

Prince Lorimel sighed and sagged in his chains. "Gudge, if we can ever find a wizard capable of analyzing and reproducing the stuff your skullbone's made of, we'll be able to create armor that *nothing* can pierce; not even common sense. Listen to me: Even the densest dunce knows that there are certain rules that govern the lives and behavior of all evil overlords ever spawned. You may have the same faith in these rules as you might put into universal truths such as *Elves are always beautiful, The sun always rises in the east, Elves are always graceful beyond the power of speech to convey, Water always flows downhill, Elves are always sexually irresistible to young women who are still living with their parents, The South always votes for—*"

"Aye, m'lud, aye, 'tis just as 'ee says, elves allus flows downhill, right enough," Gudge interrupted. "But what's that got t' do wi' our predictament?"

"Merely this, my fine bean-brain: An evil overlord's daughter will always be as wicked as she is beautiful, but she will also invariably fall passionately in love with her father's handsome, heroic captive. The girl can't help it. In fact, given how handsome I am, I'm rather surprised that she hasn't fallen in love with me already."

"She ain't even seen 'ee yet, m'lud," Gudge pointed out.

Prince Lorimel dismissed this quibble with a wave of his dainty fingertips. "Bah. You know nothing about these matters. It is now only a matter of time before the foredoomed damsel comes into this dungeon, sees me, and betrays her own father before you can say *snap*. She'll free me from my shackles, fetch me a sword, lead me straight to Lord Belg's chambers via a secret passageway known only to herself, stand by cheering my name while I skewer her father like a bunny on a roasting spit, and provide me with a high-spirited steed, a casket filled with priceless jewels, and a picnic lunch before I go galloping back to the lands of the Lofty Elves, mission accomplished."

Prince Lorimel smiled blissfully over his own words. Gudge, however, drew his bushy brows together and chewed over his master's lesson like a dog with a mouthful of nougat.

" 'Tain't me place t' be pointin' out things 'ee says as are misspoke, m'lud, nay, but hasn't 'ee made a boner er two wi' yer Exaltation's pronouns?"

"My *pronouns*?" Up until now, Prince Lorimel hadn't suspected that Gudge would know a pronoun if it bit him on the dangling participle.

Gudge nodded. "Aye: *I*. Instead o' *we*, y'know? Now th' way 'ee tells things, 'tis only yer Altitude

as'll be gallopin' away from Castle Bonecrack, back
t' th' fair elfin kingdom what yer pa rules. 'Struth,
'tis only yer Superiorness as'll be freed from these
here chains, leavin' me behind t' rot in durance
vile. I don't so much mind that, seein' as it come
wi' th' job description, but after all that the evil
overlord's beauteous daughter's gonna do for 'ee,
like 'ee says, shouldn't 'ee at least be ridin' back t'
yer pa's kingdom wi' *her* along fer th' ride?"

The elf prince chuckled and shook his head
slowly. "Oh, Gudge," he said. "Gudge, Gudge,
Gudge, will your gentle and good-hearted stupidity
never cease to astonish me? Me, run off with the
evil overlord's beautiful daughter? Me, bring her
home to meet my parents, just as if she were worthy of that inexpressibly high honor? As if she were
worthy of *me*? *Please.*"

"Then what's t' be th' poor lass's fate after 'ee've
gone off an' left her wi' nowt but her pa's body t'
bury an' a dirty great castle t' run all by her
lonesome?"

"As for the castle, she'll have no worries: As
soon the Lofty Elves hear that Lord Belg is dead,
we'll overrun his realm, take back what is rightfully
ours, and occupy those other lands which might not
be rightfully ours but which will surely welcome
our presence until such time as we decide they are
ready to govern themselves democratically. We'll
evict Lord Belg's daughter from Castle Bonecrack
in the process, of course. She'll be entirely free of
her nasty past, and won't that be a blessing? And
wherever her vagabond's life may take her after

that, she'll have the priceless memory of *me* to
keep her warm. I might even kiss her, as a more
than generous reward for her services." He smiled
complacently over his own boundless goodness.

Before Gudge could summon up the proper way
to frame his reply, a loud rattle of chains came
from the dungeon door, followed by the sound of
at least three heavy wooden bars being slid aside
and a good half a dozen locks clicking open.

"Ah, right on time," Prince Lorimel said with a
smug smile. He tossed his head ever so slightly,
sending his lovely tresses into modest disarray.
"How do I look? It's very important to present
the properly rumpled aspect, you know. For some
reason, it drives the ladies wild. Of course for the
full effect, it would be nice if I had a small bruise
on my cheek, just beside my left eye—left's my
good side. Gudge, I don't suppose you could reach
over and give me one?"

To his credit, Gudge lunged forward in his chains
most eagerly, but came up short as to fist-swinging
range. "Sorry, m'lud," he said, subsiding. "I can't
be reachin' 'ee 'thout strainin' me arm summat
fierce, nay. It'd have t' be comin' outa th' socket
fer me t' do yer biddin'."

Prince Lorimel snorted. "Isn't that just like you,
Gudge: Self, self, self. I ask you to do one teensy
favor for me and—"

"Oh, b'lieve me, m'lud, if'n I could get loose o'
these here chains, I'd be givin' yer fine face a brui-
sin' that'd be th' talk o' Intermeejit Earth, aye."

The elf prince's aspect softened. "Why, Gudge,

you *do* give a rat's ass. How sweet. Consider yourself forgiven."

"Oh, good," said Gudge.

He dropped his head onto his chest and muttered
something further which the elf prince did not quite
catch but which he presumed must be a sequence of
well-deserved thanks and praise from his devoted
lackey. Prince Lorimel might have asked Gudge to
repeat some of the better compliments had the last
lock upon the dungeon door not opened precisely
then and the door itself swung wide.

"By the four hundred and twenty-eight rings of
ultimate power!" Prince Lorimel gasped. "What vision of loveliness is this?"

Gudge cast a dour eye at the doorway where
stood a tall, svelte figure draped in a bloodred spill
of silk from shoulders to ankles, the skirt thereof
slit all the way up to both hips. This sensual confec-
tion was tightly cinched at the waist with a gold
belt studded with rubies the size of rat skulls as
well as a few actual rat skulls for luck. Glossy raven
hair artfully obscured half of a piquantly shaped,
violet-eyed face before pouring down over creamy
white arms, nor did it cease to pour until it reached
a rump of such enticing curves and proportions as
to make strong men weep.

" 'Ee k'n stop weepin' naow, m'lud," Gudge said
gruffly. " 'Tis nowt but Lord Belg's daughter,
what's as wicked as she's beautiful, aye."

The glorious apparition in the doorway turned
back and spoke to someone as yet hidden from
sight. "Are you sure this is the right dungeon,

Turnkey? There's no one in here but a man and his really ugly dog."

The troll's gravelly voice was loud enough for Prince Lorimel and Gudge to hear his reply: "Nah, that's the elf prince, right enough. He'll look better if ye take 'im out in daylight." Here he laughed.

"Did I give you permission to laugh?" Something just outside the door went *FOOM*! Acrid smoke drifted into the dungeon, smoke that reeked of incinerated troll.

"So you're the elf prince." A dainty, sandaled foot crossed the dungeon threshold. "I'm Beverel. *So* pleased to make your soon-to-be-brief acquaintance." A laugh dripping with malice and unplumbed depths of cruelty bubbled from those full, red, delectable lips as the evil overlord's offspring closed in on the helpless captives.

"Ah, sweet Beverel, if I must die, so be it." Prince Lorimel lifted his head at an angle contrived to drop a come-hither veil of golden hair across one eye. "Only swear that it will be your fair hand that rips the breath from my body, for it has already taken my heart."

"Oh, *gyarkh*!" said Gudge, who had a low tolerance for artificial sweets.

"I think your dog's sick," Beverel observed.

"That is not my dog," Prince Lorimel replied, glaring icy daggers at his companion. "If he were, he would be better bred and more useful. That is my servant, Gudge of Willowstone-Thickly. You can slit his throat if he bothers you. I won't mind."

"I'm not touching that thing." Beveral drew back

in distaste. "Still, I can't say as I care to have . . . *that* staring at me so intently while I parley with you. It's one thing to tell my victims exactly what sort of gruesome torments I'm going to put them through before death's sweet release, but I've never done it in front of an audience before, and I can't say I like it." A faint blush tinged those alabaster cheeks. "I'm just the eensy-beensy-teensiest bit scared of public speaking."

"Lovely idol of my soul, the only gruesome torment that I fear is losing sight of you." Prince Lorimel opened his luminous blue eyes as wide as they would go, which had the incongruous effect of making him look dead sexy and very much like a lemur at the same time. "Can't you get one of the servants to kill him for you?"

Beverel's succulent lips pooched out in an adorable pout. "If Daddy finds out I got one of the servants to lend a paw, he'll never let me hear the end of it. He thinks I'm soft."

"And so you are, in all the most scrumptious places," Prince Lorimel drawled. "But you know, you could always kill the servant, afterward."

"Oooh, aren't you the sweetie to think of that. But no, no, Daddy would figure it out. He keeps *very* detailed household accounts." Abruptly, Beverel's face brightened. "I know! I'll get Vug."

"Vug?" Gudge echoed. "Wossat, some manner o' foul an' lethal venom as yer Evility'll try'n make me drink, aye?"

"Well, you got the *foul* part right. Vug's my sister." Beverel raised one elegant hand for amplification's sake and shouted, "Hey, Vug! Get your fat butt down to Dungeon Seventeen *now*!"

A fresh magical *FOOM*! sounded from the corridor, followed almost immediately by the entrance of a short, plump young woman whose mousy hair was confined to a pair of untidy braids. Her round, plain face was distorted with distress and revulsion as she picked her way down the dungeon steps. "Beverel, what did you do to poor old Thungil? He's nothing but a puddle of troll fat, and him with just one more day to go before retirement, too!"

Beverel shrugged. "It saves Daddy money on pensions."

"Yes, but you even liquefied his keys! Daddy's *not* going to be happy if we can't lock and unlock the dungeon doors."

"Shut up, Vug," Beverel said casually. "It's not as if we're going to need to lock or unlock anything once I see to it that our prisoners are . . . *taken care* of. Mwahaha!"

"*Taken care* of? But Daddy said—"

"What Daddy doesn't know won't hurt him," Beverel replied suavely. "And what Daddy doesn't find out from a certain tattletale little sister I could mention, won't hurt *you*."

Vug's eyes brimmed with tears. "You always ruin *everything*."

"Stop your namby-pamby whining, you puny excuse for an evil overlord's daughter!" Beverel snapped, slapping Vug smartly across the face for emphasis. "I'm your elder *and* your better; you'll do as I command you. Now take this wretched object—"

"That'd be me," Gudge said stolidly.

"Shut up, Gudge," Prince Lorimel put in for no better reason than to keep in practice.

"—put an iron collar and a pair of cuffs on him, take him out of here, and get rid of him," Beverel went on. "I don't much care how you do it as long as you have the castle limner make detailed sketches of the really *juicy* bits, afterward."

Vug's shoulders slumped. "Yes, Beverel," she said. "As you command." She went about freeing Gudge from his fetters and saddling him with the prescribed iron collar, leading chain, and traveling manacles, according to her received orders, then gave him a shy look. "Er, shall we go?" she asked timidly.

Beverel uttered a loud growl of impatience and demanded of Prince Lorimel, "Do you see what I have to put up with?"

"My poor, suffering darling," the elf prince replied, batting his eyelashes madly. "Tell me all your troubles. Let me share your pain." He turned a glowering visage to Gudge and in a voice of fiery wrath bellowed, "Don't just stand there, you moron! Help that stupid girl get you out of our sight before she upsets my beautiful Beverel any further. Go!"

Gudge eyed his master with a look of cool disdain worthy of a Lofty Elf. So perfectly belittling was that glance that it gave Prince Lorimel the optic equivalent of being smacked right in the chops with a sizeable halibut. Even the lovely-but-cruel Beverel was shocked to see an expression of so much authority upon the countenance of such a previously underestimated supporting character.

But all Gudge said was, "Well, we'll just be off then, m'lud," and he headed up the dungeon steps with a bemused and doubtful Vug in tow.

Once they were beyond the dungeon door and had stepped gingerly over the puddled troll in the corridor, Gudge turned to Vug and said, "Beggin' yer Depravity's pardon, but this be as far as I can go 'thout 'ee gives me some d'rections, seein' as how I be a stranger to Castle Bonecrack."

Vug blushed a becoming shade of rosy pink. "Of course; how silly of me. This way, if you please." She gave Gudge's leash a tug, but it was really more of a gentle waggle that didn't even make the links clank together.

By way of fetid passageways, dimly lit and vermin-haunted stairwells, musty rooms rank with the stench of ageless evil, and the back door to the kitchen, Vug at last brought Gudge out into the light of day. The elf prince's castoff servant blinked to accustom his eyes to the long-missed brightness and filled his lungs with the sweet air of the little herb garden whither Vug had conducted him.

"Ah, 'tis true as they say," Gudge opined, a look of beatific calm and resignation on his face. "A garden's a lovesome thing, th' gods wot, where t' be cruelly done t' death by an evil overlord's daughter what's as wicked as she's beautiful. All right then, young lady: I be as ready naow as ever t' perish, aye. Just say t' word as to where 'ee'd find it most

cornveenent fer me t' stand whilst 'ee rends me
limb from limb, if that's yer pleasure."

"Rend you limb from—? Oh my, no!" Vug
dropped Gudge's lead chain and clapped both
hands to her face in an access of dismay.

"Nay?" Gudge gave her a speculative look.
"Then I'm t' die by murd'rous sorcery, aye?"

Vug shook her head in the negative so hard that
she whapped herself across the mouth several times
with both braids. "Not that. I couldn't stand doing
that to anyone."

By now Gudge was truly flummoxed. "Not death
by steel nor death by sorcery? What's left, then?
Ah, wait, I knows th' answer! 'Tis poison as must
send me into th' shadows." He slapped his forehead as best he could without breaking his own
nose with the manacles binding his wrists. "How
could I've forgot summat that simple? An' this here
garden where 'ee've brang me, m'lady, no doubt's
the source fer the venom as'll be my doom, aye?"
He bent over and plucked a large tuft of leaves
from the nearest plant. "Well, as me old slut of a
Mum used t' say, don't be shy, no one's gettin' any
younger, no time like the present, and bottoms
up!"

He stuffed the leaves into his mouth, chewed
lustily, and swallowed, then stood by with a look
of uncomplaining anticipation.

"Er, sir?" Vug tapped her captive lightly on the
shoulder. "That was basil."

"Oh, aye?" Gudge ran his tongue over his teeth,
dislodging a few clingy green shreds. "An' what'd

poor ol' Basil do wrong fer 'ee t' be turnin' 'im inter a poisonous shrub?"

Vug patiently corrected Gudge's misapprehension. He listened attentively, then said, "I see. Well now, in that case, I'd be obleeged if 'ee'd point me at th' nearest properly lethal veggie. Meanin' no offense t' yer Dread Badness, fer 'tis not yer comp'ny as I'm findin' teedjus, but on th' other hand, there's no sense puttin' off th' inevitable, nay. Th' sooner I'm dead an' gone, th' sooner I can stop bein' scairt a mere halfway t' death o' dyin', as is me present state o' mind. So . . . got any henbane?"

Vug began to weep. "Oh, please stop being so nice about this!" she wailed. "It's bad enough my having to kill you without your being helpful about it. Really, it's too cruel!"

At this point, Gudge's bewilderment had reached that level where the bewilderee begins to question his own sanity. In such cases, matters have come to such a cognitively dissonant head that the only two possible explanations are:

1. That the whole world has gone mad or:
2. That the witness to such alleged madness is himself irredeemably 'round the twist.

Most people placed in such a lose-lose situation tend to get rather testy about it. Gudge was no exception.

"Naow look'ee here, Missy!" he exclaimed, rattling his manacles in a monitory manner. "What's all this blubberin' about? Ain't 'ee heerd th' rules

what governs dark an' evil overlords an' th' fruit
o' their dark an' evil loins? Yer th' daughter o'
Lord Belg, aye?"

"Aye. I mean, yes," Vug said in a miserable
voice not much above a whisper.

"An' 'ee knows yon rules of which I speak?"

This time Vug merely nodded.

"Then what's holdin' 'ee back from slaughterin'
me, seein' as how th' rules says 'ee've *got* t' be as
wicked as yer beautiful? Fer if that's so, 'ee must
needs be th' wickedest creetur as ever breathed."

It was now Vug's turn to put sanity on the witness stand to determine when it had left the
premises.

"You . . . you think I'm that evil—I mean, that
beautiful?" she asked Gudge.

"Aye, m'lady." Gudge's face broke into a raptur-
ous smile. " 'Ee be th' fairest thing as I've ever
seen, an' 'tis me one consolement, here on th' brink
o' death hisself, t' have been able t' get me an
eyeful o' such pulchritude as yer own. Now let me
die, fer 'tis me sad and sorrowful fate that—"

"Shut up, Gudge," said Vug, and she threw him
down and had him in the basil.

Some time later, Gudge sat up and scraped im-
promptu pesto out of his hair. "You know, if this
is the way you're going to kill me, my lady, I feel
honor bound to tell you that it's not working," he
said. "Not that I'm complaining, you understand."

Vug sat bolt upright and stared at him as though
he'd sprouted radishes. "You can talk?" she exclaimed. "I mean, you can talk like *that*? Did I

just break some kind of evil enchantment on you?
Usually it only takes a kiss. Daddy always did say
I was an overachiever."

Gudge shrugged. "This is the way I speak. It's
not much help in the job market, though. Outside
of their house-and-palace domestics, the Lofty
Elves only hire servants who speak fluent Bump-
kinshire, for some reason. Ooo, arrh, aye," he
added for effect, and tugged his forelock is the approved Rustic Underling manner.

"Then the Lofty Elves are all a bunch of smug,
affected, bullying twits," Vug said grimly. "Just like
Beverel. That mean, greedy thing knows that *I'm*
the one who's supposed to take care of all our prisoners, but did that stop h—"

Gudge stemmed the flow of her complaints
against Beverel with a kiss. "My sweet Vug, I'm
beginning to realize that your definition of *taking
care* of prisoners is not one to be followed by
'Mwahaha,' true?"

Vug smiled and kissed him back. "I should hope
not! The only proper way to take care of prisoners
is seeing that they've got enough to eat and drink,
that their cells aren't too dank or too warm, that
all the dungeon rats have had their rabies shots,
that their manacles aren't too tight or too—Wait,
let me get that for you."

She spoke a word of power and Gudge's irons
dropped away from neck and wrists. "That's better." She favored him with a smile. "Anyway, that's
how *I* take care of prisoners. Beverel makes fun of
me, but it can't be helped. There's no getting

around the rules: the evil overlord's daughter must always be as wicked as she is beautiful, and just *look* at me! Once I put on a little bit of lipstick and kicked Daddy's favorite hellhound, but I felt terrible about it afterward."

Gudge took her in his newly freed arms. "Bother the rules," he said. "I say you *are* beautiful, even if you're nowhere near wicked. Your father's minions can recapture me, drag me back down into that dungeon, torture me, and I'll still say so."

"Oh, you're not going back to any nasty old dungeon, dearest Gudge," Vug said, kissing the tip of his nose. "I'm not finished taking care of you yet, and the best way to do that is to make sure that you escape from Castle Bonecrack safely. We don't want Daddy getting his paws on you. He's a lamb, once you get to know him, but he's just not a people person. Or an elf person. Or a troll person. Or a whatever-the-blazes-you-are person. Now just say the word and I'll fix you up with a spirited horse swifter than the wind, a casket of jewels beyond price, a nice picnic lunch with extra pickles, and a map showing the fastest way out of Daddy's realm."

Gudge kissed her again. It was getting to be a very pleasant habit. "Can I make a request about the lunch?" he asked.

"You don't want pickles?"

"Pack enough for two."

"You . . . you want me to come with you?" Vug couldn't believe her ears. "None of the other prisoners I've freed ever—" She blinked away tears.

"Beverel always said that was because I was far too ugly for any of them to—"

"Darling Vug, do you think I give a fig for what your spiteful sister says?" Gudge demanded. "My fool of an ex-master's in the middle of seducing that vile wench as we speak, and I hope he succeeds because those two deserve each other."

"Sister?" Vug's brows rose in perplexity. "I don't have any sisters. Beverel's my bro—"

The shriek that blasted from the dungeon depths to the topmost pinnacle of Castle Bonecrack interrupted Vug's revelation. It embodied equal degrees of discovery, shock, incredulity, and despair, together with a string of impressive curses in the tongue of the Lofty Elves. (These were rather specific curses, usually reserved for merchants who sold gilt for gold, nutmegs carved from wood, or beef potpies that had once answered to the name Fido.)

It ended with a different voice cackling "Mwahaha!" just before the final *FOOM!*

Gudge turned to his beloved. "So . . . about that horse?"

THE MAN WHO WOULD BE OVERLORD

David Bischoff

The time has come in these memoirs to discuss the nadir of my career. I, Vincemole Whiteviper, have had my ups and downs, my ins and outs, my evenings before and my mornings after. However, say what you will of me, I am intelligent enough still to appreciate the bitter wormwood-flavored irony of the fact that I fell to my deepest under from my biggest over.

Pah! To think! I stood then on a vasty plateau of grandeur, master of men, elf, fairie, and other ilk, up to my earlobes in delightful atrocities and fiendish plots, in my physical prime and indulgent in decadence and debauchery beyond mere pleasure. To think that at such a zenith of my star's rise I should suffer the lowest blow of a life battered and torn by fate.

Need I tell you, Rotvole, that there was a woman involved in this indignity?

I'm drunk as a vat-worm, so the transcription will be difficult. Why do I hold this different sword from my collection? Why do I swing it around so? This was the weapon with which I have judged in the past. This was the weapon that lopped off the head of a god. I clutch it, and the memories gush forth.

Bring that dictation-gem closer, for my mournful words will sometimes be low and mumbled. Please, and pour yourself a brandy, and avail yourself of these fresh handkerchiefs for weeping. It is time to tell sad stories of the death of . . . things.

I wish I could say I achieved my high position, my power over so many lands, so many lives, and so many riches through cunning, intelligence, machinations, or even a backstab or three.

Alas I came by my good fortune in the same manner I came into so much in my picaresque career—I blundered into it.

Readers of these memoirs will remember that for the portion of my life that I was not apprentice to a master hooligan or lying low in some godforsaken inn somewhere, drunk, I was a soldier. Call me a mercenary if you like, call me a multiple patriot, but there being many kingdoms in this vast world, I have served many kings—and served them well, I might add.

However, after an unfortunate incident involving a princess, a chastity belt, a file, and the vengeful fury of one of these selfsame kings, I thought it best to retreat to the nether regions of this world, the far, undisciplined reaches to seek something that military service had not yet given me: a vast amount of loot. Yes, I became a soldier of fortune, and it was in the weird and mysterious land of Worpesh that I found myself as far from that afore-mentioned king's wrath as geography would allow.

Now as my speedy flight had prevented me from taking much in the way of revenue, I had to pick up what I could along the way, through odd jobs and dark alleys. Not a glorious life, but there's no place like the streets to pick up skills and sharpen one's survival mechanisms. Once I'd made it to Worpesh, though, on ship and camel, on coach and steed, I was disappointed to discover that while the pickings were actually less (dark alleys were inhab-ited by nothing but the poor and other cutpurses) the dangers were more. Oh, it was a dreadful place!

Yes, supposedly there were lost cities piled with treasure—plenty of farthing maps to them for sure. But you had to traipse through steaming jungles full of quicksand, giant prickle-snakes, and saber-toothed werecats to achieve them. I fully suspected that perhaps it was the snakes and cats who made the maps to lure supper into their jaws, so I was not terribly tempted. Moreover in the humid and foul land, half the populace was leprous or diseased in some fashion, and in truth where it did not stink to high heaven it stank to low hell.

One night, I took my disappointment and depres-sion to a bar, and there drank the sole alcoholic offering: some kind of fermented milk. Nasty, but with enough nutrition that some of the natives lived on it, I think. I was half in my cups, plotting some method of returning to lands of proper dank shivers and warm soothing beers, when a voice called out to me from the depths of a large booth.

"Ahoy there, matey. Be you from more northern climes?"

"Aye," I said.

"From the cut of your jib, I'd take you to be a soldier. And a strong, fine one at that."

"That I am," I said. "Fought in many a battle, skirmish, and war, with scars enough I suppose."

"And you're here in Worpesh to seek a better life."

I hiccuped and laughed. "Is that written on my forehead?"

A rueful chuckle. "No, I see myself hunkered at that bar. Come and join me, and drink something a bit better than that swill in front of you."

Well, I had a dagger in my belt and a knife in my boot, so even though that booth was dim, I had protection. And as I felt that I was growing cheese in my gut now, I longed for anything better than what I was drinking. So I abandoned my swill and approached, albeit warily.

"Come, come, my friend, I won't bite!" called a hearty voice. A candle flickered within and by its light I saw a man in a hood sitting back nonchalantly. One of his hands was on a lifted knee and one was around a bottle. "Come and have a drink with one of your countrymen from the land of swords and honor."

He lifted the bottle and poured out an amber liquid.

"Whiskey?" I said, astonished.

"Aye, sir. And good whiskey at that. Won't you have a glass?"

He threw back his hood, and I saw blue eyes, pearly teeth, dimples, and a jolly smile. He pushed the glass over to the other side of the bench.

I sat down, lifted the glass, sipped it. I tasted poison. However, a fine and beautiful poison.

I drank it down in a gulp, and was rewarded with feeling good for the first time in months.

"Thank you stranger. The name's Whiteviper."

"And mine is Divort. Dinny Divort. Would you care for a cigarillo?" This selfsame Dinny Divort produced a humidor from the darkness. The aroma drifted over, a gentle and perfect complement to the whiskey. I availed myself. Ah, the rasp of crinkling leaves between thumb and forefinger. "Thank 'ee."

He selected one for himself, stuck it in his mouth. He snapped his fingers, and his thumb came alight. I jumped back a bit, then grinned. "Again, thank 'ee," I said, leaning into the flame. The plumes of smoke that arose twirled with subtle shades of alabaster, cerulean, and cinnabar. The taste of the smoke was wonderfully superb.

"A magician, then," I said.

"A know a few things about the arcane arts, yes." And when he brought the flame up to light his cigarillo, I saw that he had a star tatooed upon one pale cheek. "But I too am a soldier."

"Of fortune?"

"Of fate. Of destiny." He blew out a flume: it

twirled into shapes of spangly coins, glittery gems. "Rich fate, rich destiny. This is why I have called upon you, Sir Whiteviper. I sense we are two of a kind. You have need of me and, without a doubt, I have need of you."

I raised an eyebrow. "I may look naïve, sirrah, but I may tell you, I have not had good luck in my dealing with beings who know magic."

He shrugged. "I know not magic. I am no true magician. I served, Whiteviper, as a carny in a traveling bazaar. Aye, I know a little bit of the true arts, but in truth most of what I do are show tricks." He blew out his thumb. "I keep myself well away from the deeper magic that would steal men's souls."

"Sorcerors are often liars."

Again a shrug. "Why don't we talk a bit, drink some drink, smoke some smoke. I would like to work with you, sir. But don't you think if I were a true sorceror, dark or white, I would seek to enchant you rather than persuade you?"

"You flatter my intelligence, Dinny Divort."

"There is much to flatter, Whiteviper."

I allowed that I would stay and listen for a couple more drinks, knowing full well that I was captured by the mere promise of the jingle of coins in my pocket. Clearly this fellow could avail me that much. If I chose not to go along with his plan, I could just follow him to a back alley and take his money in return for a lump on his noggin.

If he knew of my plans, he made no sign of it.

I listened.

Three or four drinks later, I agreed to his plan.

The next day, we were on our way to the outmost of the Outer Territories, in the tippy-toppy reaches of Just Beyond Beyond, to take our destined positions of High and Rightful Overlords.

"You see, Sir Whiteviper," Dinny Divort had said, leaning forward into the miasma of smoke back at that tavern of our meeting. "All my life I have sought money. I inherited the want from my carny background. But in fact, during my days slogging and grogging about on the borders of things, it started to occur to me that what I really was in want of was power, for power can create riches and more. And in my heart of hearts, I realized that since I am no ordinary man—no, nor are you, Sir Whiteviper—I need no ordinary power."

Divort diddled his fingers. A rainbow extended from hand to hand, imbued with tinkling musics. Insense seemed to writhe from the emerald, perfume from the crimson. Herein was an intimation of the Fantastic, the Wholly Marvelous that I had witnessed before in my checkered career, and in truth yearned for above all else.

In a breath, it was gone.

I felt a grave sadness, for these glimpses of something Wonderful Beyond always seemed to thus disappear. I felt empty, and was made aware of my abject poverty.

Again, as though reading my mind, Divort reached up into the dimness above his head. He seemed to pluck something from thin air. Drawing it down, he displayed his catch: a pouch. It banged and jingled metallically upon the wooden table between us.

"Half of all the money I have, Whiteviper. We share and we share alike in this venture, sir. Take your half and join me."

I raised an eyebrow. "Naturally I wonder if I can trust your purposes here. Why me?"

"Take the money, Whiteviper. Easier than stealing it, don't you think? Don't you truly wonder, why does this fool think he can trust me?"

By turning the tables he caught me by surprise. I laughed heartily. "You're calling me a rogue, sir. Aye, that will cost you!"

I snatched the pouch before he could take it away. Inside were nine gold pieces, just enough to make my way back to healthier climes.

"Ah, but the rogue I see has dreams. I see myself in you, Whiteviper. Come and find your heart's desire. Come and find the power you crave. Power and glory shall be ours. You see, where I take us, there is a prophecy of brother gods—a duo—that will come and inherit a vast prize. I have magic, but I cannot create a brother, Whiteviper."

Another drink of whiskey was enough to convince me and we drank the bottle down. The exact details of our talk escape me from that point onward, and I must have passed out, for I found myself in a delirium later, lying in a pool of my own sick, daylight creeping through the cracks in the window. I gasped and reached to make sure there was no knife in my back. I was alive, and still in possession of all nine pieces of gold. Above me, eating breakfast and drinking a steaming cup of the local tea, was Divort.

"Oh, two more details, Whiteviper. For the magic to work, sir, for the duration of our power and glory, you must swear off alcohol and women."

The very notion of either made me retch. My only comfort were those pieces of gold my new friend had bestowed upon me.

My first decree, to my own self, was that during the rule of Vincemore Whiteviper, there were to be no hangovers!

And in truth, a few days into our journey up toward Beyondastan, I woke up with the taste of fresh mountain air in my lungs and nary a pain between my temples. Dinny Divort had proven to be a fine partner, full of jolly stories and good cheer. Away from the damp and warm and stink below, I felt my own self once more.

In fact, I felt very well indeed!

"You look good, Whiteviper. Your foreswearance of strong drink does your constitution well, I think."

"Perhaps, " I said, stretching. "But even now I'm thinking of the pleasures of lying in furs with a naked and nubile female."

"Ah, nothing wrong with desire for either drink or women in our promise. Just in the taking. Besides, consider: perhaps a time without women will make you feel even better than a time without strong drink. Indeed, there are philosophies that state that when a man evacuates his seed into a woman, he loses his power. Properly controlled, that power, still inside the man, builds up keen perception, control—power. It is a gnosis—an inner light that burns from the essense of his being!"

After some nice tea and bacon and hardbread, I forgot about women, lost in the scenery. For glorious indeed were the mountains upon which we were stumpy, snowy legs of gods lifting up to majestic peaks, or sometimes, just peaks.

Divort had an old map he said was drawn up upon human skin. And a good thing too, for there were many forks and intersections of paths in this mountains.

We had a couple of pack mules to carry supplies, fortunately—and me as well at times, for in truth I was never a traveler with much stamina, usually traveling only from one tavern to another while between soldiering bouts. However, by the third day in the mountains, when I was accustomed to the rarefied air, without the drink, I found I had more strength and preferred to walk instead of suffer donkey stench.

It did not take long to see why no one made this trip often. In the nooks and crannies of this trail lived not just brigands and thieves, but creatures of marvelous horror. Furry snakes slithered and abominable stick folk hobbled, fully half their bodies claws and fangs, the rest hunger. However, here too Divort's bag of tricks broke the way for us: He flashed fires of intense strength at them, burning some to piles of ash, singeing others. By night the most awful sounds gurgled and spat around our campfire—but nothing seemed to dare venture beyond the sparkle of the protective spell that surrounded us.

"You well may wonder from which power is drawn this source of this magic—and I tell you," said Divort one morning, after smoting a weregoat with lightning blast. "It is you."

"Me?" I said, looking down with distaste at the scorpion tail that writhed poisonously from the beast.

"Aye! Your puissance grows! Unmanacled from the drink that sapped you, and with your chi stoppered up and not serving women, you are a factory of power. I salute you, sir."

In truth, for all of that, I still felt a want, and wondered aloud if I might try drinking women and rogering ale. Divort's laugh was so hearty, and he slapped my back in comradeship, I hadn't the heart to tell him I was not jesting.

Oh, I could bog down this tale for a space with tales of the cat-dragons, the gnarl-critters, the brouga-brougas we fought. Alas, our donkeys were caputured and eaten alive by a cyclops, whom we managed to prevent from eating us by dint of a vast expenditure of Divort's magic fire.

Two weeks of travel! Two whole weeks, and our supplies were gone, so we lived on any creatures Divort could cook and on melted snow.

And when I saw that we had to scale a snowy mount for the last leg, I nearly lost faith. But it was Divort's jokes and good cheer that goaded me onward despite myself. That, and my own dreams and fantasies, considering what I would do with this vast power that awaited me. To think, no longer to take orders, but to give them! To think, no longer to be forced to work for my keep, but to rest if I liked, wander if I liked—to kick the behinds of vassals, if I liked.

At the crest of the hill, there in afternoon glow, at an elevation higher above sea level than I had ever yet attained, I saw the turrets and towers of a diamond city, awash in gold and sapphire.

Divort grinned and chuckled.

"Aye, Whiteviper. Our goal is near. There, my new brother, is our goal, finally—The OverEye."

Ah, yes, and a beauteous city it was too, Over-Eye.

A dazzling sheen arose from its stone walls to its lofty spires, coruscating with glinting color. Prisms echoed spectra of ocher, brilliantine, and topaz in a most aesthetic manner. All in all, it seemed indeed a city of glass. And yet, with the feeling of both magnification and dimunition in this city, the impression that most swept over me as we gazed upon this wondrous places was that it was a collection of lenses.

I said as much to Divort.

"Aye, that is the reputation of OverEye," he said beneath his breath, also caught up in the majesty and the grandeur of the place. "It is said to be caught at a juncture of worlds, like the central sphere of an infinite bubble cluster—and through its walls seep images of those worlds." He nodded. "Aye, and portals there be." He sighed and grinned. "And puppet strings as well."

The implication of his words sank in, underscored by the otherworldly nature of that which I beheld.

"The power that can be ours," I whispered. "I believe I had limitations on it before now."

"Indeed," said Divort. "I advise you, this place will outstrip imagination!" He clamped a hand on my shoulder. He winked. "But come, brother. It's time for acts of gods!"

We made our way down to the city, pausing at a gaily babbling brook to wash and primp, that our visages might not be so ragged and dirty.

From his pack, Divort took out fresh clothing, which he bade me wear. After shedding my rags for these fine, fresh breeches, and a starched white jerkin and tunic, I indeed felt like a king, or overlord, and my haughty spirits rose up accordingly.

There were no guards as such at the gates of OverEye, but rather a sign in a language hat I could not decipher.

"What does it say?" I asked.

"Why, I do believe it says, 'Gods Needed' Whiteviper!" said Divort, chortling. "In truth, I cannot read it myself. But there's nothing barring our entrance. So let's make haste and assume our rightful place."

There were peoples of various sorts moving through the clean and orderly cobblestoned streets of the city, but in the main the men of OverEye seemed much shorter than ourselves, runty little fellows, uniform and bland of feature. The women, though, oddly were taller than I'd generally observed women to be before, and beautiful beyond measure, each in her own unique manner. And on every corner of the neat blocks of this city, there was a tavern, outside of which laughing people drank sudsy beer, perfumed with heaven's own hops.

My mouth began to salivate. Over the beer or over the women I did not know.

At first we were roundly ignored. It was almost as though the citizens did not see us. Divort did not seem to be bothered at all by this. From his pack, he drew out a stool and he sat on it, paging through an old, musty tome. I sat down on the curb beside him after tethering my mule, feeling entirely too sober and entirely too celibate.

Divort clamped the book shut with finality.

"Just sit there and do not move, Whiteviper. No matter what happens, do not move, and soon we will be Overlords."

"Perhaps," I suggested, "I should sit over there at yon tavern, beside those tankards."

"Temptation does not suit you," he admonished. "No no, you've had patience yea these weeks, have patience for a few more minutes."

Thus saying, he set up a stand, from which he performed feats of magic. By this time I, of course, was wondering how Divort expected these people of OverEye to be diverted by a bit of fire and thaumaturgy when they had but to peer through the multitude of lenses into other worlds to see far more wondrous marvels.

Yet, from the outset of the performance, I saw that these tricks were different. Divort began by pulling off his cap and extolling the people to observe; from the hat, he pulled out a rabbit. It scampered off beneath their legs. Then Divort produced a pitcher filled with milk and poured this milk into a rolled up bit of paper. He then crumbled the paper, which was as dry as the desert.

By then, a large crowd of the OverEye folk had gathered, all agog, and from the fire in Divort's eye, I saw he was about to produce his *piece de resistance*. From his back pocket came a pack of playing cards.

Ah! I thought. Cards, and wished he had produced them by our campfires, so that I might have fleeced him of some more of his gold.

The people of OverEye surrounding us gasped. These cards struck some sort of resonance with them. All eyes were on Divort, who proceeded to perform all kinds of tricks with these cards, acquiring help from members of the audience. By the end of half an hour of simple card tricks and bout of applause after bout of applause, Divort bowed, and bade me stand up and take a spot beside him.

"This is my dear brother, Whiteviper. I am Divort. We have come to fill the positions of prophecy. We are the new Overlords!"

A moment of awed silence swept over the audience. Then a man cheered, and a woman swooned for joy. Soon the approval was unanimous. A man

wearing a velvet cape and mauve pantaloons
stepped out and bowed, to us, "My Lord, I am
Artmus Pedercaster. I am provost of this sector and
thus have the supreme honor of ushering you to
our mayor. Will you accompany me, O Great Gods,
Long Foretold?"

"That was easy as falling off a log," I said from
the corner of my mouth during the celebratory parade to the mayoral mansion.

"Thank you, Whiteviper. Your visage was the
most vital part. And your chi imbued my magic
with its glamour."

Well, I wasn't going to argue with him. The
promise of becoming Overlord, after all, promised
also a hot dinner, a warm bath, and a safe place to
snore. We were taken to a large building replete
with marble steps and marble pillars. Beyond the
doors, we found ourself ushered into a superb room
with high ceilings and festooned with magnificent
draperies and huge murals of scenes of a fantastic
and heroic nature from different worlds. Our footsteps echoed in the greatness. The scent of snuffed
candles and insense sanctified the sensations.

Through another door, we found ourselves in another magnificent, if smaller, room occupied by a
golden desk and a high-backed silver chair behind it.
Upon this chair, wearing a pair of bejeweled specta-
cles, was the most stunning female of her uniformly
luscious breed. As tall as I was then—and Rotvole,
believe that I have shrunk indeed—she had a halo
of golden hair, a figure an hourglass might envy, and
a perfect oval face, with huge azure eyes.

She gazed upon us rapaciously, and I would like to say lustfully, save for her first words:

"Gentlemen. I am Cordinia, Continuum-Governance Administrator. What has kept you? We have been waiting for you, yea, these last few millennia!"

"Odd are the ways of the gods," said Divort. "My brother and I were detained by small, niggling matters."

"And you have indeed come to serve as our Overlords?" she continued, looking at us with what can only be called awe.

"We have come to claim our due!" I announced arrogantly, getting into the spirit.

"Well, then, oh lords, you look weary from your trip. I will summon servants. You may bathe and eat and rest, and afterward you may take up your duties."

I need not tell you that I accepted all that pampering as though I was born to it! I bathed in silky bubbles, I ate a delicious stew and sweetmeats, forsaking the wine and joking with Divort as we feasted. In feathers and softness I slept. After a breakfast of brisk tea and fresh-baked bread slathered with honey, we were again ushered forth to Cordinia.

"Now then," she said. "There is a small matter. Who is to be the Light and who the Dark?"

"Pardon?" I said

"That is why there needs to be two."

"Oh. Of course," I said. "Well—Divort is always one with the ready joke. So I suppose he shall be Light."

"Such was my intention," said Divort.

My brows furrowed a bit. "But the Dark . . . what different duties does that entail?"

"Trifles!" said Cordinia. "Trifles, I assure you. Come this way, gentlegods."

We were led up a spiraling stairway to the largest, highest tower in the city, the top level of which sat like a huge saucer upon a needle. I expected from this summit to witness a view of the panorama of the city and the mountains without. Instead, the walls were dark.

"Here are your command thrones, O great Overlords. We are in the cycle of the Dark now, so you, Lord Whiteviper, have command." She smiled at Divort, and took his arm. "Come, Lord Divort, I have some other duties for you."

"Pardon me," I said, confused. "What am I to do here?"

"Oh, Ygor will be very happy to tell you!" She clapped her hands. "Ygor! Excellent news! Your long-promised Dark Overlord has arrived to give you aid!"

A grating giggle of joy arose among the dim rafters. A creature unwound itself down on a thread. At first it seemed to be a spider, but a closer look showed it to be a man with several legs, several arms, and a bulbous head. His entire body was twisted unnaturally—no symmetry here!—and blisters and buboes rose up from its pasty skin. It mumbled gleefully through crooked fangs: "Agack! Agay! My dear lord. You have arrived not a decade too soon!" I found my hand suddenly drawn up—

the thing drooled a kiss upon my hand. I hastily withdrew, shuddering.

"We will leave you to your destined duties, Dark Overlord," said Cordinia. "As there is much to deal with, your meals will be delivered to your quarters here." She pointed to a corner, where on a mat, a chair and a table sat. Upon the table was a large leather-bound tome with gilt edges and a candle.

When I turned my attention back to Divort and Cordinia, they were gone, leaving me alone with Ygor.

"My lord!" said Ygor. "Here is the dilemma. The world of Obscuse in the galaxy of Narvar wobbles out of balance, overpopulated and oversecularized. They no longer pray to the Ubergods, and are puffed up with great hubris. Should their number be stricken with plague, pestilence, alien invasion, tornadoes, cankers, infernal explosions, or do these haughty beings deserve protracted and exacerbated individual torture? I have randomly selected the Spell of the Bee Swarm as a possible measure."

My attention was immediately thus achieved. "Hmmmm," I said. "To bee or not to bee! That is the question!"

And thus did the best days of my life begin!

Ygor ushered me up to the command barge, from which we commanded purviews of the many worlds intersecting herein, within reach of our control.

"You see, my lord," said Ygor, hobbling up the crooked stairs. "Lo, these many centuries I was only intended as temporary help. I have done the best as I could, but alas, the universe has fallen out of balance."

"Oh?"

"Witness our present case! Because of my huge caseload there are hundreds and hundreds—perhaps thousands—of worlds and peoples out of balance. In existence, there is light and dark, there is good and evil, there is fortune and misfortune, order and chaos. But for one to exist, the other must also exist." He shook his head sadly. "I should be whipped! Now there is too much good, light, and order. The universes hobble and cavort toward certain doom."

"You seem to dwell on doom."

"Oh, my Overlord. Balanced doom, not bad doom, which is nothingness! Obliteration!"

"Ah. I see!"

From the perch of craggy thrones, I looked down upon a plethora of lenses. Ygor danced and swung upon levers and cranks. An iris opened, and I was able to peer upon a series of friezes representing the people of a world. They seemed smiling and content people. My stomach churned.

"Some cataclysm perhaps, my lord? An earthquake?" quavered Ygor indecisively. "That is always what I fall back upon."

I shook my head. "I see two moons in their skies. The moons shall fall upon the world."

Ygor's eyes lit. "Yes! What a splendid spectacle!"

I pointed decisively. "Make it so!"

The sounds composing the wrenching desmise of this previously happy planet were most satisfying, to say nothing of the screams of the people. They'd been rather elfin looking, and as I have made it known before, I despise elves.

And thus began my too-short career as god. I am happy to say I was more than up to the task. Wholesale destruction was seldom needed: Small calamities upon planets and peoples sufficed. As the backlog of worlds deserving evil luck dwindled, I was able to focus more on smaller, even more satisfying matters. Battles. Wars. Rape and pillage were great fun, and I soon found favorite ogre and troll races to do my bidding in a veritable poetry of violence.

Such was the entertainment aspect of my new job, that for a while I slept and ate little, absorbed in the intricacies of the tasks at hand. Ygor noticiably relaxed, and was able to take time for himself in his little warren of cubbyholes, relaxing with his hobby of spider-wrangling.

One day, however, after a particularly satisfying guillotining of a beautiful princess, I felt odd. Stirrings of old hankerings flickered inside of me, and I realized that I'd been cooped up in this tower for weeks on end. I felt the need to receive some sort of praise for my hard work, or at the very least some mild acknowledgment. The music of the spheres was again in harmony, with evil's song properly placed, and I was responsible.

Letting Ygor have the conn, I managed to find my way back down the winding staircase to the lower parts of the city. The first person I saw was an attractive young woman. I went to her to announce my presence, and offered my hand. "You may kiss the hand of a new god," I said. For while I'd forsaken women's more erotic charms, I saw no harm in their lips worshipping me in substitution. The young woman gasped, gave me a look of horror, and fled. There was a mirror nearby and I looked in it. My handsome features now were gnarled, twisted, and blackened with the evil of my duties. I snarled and hissed at myself, and covered my face with fingers that had become claws.

To reject women is difficult enough, but to have women reject me was too much. I felt for the first time a dreadful need for strong drink. However, I took a deep breath inside me, and thought for a moment: should I drink of alcohol, I might lose my Overlordship. No more would I be able to lord over puny beings lost in their own selfish stupidities.

Then again, I thought, what if I spoke with Dinny Divort! Surely some kind of arrangement might be made to allow a god a little sport with wine and women. A small thing surely for one with Divine Powers.

I went to the desk where first we saw Cordinia. It was empty. I explored associated chambers again. I felt as though Cordinia might indeed know where Dinny was, and so inquired after her personal quarters. Fortunately, the evil upon my face was growing less ugly as time passed, and my questions were met with answers: upstairs, I was told.

Would I had not ascended those steps!

However, I did, and upon the topmost I heard Divort's rolling tones, singing some silly song.

"Divort!" I cried, bursting into a room. "We must have words!"

Well, upon viewing that scene before me, I indeed needed words, because words were stolen from my throat.

There, lying upon a vast bed of amber pillows and ivory sheets lay naked none other than Dinny Divort and Cordinia. The scent of after-coupling hovered in the air like spring, and both sported huge crystal tumblers of wine, from which they were drinking.

"Zounds, Whiteviper! Have you insuffecent courtesy to knock first?"

I stood there for a moment, aghast at what lay before me. For her part, Cordinia looked no less upset.

"Please, if you insist on staying, do close the door."

I ignored her. "You blackguard! You bounder! What about our pledge?"

"Your pledge, dear boy! Never said I would have to swear off the fun bits of life! I say though, you are looking a bit piqued. Perhaps you should go back and have a nap."

I reached down and grabbed him by the neck and started shaking him. "I am the Dark Overlord!" I shrieked. "No one goes unpunished who betrays me!"

"Trifle melodramatic, don't you think, old boy?" choked out Divort.

I tossed him back into his bed of sin and stepped back, overwhelmed by vexation. Seized by an apoplexy, I could not speak. However, events proved I did not have to speak, for who should enter the room through the door I'd opened but Ygor. He carried this very sword I wave now.

"Cordinia? My love. Why?" He turned on Dinny Divort. "Bastard! I strike thee for this adultery!"

Thus saying, he struck at Divort, thusly—and with such force lopped off his head! Oh, the look upon that bouncing head! The body itself geysered blood messily onto the sheets and then tilted forward.

Both Ygor and Cordinia looked aghast upon this occurrence.

"This was no god!" said Cordinia "I wondered as much."

She turned to me. "And you are no god either, but a partner in this trickery. Ygor—the sword!"

In truth, that was almost the end of me. Fortunately I finally found words, and Ygor remembered that for all my humanity, I'd been the best damned Dark Overlord they could have wanted. However, with my lack of godhood, I was now considered unfit. And so I was banished, with two mementos of my time there in OverEye.

You see the first now, the sword I have been waving, given to me only because it had been tainted with Dinny Divort's human blood.

And look now, Rotvole—here's the other memento at my feet. I lift it up by its scraggly hair. A bodiless head. The head of Dinny Divort and—

Oops! Dear Rotvole! Hah hah. The Evil Over-lord strikes one more time for posterity! Dinny's still in the basket under the chair. My swinging, drunken sword lost its way.

I'm holding you!

ENSURING THE SUCCESSION

Jody Lynn Nye

The tropical island was a bright green and tan dot in the middle of an endless aqua sea under an equally endless vivid blue sky. Rainbow-colored birds emitted their raucous cries and were answered by the shrieks and honks of the tree-dwelling wildlife. All was still, but for a gentle rustling in the bushes caused by a body perceptible only to the watcher viewing the scene through a remote infrared camera.

The pristine vista was suddenly marred a tiny black, elongated dot that approached rapidly from the eastern horizon, accompanied by the loud humming of engines that quickly swallowed up the natural sounds. The rocket-copter steadily descended until the wash from its steering rotors stirred up a miniature maelstrom in the waters of the peaceful cove. It landed inside a twelve-foot circle marked out by basketball-sized stones above the high-tide line.

Two men climbed out of the chopper, one from either side. They wore dark glasses and black boiler suits with red cuffs and collars, with the insignia of a knife piercing a tilted ring on each shoulder. The first man, a tall, hefty individual with very dark skin, flipped up the latch on the hold behind the passenger compartment. The pair began to unload the cargo: large, gray-painted crates stamped with the same blood-colored dagger-and-ring logo.

The moment they turned their backs, a young man burst out of the undergrowth. His long, light brown hair was wild, and his bright blue eyes burned in a tanned face. He moved with such silent deliberation that he was upon the large, dark-skinned man before the man could turn around. The youth pulled the gun out of the pilot's holster and shot him in the throat with it. The man fell. The youth leaped into the pilot's seat, entered a code in the keypad on the navigational computer, and strapped in as the rotors began turning. He hauled back hard on the stick and lofted the copter up out of the reach of the other man, who jumped up and tried to hang onto the landing gear. He missed. The aircraft was out of reach in seconds, and, as the jets kicked in barely ten feet above the treetops, out of sight over the horizon in minutes.

The watcher, a thousand miles away in an underground bunker, the communications center for Alkirin Empires, Inc., turned from the first screen to a second and touched a red button beneath it. The image of a man's craggy face with bright blue eyes and bushy black eyebrows in vivid contrast to his shock of white hair appeared.

"He did it. He's on his way, sir."

"Thank you," the older man said. "Out."

Vaslov Alkirin closed the connection and swung away from the console. How satisfying to know that years of planning were about to come to fruition. He had hoped, but hope was less than one percent of how things came to be.

He looked up at the map that adorned the far marble wall of his "office." Others had referred to the thirty-meter-square chamber as a throne room. If his employees suspected that he could hear them at all times and in all places they never let on. Alkirin assumed that they did not. They believed he trusted them. He did, and didn't. *Only a fool trusts all of the time*, he thought, surveying the boundaries of his empire. Or never.

His was not a country as the historians thought of one; rather, it consisted of large parts of several traditional nations that he had conquered through economic ploys and other means, plus other nonadjacent territories that belonged to him as outright purchases or gifts from the former owners. The continents in the sea of slate-blue marble were of silver. The lands that he controlled were covered in a layer of gold. Ashoki, for example, there on the eastern continent, was almost totally under his domination—except for two flipperlike provinces at the eastern edge of the oval country, and those two

were dependent upon his holdings for vital resources. Soon they must fall under his command
for mere survival's sake. He was ready to accept
their capitulation. Only the stupidly proud premier
was holding back on giving consent. Alkirin was
content to wait. That consent could not be long in
coming, not with the drought that had dessicated
the country for the last five years, and Alkirin's
water reservoirs the only nearby source, the only
reasonably priced source.

He had similar plans under way everywhere. He
had taken a world under threat of war and was
gradually joining it together under one flag: his.
One day all the nations of Ployaka would be gold.
Ah, but he wouldn't live to see it. That was the
purpose of the test today. If it succeeded, he had
no fears for the future of his empire. If it failed . . .
was he too old to begin again?

Alkirin was not immortal. The presence of the
clinical white tray full of bottles and vials at his
elbow was testament to that as was the gray-
uniformed nurse, a middle-aged woman who
brooked no nonsense from him, no matter how
many countries he controlled. She shook out three
pills and handed them to him with a crystal goblet
full of 90 percent water and 10 percent brandy. He
took his medicines when and as she said. He liked
Mlada Brubchek. Young, attractive nurses with
firm breasts and tiny waists had been tried and
found wanting. They were either too afraid of him
to make him take his treatments, or gossiped about
him and the workings of his personal estate when

he allowed them leave to go home. Brubchek considered everything about her work to be confidential. Alkirin had planted listening devices in her home and her possessions, but in twelve years, not one word about him had ever passed her lips to anyone else not directly concerned in his care. He didn't worry about her, but occasionally he still checked. *Trust, but verify,* as a wise old man of Earth had once said. Brubchek had seen to it that the illness that consumed him was as pain-free as possible. For that she was amply rewarded, and would continue to be. Brubchek nodded sharply to him, and retired to her quarters, through the door in the wall behind his "throne." Alkirin watched her go, and listened for the snap of the automatic door as it slid into the wall and locked behind her.

He poured himself more brandy. He had been fortunate over the years to acquire a few employees such as Brubchek, but on the whole, people were sheep. Steeped in blatant self-interest, they saw nothing beyond their next mouthful of grass. He preferred to let them live their lives, with only the occasional reminder that he was their master. They were happier that way, and he did not have to devote a moment's worth of concern to them. Once in a while a youngster would rise up from the peasant or merchant class and declare that his or her people must not be ruled by an unelected dictator. Alkirin enjoyed listening to them. They all said the same things. It must be hardwired into human DNA that when certain recessive genes combined, a bad, bombastic speech resulted. His response, therefore, was hardwired as well: the youngster was brought to him or one of his few lieutenants. If that energy could be converted to the service of the Alkirin empire, then he had a new and energetic employee for life. If not, then the rebel would vanish at once, leaving the other sheep to return hastily to their grass. Presidents, kings, emirs, lordships all made attempts to deter or destroy him.

They had a saying in Birreshalov, on the western continent, where he had been born: you nod and nod your head, and all is well. One day you shake your head, and it falls off. He had made that come true many times. Between threats and friendly persuasion, subtle poisons and very public murders, he had enforced his grip upon his holdings. Worldwide domination was in his grasp, if he lived long enough, but since he would not, other preparations had had to be made. A child, one born of Alkirin's design and brought up to have all the necessary skills would be the one to carry on Alkirin's legacy. Or would he? His enemies had accused him of having a God complex, enjoying holding the power of life and death over his minions. Perhaps he did; at the moment he was reveling in having created life. He would only be disappointed if this Adam did not bite the fruit offered to him.

The desperate flight from the island far out in the Msovich Ocean had been years in the planning. Alkirin had laid down the steps with great care. It had taken time to establish a random pattern of visits of the supply vehicle, a jet-copter capable of flying over one hundred kilometers per hour, then slowly regularize it to a monthly pattern: first, flights on the same day each month, then at the same time, until only a fool would fail to realize their schedule was more regular than old Earth's celebrated Swiss trains. Months to drop the contingent of heavily-armed guards on delivery detail down to two whose habits were easily observed and learned. Alkirin had chosen the final two deliberately because one of them was night-blind and the other had poor peripheral vision in his left eye. They'd been well paid. They knew they could be killed while in his service, and now one of them had been. The second would retire, if he was smart, and never tell a living soul what he had done. That would be backed up by computer surveillance for the rest of his life.

"Sir." Colebridge's voice interrupted his thoughts. Alkirin checked his verification program in the console at his side and waved a hand. A door in the wall to the right opened up, admitting his major-domo. Colebridge, a lanky, sallow-skinned man whose thin limbs belied their strength, had started out in Alkirin's employ at the age of twenty as a hired gun, but the way in which he handled his assignments, while obeying every stricture laid down by Alkirin's captain, still managed to show such a spark of creativity and economy of movement that Alkirin himself was moved to take a closer look. Colebridge was fantastically intelligent and inclined to give his total loyalty to his new employer. He had been repaid with bonuses and promotions commeasurate with his growing skills, and now was second in command worldwide to Alkirin himself. He was a good number-two man. His character was such that he never could command, as Alkirin did, but he carried out orders and got the best out of those who worked for him. He would do that no matter who he worked for. For that alone, Alkirin would have paid well. For the whole man, price was no object.

While he was waiting for the black craft to arrive, he dealt with other matters demanding his attention. The stock market in Illisov City in the southern nation of Blen was bullish on a stock that Alkirin felt had not yet lived up to its potential. He had his chief accounting officer leak an announcement to a financial reporter (that the corporation had bought and paid for) that they were about to sell a majority holding—a catastrophically large majority. Within minutes of the release the stock fell to a satisfactory level. Alkirin permitted the executive to purchase another large percentage of the remaining shares at a substantial savings. So what if it bankrupted countless other buyers? Had no one ever told them that the market lost as many fortunes as it made?

Alkirin also ordered the summary execution of a member of his security force. Colebridge had brought him proof that Estarina Tolokombe had been prepared to embezzle a portion of the output of the diamond mines her staff protected. At least a dozen others were in on the scheme, but the sudden and violent death of their leader would certainly cause them to give up their plans and be good little soldiers again. *If not*, Alkirin reasoned, switching off the screen after watching his hand-picked guard carry the body away from the pock-marked wall, *bullets were cheap*.

He hoped the boy could be ruthless; no one respected a weak leader.

At last, five hours after the communications center sent him video of the takeoff, his console beeped again. Alkirin waved a hand over the controls just in time to see the black jet-copter hovering over the mountain ridge that surrounded the valley in which Alkirin Headquarters was located. It landed safely and almost silently just beyond the top of the ridge. Little detail was available at that range, but sensors indicated that the craft was intact. Alkirin waited.

Whoosh! Snow sprayed out in a circular pattern when the emergency jet-assist escape pack lifted the youth a hundred meters into the air. The fuel cell was only large enough to get him over the mountain to the edge of the estate. Alkirin's scientists had calculated the quantity exactly; not another erg was left in the tanks by the time the boy landed just inside the six-meter high electronic barrier, less than two meters from the nearest security camera.

For the first time he saw the boy's face clearly. Sergi! At once he could see the similarities between him and his son, and the differences. Alkirin had been too busy in recent years to pay close attention to him. At twenty-three, he was slimmer than his father had been at that age, and his hair was the

honey-brown of his mother, but the eyes were the
Alkirin eyes, blue as a clear sky, with a bright fire
and intelligence behind them and that went into
turbo drive whenever the body was under attack.
Now he would see whether the long grooming had
produced the results that the father wished.

The old man leaned over his opulent chair's arm
and touched a lighted patch.

"Intruder alert," he said.

Sirens began to blare and security lights blazed
into life. All over the compound, dogs and soldiers
with guns burst out of their guardhouses. They
would give Sergi, as the Earth saying had it, a run
for his money. Trained serpents with maws as wide
as a man's chest slithered up and out of their sub-
terranean cages and undulated around the enclosure, hunting for helpless prey. Occasionally one of
the dogs, and very occasionally one of the men,
had gone missing, but that was the price of keeping
valuable guardian animals, imported at great difficulty from another planet.

Sergi heard the frenzied barking and the clanging
of metal doors flung open, and scanned around him
for an escape route. There was none. Alkirin
leaned back in his chair to see what he would do
once he realized it.

The boy had lived with his mother for the first
seventeen years of his life. Alkirin's wife, Tamica,
was a biologist. Alkirin had not seen her in six
years. He doubted that she devoted many hours of
thought a year to him. She was consumed with her
research. Those were two of the things that had

interested him in her: her dazzling intelligence and her single-mindedness. Twenty-five years before, his staff had prepared for him lists of likely women whose brains and character suited his purposes. Tamica was far and away the best prospect. He had proposed marriage to her, talked of children, and offered her unlimited research funding. He would have threatened her or kidnapped her to impregnate her if necessary, but it simply wasn't. She was not entirely unworldly for a scholar; the third offer had definitely made the other two more interesting.

Tamica visited him once in a while, but she was not highly sexed. Alkirin did not care; he had doxies to serve his sexual whims. Nor was she smotheringly maternal. Her offspring was interesting to her, but not quite as engrossing as her latest study of synapses or brain chemicals. She saw Sergi as more an undereducated colleague whom she enlightened when he proved curious. What she had in abundance were traits that Alkirin wanted to make use of in the next generation. He had made sure the child had nannies and tutors, every one a genius who was also an expert at child psychology, but he never maintained contact himself. That would never have done for his purposes. He did not want to establish himself as a cosy presence.

When the boy was seventeen, Alkirin had him kidnapped and taken to the lonely desert island. Alkirin had watched him through monitors planted in his house and school. He believed him to have too trusting and friendly a nature. That needed to be adjusted. Men in black hoods had broken into his room that autumn while his mother was away at a seminar.

The mother believed that Sergi had decided not to wait for her and hitchhiked his way to the college he had chosen for his higher education. Alkirin's staff had sent messages purporting to be from the boy, even occasionally throwing in the photo of a girlfriend or a blatant plea for money, all judged to be dismissed as a bore by his mother, who was more interested in her current biomedical research, dedicated to ridding humankind of the scourge of brain decay.

On the island, Sergi's life was an unpredictable medley of peaceful education and terrors. He had tutors to give him lessons on statecraft, science, psychology, finance, and many other topics that he needed. Every one of the tutors was well-compensated, intelligent, at the top of his or her field, and every one with a terminal illness who had been promised that they could spend their remaining days on a tropical island with one highly-motivated pupil. Alkirin kept that promise. Some were so ill that they were able to last only a few months, and were buried there, but died happy. He did not, as the local media had it, always kill his employees out of hand. Some of them died on their own. None of them knew precisely where they were. The astronomy professor was the one risk, since he could work out the island's location by the stars, but he kept his promise not to reveal it to the boy.

The servants on the island were poor, uneducated men and women from villages that had no electricity or clean water and were located in undeveloped nations that the overlord had not yet taken over. In exchange for generous wages paid directly to their families, they were happy to serve the "young master," and kept the island mansion perfectly clean, cooked wonderful meals from local and imported ingredients, and did all the menial tasks with which no self-respecting despot need concern himself directly. As far as he knew the boy had never made his own bed or swept a floor in his life. That was appropriate. Even more appropriate, Sergi knew exactly how one should do a task properly, and could point out errors in execution, whether it be making a delicate sauce, repairing a drain, or assembling a complicated weapon.

At other times, Alkirin made the boy the target of live hunts. Sergi never knew when he would wake up from a drugged sleep, stark naked in the middle of the jungle, with or without a weapon, and the shouts of hired beaters and skilled hunters pursuing him. It was to make him ruthless, as he learned woodscraft and survival and how to fight. Alkirin believed Sergi came to love the thrill of the chase. He had killed five hunters in the past two years, and had become an expert in reading terrain.

Alkirin watched with avid interest as Sergi laid a false trail. The boy tested the ground and judged, quite rightly, that it was too firm to take footprints, but the hounds hunted by scent. He ran for several hundred yards in one direction, looping in between trees and up over blind ridges. Suddenly, he doubled back and hurried the other way, careful to plant his feet in the same flattened grass that he had just passed over, then hoisted himself effortlessly into a tree to wait.

The hounds came baying over the hills, with their handlers behind them in nimble, four-wheeled cars. Sergi withdrew into the canopy of leaves. There were sensors in every tree. The security overseers would have spotted the infrared signature by now. Ah, he was tearing them out! Sergi leaped from tree to tree, finding the hidden monitors and wrenching them out of the circuit. Soon there was a dead spot in the zone. Without seeing him alight in the last tree of his choice, Alkirin would not have a clear picture of where he had gone. In a fair battle of wits, Sergi would have made the first score.

The dogs found the discarded rocket pack and began baying. They ran down the scent. The dogs quickly came to the end of the trail and dashed around in circles, howling their frustration in the middle of the field. The handlers herded them back, insisting they try again.

They drove back again to the beginning, keeping the dogs at a slower pace. While they were questing to and fro, Sergi leaped out of the farthest treetop, landing on all fours, then ran over the nearest blind ridge to where the lizards were waiting.

He'd met them before. Alkirin had sent them to the island twice . . . no, three times. The first time Alkirin had used toothless, old animals, just to frighten the boy and teach him about the creatures. They had very poor sense of smell, but unusually

keen eyesight. They would chase down and eat anything that moved.

As soon as they saw him, the three lizards, each
twice the length of a man, swarmed toward him.
Sergi's face tightened when he saw how big they
were. He had only the gun he had taken from the
jet-copter pilot. He looked around for a hiding
place that they could not fit into. Ventilation ducts
for the underground facility poked up through the
earth at intervals, surrounded by a haze of electrical filaments as fine as hair. There was always a
dead animal or two lying by the intake, electro-
cuted when it tried to land on the spongy mass. It
was the gardeners' responsibility to move them before the stench suffused the lower levels of the castle. Alkirin had had four of the ducts widened
enough for a human body to fit through, but one,
and only one, gave passage into the castle. Sergi
kept running, dodging back and forth. The lizards'
ungainly waddle was deceptive. They moved far
faster than one thought they could, but Sergi knew
exactly what they were capable of. He led them
toward the first of the protruding ducts. With a
mighty leap, he dove over the first mass of wires,
landing on top of the duct. The lizards came after
him. The leader piled into the invisible filaments.
A loud *crack*! and a blaze of blue light, and the
lead lizard fell dead, twitching. Its companions,
smelling cooked meat, began to tear into it with
their dagger-sharp teeth. In the meantime, Sergi,
his face shiny with sweat, swung down over the top
of the duct. It was wide enough for him, but this

one, alas, terminated in a dead end. Alkirin clicked his tongue as Sergi, using very juvenile bad language, backed out and went looking for another one.

The dogs came yelping over the crest. They made straight for Sergi. The youth went on guard with the stolen sidearm in one hand and a belt wound around the others. The dogs surrounded him as the men poured out of their little vehicles, shouting. Sergi spun and snapped out a foot, kicking in the throats of the nearest two dogs. They collapsed, coughing blood. A guard leveled his weapon. Sergi was quicker. He shot the man in the forehead. The guard fell. Sergi ducked as the others responded, filling the air with bullets.

Alkirin watched with pleasure as Sergi destroyed the guard squad and its animals. With only thirteen bullets left in the magazine of his gun, he had to make every shot count. When they were gone, he waded into unarmed combat using the martial arts techniques of the best of the Skonzi-ka masters. All nine men fell, dead or wounded, and the lead hound died from a shot between the eyes. The others lay on the ground, wounded and whining. His opponents vanquished, Sergi discarded his useless gun in favor of one of the guards' weapons, then went looking for another way in. Alkirin nodded with approval.

After two more false leads, Sergi found the air passage that led into the castle cellar. He crawled on elbows and knees through the ventilation system. He emerged into the darkness of a dusty

storeroom. Alkirin continued to watch Sergi's progress on infrared. More guards were being dispatched. Sergi must know he had little time to
accomplish his goal. As if he were inside the youth's
mind, Alkirin followed every step of his progress.

Tamica had brought the boy to meet Alkirin for
the first time when Sergi was eight years old. The
old man sensed the keen, inquisitive nature Sergi
got from his mother, and permitted himself to answer any questions the boy had. Once engaged
upon a topic, Sergi could not be deterred from elic-
iting every fact, and got impatient when those facts
were slow in forthcoming. Alkirin admired the
single-mindedness, and a ruthlessness that reminded
him of himself. Sergi had a facility for memorization,
and retained every fact he was given, even correcting
the old man when he made deliberate errors to test
Sergi. Alkirin almost felt sentimental, as he answered unflinching questions from a small, bloody-
minded boy about torture, murder, and conquest,
assuring the boy his reputation for terrible reprisal
was true. He told Sergi all about building his empire from a single village, how he now controlled
the fate of nations, the very lives of all its citizens,
and kept the rest of the world guessing how, and
all from the humble origins of a mercenary soldier
younger than Sergi was now.

He had gone further, showing the boy his headquarters, describing in detail all the places where
enemies had perished, the archives where information on government finances were kept, and most
especially, he led Sergi past a short hallway on the

second basement level that featured a dead-drop door that he claimed was meant to trap invaders. The room was a dead end from which there was no possibility of escape. An intruder locked within would surely die there of starvation, hunger, and madness within days. He took Sergi past that hallway every time he visited, making certain that it was impressed in his memory.

It was. The first thing the boy did on entering was to ensure that the hallway was still where he remembered it to be. At the risk of being discovered by a security patrol, Sergi felt all the walls and examined the switch on the panel outside. Alkirin approved. The military scholar who had educated the boy in strategy and tactics was worth every credit he had been paid.

Alkirin had also made certain that the boy had overseen a guard captain opening one of the armories on the same level and memorized the locking codes. Those had been changed a thousand times since Sergi's last visit, but carefully reset to that set of numbers and symbols as the black jet-copter was landing. Nothing must be left to chance.

The new guard patrols combed the levels one by one, trying to discover the invader who had come in through the vent. Alkirin had told none but his "trusted" few who it was. He didn't want Sergi to feel that he was being manipulated, even if he was.

The youth's jungle training had served him well. He managed to squeeze into unbelievably tight niches or cling to the ceilings of corridors as patrols jogged through in search of him. He broke into a laboratory and stole a handful of chemicals, which he mixed up and spread on the floor. The first dog handlers to lead their animals through the corridor were astonished as their charges howled and broke loose, their brown eyes tearing. Alkirin hoped the chemicals' effect was temporary. Those dogs were highly trained. Besides, he was fond of dogs. It was one of his soft spots.

Sergi moved from place to place, picking up an item here, breaking into computers and changing settings there. He must have planned his incursion to the very last letter over the course of the years. It cost the lives of seven scientists, two computer programmers, an innocent file clerk who was in the wrong office, and a dozen lower-level guards.

Alkirin allowed the hide-and-seek to go on for five or six hours, then called for his personal body-guard. The seven men and one woman who answered the summons were the best-trained, most deadly fighters that he had ever had work for him.

"I wish to visit the financial center in the third basement," he said.

None of their faces changed, but he knew their minds must be racing. All of them must have been thinking that there was something wrong; he must know that the invader had not yet been captured. But they did not question Alkirin. No one did. All of them drew weapons. He took his place in their midst. The first two guards scouted outside the room, then gave the signal to the others to escort Alkirin out. He allowed himself to look sedate and calm, but his mind raced, ensuring that his calcula-

tions were all correct, and all preparations were
made.

Now, for the confrontation that Sergi must de-
voutly be praying for.

For the first time since he had been a foot soldier, Alkirin felt the frisson of physical terror crawl
coldly down his back as they marched. The youth
was following them. Alkirin knew Sergi had
shorted out the security monitors in this section,
and had looped a file showing the passage empty.
The boy did not know about the secondary cameras
that fed into Alkirin's personal console and Colebridge's computer. He did not realize his every
move was still being watched.

Here. It must be here, Alkirin thought as the
guards escorted him onto the private elevator. It
was what he would do under similar circumstances.

He was not wrong. The elevator moved downward smoothly, then jerked to a halt. The chief
escort barked orders. One guard spoke into his
communications link, trying to raise the engi-
neering department. The others pried open the
doors to discover that they were nearly level with
the second basement floor. The guards decorously
assisted Alkirin out and up to the floor when the
explosion came.

Head ringing, Alkirin found himself on the floor,
covered by the bodies of four of his bodyguards.
The others were dead, blown to pieces. Those remaining alive tried to cover him, but they were shot
dead by the powerful hunting rifle Sergi held.

Alkirin was not unprepared. From his sleeve he

flipped a flash grenade at Sergi. Shielding his eyes from the glare, he ran up the corridor.

The exploding light cast a long shadow before Alkirin. He wondered if Sergi had ducked or if he had been blinded. Ah, footsteps! The boy had protected himself.

The pain came almost at once. The doctors had warned him that his heart was growing steadily weaker. A transplant, they suggested, or perhaps a cloned graft. He had turned them all down. If only his tortured organ would hold out long enough to finish this matter correctly!

He could not stay ahead of Sergi for long. The boy overtook him swiftly. A hand grabbed his shoulder and turned him around, shoved him against a wall.

"Unhand me, boy!" Alkirin shouted. Sergi leaped back. The authority in the old man's voice made him obey automatically. His handsome face screwed up with petulance. He was still a child in so many ways.

"You!" Sergi burst out. "You were responsible! Why? Why did you make me a prisoner on that island? Why? You tortured me! My physics tutor told me it was you that took me to that island! Why? Why?"

Alkirin remained calm. "Allow me to introduce myself."

"I know who you are," Sergi interrupted.

Alkirin held up an imperious forefinger. "You know who I am, but not what I am. Sergi, I am your father."

The boy let out a snort of disbelief. Alkirin merely smiled.

"Oh, I can give you proof. Your mother could. She is a biologist, but you are also trained in the sciences. You can examine our DNA signatures. We are close flesh and blood, you and I. You are my son and heir."

It was a lot to absorb. Sergi's face showed the struggle to understand, to accept, but his mind refused to release the question until it was answered. "But why? Why did you do all that to me?"

"To test you. To make you the strongest man you could be." Alkirin held up his hands in admiration. "And look at you!"

Sergi gaped for a moment, then pulled himself together. His expression became scornful. "I overcame all your tests, old man. You are not so formidable."

"Ah, you still think you are the architect of your own rescue. Oh, no. Everything you did, I set up for you. I engineered your opportunities. True, you took them. That was the test: whether you could see and take advantage of situations. I made the pilot leave the departure point in the jet-copter's memory. I changed the schedules so that you would know when to take advantage of the craft. I left the way in here open so you could take it, made all the rooms and safes the same as you recalled them from when you were a boy. If you had thought about it, you would have realized things do not remain frozen in time. They change. You will learn."

Sergi could no longer conceal his astonishment. Akirin's point was made. "*Why?* Why all this?"

"Because you are my heir, Sergi, but I have no intention of allowing you to live if you are unworthy. I wanted to see for myself. And now, I," he added, allowing his eyebrows to droop sadly, "I have decided that you are not worth the trouble I have gone to."

From the sleeve of his tunic Alkirin whipped a slender gun and fired it. Sergi saw the movement of his hand. He dropped and rolled. He was remarkably fast. The explosive charge Alkirin fired blew a huge hole in the wall behind him exactly where his head would have been. The boy sprang up. Looking alarmed, Alkirin took to his heels and ran. Slugs winged past him with a noise like angry hornets. He was running. Brubchek would be furious.

He was being steered, Alkirin realized, as he fled down the hallway. Every time he tried to duck into a side corridor, the bullets on that side would increase in number.

Alkirin, too, tried to kill his son, triggering traps that had been set in the ceiling and walls of every room of the fortress. The youth was superbly trained, and his memory of his previous visits was clear. He eluded the weapons that sprang from hidden emplacements where he had not already disabled them.

A lone soldier sprang out of the safe room he had been guarding. Fearing for the life of his master, he drew a knife and rushed at the boy, shoving him face-first into the opposite door. Sergi leaped up, wall-walked upward over the man's head, dropped down behind him, and shot him before the guard could turn around. Alkirin took the opportunity to flee around a corner. Sergi followed. Alkirin saw his eyes light up with manic pleasure as he saw which corridor the old man had run into. He had *not* forgotten. He rushed for the controls.

The door slammed downward as Alkirin lunged for freedom. It snapped shut so fast it took the tip off his boot.

"Let me out of here, you brat!" Alkirin pounded furiously on the door with both fists. The steel boomed, but all his blows were in vain. "Let me out! Unlock this door!"

Through the solid wall he heard footsteps retreating hastily down the corridor. Silence. Alkirin turned and collapsed with his back against the wall, gasping at the effort. The pain returned, sending daggers of agony stabbing in his limbs and chest. Without his medicine he did not have long to live.

In a moment, he got his breath back. He rose slowly on hands and knees, then gradually attained his feet. His back proudly erect, he paced to the center of the northern wall and waved a hand across a concealed section the same texture as the wall. Sensors beeped as they recognized his palm print, and a panel slid back to reveal a small comm screen.

His majordomo's anxious face appeared on it. Alkirin nodded at him.

"He's done it, Colebridge. He's on his way up

now. You had better intercept him before he tries to leave the estate."

"I will, sir," the man said. There was a long pause, as Colebridge's usually iron jaw quivered slightly. "Sir, good-bye."

Alkirin smiled. "Good-bye, Colebridge. He'll do well. Just do for him what you did for me."

"I will, sir. I promise."

"Yes, you will. Ah, yes." Alkirin waved his hand to close the link. He pressed his hand to the square of wall beside the screen.

This time an enormous panel opened. A couch-like easy chair rolled out and opened up. A padded footrest rose. Alkirin sank into it. Comfort, a luxury he rarely allowed himself to indulge in. Very restful for his old bones.

Outside the locked chamber, the staff, led by Colebridge, would be swearing fealty to the new young master, and educating him as to his new place in the world. Sergi would be overwhelmed, but Colebridge would guide him until he had his feet under him. Sergi had proven to be just as intelligent and ruthless as he needed to be, and would make a good master. Once he had calmed down the staff would help him locate his mother. Whether he would believe it when Tamica told him that she had no idea how Sergi had really spent the last seven years or forgive her Alkirin did not know, but that was of no moment. She had no defenses against him, and was no threat to his newly-won empire.

Another small panel opened up. From it Alkirin

took a cup and a blue pill, both of which had been replaced regularly for the last six years for just this moment. The pill contained an untraceable, flavorless, and above all, painless poison. Alkirin put the pill on his tongue and washed it down with the excellent brandy in the glass. A fitting end, he thought, sensing the torpor beginning to creep slowly from his extremities inward. He was no longer afraid to go. Allow the boy to think he had disposed of the old man. Only Colebridge and a few trusted associates would know the truth. Having killed the previous master would give the boy a reputation to fear. Such a defeat couldn't hurt Alkirin, not now. He got what *he* wanted. His empire would endure.

"And on the final day, I created Man in my own image, and I saw that it was good. And then," Alkirin murmured, as the darkness began to gather in his vision, "I rested."

THE LIFE & DEATH OF FORTUNE COOKIE TYRANT

Dean Wesley Smith

You will live your life by direct instructions.
—Chinese fortune cookie

The origin of a tyrant is often a mixture of common sense, wild strangeness, and a lot of luck. Those three factors led to the creation of one of the world's most feared and misunderstood dictators, Fortune Cookie Tyrant, or just FC among his minions when speaking of him in private.

Every great ruler's story usually starts with a single event. Seven-month-old Fortune Cookie Tyrant, then named Steven, had just soiled his diaper while strapped into his high chair near his mother, Betty, at the end of the table at Fon Wong's Emporium and Lounge. The smell of Steven's little event mixed well with the smell of the last few bites of fried rice and overcooked chow mein, so, for a while, no one noticed.

Steven's dad, Frank, burped, pushed his plate aside, and leaned back, patting his growing beer gut. "Good food."

Every Wednesday night he said the same thing after eating the same dinner at Fo Wong's, so Betty just nodded and kept eating. He always finished ahead of her and then wanted to leave, so her only hope now of enjoying the last few bites of food was to work fast.

Steven, being somewhat uncomfortable with the nature call, started to "fuss," as his mother called it.

Sensing that Steven was going to be a problem, and wanting to just finish the last few mouthfuls of her dinner, Betty reached over and gave Steven a fortune cookie that had been left on top of the bill. It had been her cookie, but at this point it didn't matter.

Distracted for the moment from the loaded diaper, Steven played with the cookie, finally managing to crack it open before putting it in his mouth, fortune and all.

"Whoa there, big fella," his dad said, reaching over and pulling the paper and most of the cookie from Steven's mouth. "You gotta read the fortune before eating it."

Betty laughed and just kept eating, glad for the few extra moments, as Frank opened the fortune and read it aloud. "Big fella, it says you will live your life by direct instructions."

Steven's father grunted and glanced at Betty before tossing the slip of paper on the table between the dirty plates. "What kinda stupid fortune is that?"

Actually, unknown to either Frank or Betty or the growingly more uncomfortable Fortune Cookie Tyrant, it was a charmed fortune, cursed by the magic of an angry Chinese man whose brother had slept with his wife.

The cookie had been specially made for the man's brother, with the curse on the fortune intended to let the angry man push his brother around and pay him back for his deed by giving him fortune cookies with really nasty instructions inside. But as luck would have it, the charmed cookie that was to set the entire process in motion was lost in the packing process. Instead of being sent to the angry man who could then give it to his brother, it was added to a shipment headed for the United States, where it ended up in Steven's hands at Fo Wong's Emporium and Lounge.

Common sense, wild luck, and a strange curse had come together to change Steven into Fortune Cookie Tyrant, a man whose entire life and therefore the future of the entire world was to be steered by the fortunes included in small desserts.

As life would have it, Steven's parents were killed the following weekend in a tragic deer hunting accident. Steven was sent to live with his wicked and uncaring aunt who hated Chinese food. Thus it was twenty years and five months before Steven got his next "fortune" and came to realize his true powers for evil.

*   *   *

The date with Amy wasn't going well. They had met in a freshman United States history class at the university and smiled at each other for a few classes before Steven had had the courage to talk to her, and eventually ask her for a date. Steven, at this point in his life, was not an attractive man. He looked like a bad cross between a nerdy scientist in a movie and Ichabod Crane. He had just finished into his last growth spurt and had the social skills of a stumbling tenth grader, even though he was in college.

Amy was no real catch, either, but for Steven, any woman who agreed to go out with him was someone special. He had fantasized for days about making love to her.

Now, sitting in Amy's favorite Chinese restaurant, the conversation had lagged and become strained toward the end of dinner, and all Steven could think about was how he was going to get her back to his dorm room and into bed. He had no idea what she was thinking about, and had no idea how to ask her. In fact, he had no idea at all what to even talk about next. It was *that* sort of uncomfortable moment.

She picked up the tray holding the two fortune cookies, smiled at him from behind her thick glasses, and said, "You first."

He took the small cookie, she handed him the tray, then she took the second. He was about to pop the entire thing into his mouth when she broke hers open and took out the little slip of paper.

He did the same, puzzling at the strange feeling

that came over him when he read the words, "Intuition will help you solve puzzling problems."

He glanced up at her as she shook her head at her fortune and then flipped it toward him. "Dumb, really dumb. I'm supposed to come into money shortly. Yeah, that's going to happen. Why can't they ever do anything original with these cookies?"

Steven wasn't listening. He knew instantly how to solve his problem, how to get her back to his dorm room, and into a position they might both enjoy. He didn't know how he knew, but with one look at her, he just knew.

Not allowing himself to stop and think about what he was doing, he reached his hand past the half-eaten plate of pork fried rice and touched her hand, looking into her startled eyes.

"I've got a confession to make," he said, letting himself smile just a little to not make his words seem threatening, "I've been sitting here this entire dinner trying not to stare at you. You're the most beautiful woman I have ever seen, and I just had to tell you that."

His words were smooth, smoother than he had ever spoken in his life, his voice deeper, his tone perfect, his eyes focused and caring. Steven marveled at himself as this new power took over his body, smoothly talking to Amy, making her laugh, making her squeeze his hand with the promise of the night.

From that moment on, he said the exact right thing at every exact right moment.

And considering that he had never been with a

woman his entire life, and had only watched a few porn films, he was a perfect lover as well. It seemed that the power to know how to solve her needs, as well as his own, stuck with him long after the dinner was gone.

The next morning, after she had left with a long kiss and a hope for more time with him, the power didn't go with her. He just sort of knew how to solve problems, how to deal with things that just the day before would have left him puzzled and lost.

And from that day forward his classes, once challenging, were insanely easy. He knew how to get extra money when he needed it, how to make himself look better, and how to talk a woman into bed. Within a few months, he had a new wardrobe, had moved into an apartment, had bought a nice car, and had a perfect grade point average.

Fortune Cookie Tyrant had taken his first step toward world domination and control, and not once did he link it to the fortune in the cookie; thus it was over a year before he took his second step toward his true destiny.

The football game had been awful, and the team had lost badly, making Steven's mood at the Chinese dinner more somber than excited. He had never played football because he had always been too skinny and uncoordinated and his aunt had hated the game. But that didn't matter. He loved watching football, and over the last year had become one of the university team's biggest fans.

Across the table from Steven was his date, Jane, a woman with few brains, long legs, and a sexual appetite that needed to be fed often. At first the combination had attracted him, along with the fact that she was way out of his class in looks. But now, after dating for almost three weeks, he had to admit she was starting to wear him out.

Besides that, the conversation with her when they weren't making love was deadly dull.

"Oh, I love fortune cookies," Jane said, clapping her hands like she was kid and reaching for one as the waiter set the bill down on the table.

Steven just shook his head, took the leftover cookie and broke it apart. Then he read the fortune. "Your natural ability with words will make you a leader that many will follow."

"Yeah, right," he said, flipping the fortune back onto the table. But he could feel that something around the table, around the entire restaurant had suddenly changed. Everyone was looking at him. It creeped him out.

He checked to make sure he didn't have a big hunk of pork hanging off his nose or a noodle caught in his hair. Nothing. Even his zipper was up and tight.

"What shall we do next?" Jane asked, her eyes peering into his like his every word suddenly mattered. She was leaning forward, showing him a nice view of one of her best assets.

Steven glanced around at everyone watching him as the silence in the restaurant settled in.

Creepy.

He glanced back down at the table and the fortune caught his eye. ". . . a leader that many will follow." His intuition sense told him that he had gained something special tonight.

But for the first time in a long time, he wanted to test that sense.

He looked directly at Jane. He'd had a great dream the other night about watching her dance naked. Why not try that? "I'm up for some dancing naked in the street."

He said it just loud enough for most of the patrons in the small restaurant to hear. He wanted to just shock those staring at him, make them look away. But actually, more than anything, he wanted to see Jane dancing naked in the street. That would be a lot of fun.

"Great idea!" Jane said, again clapping her hands together like she was ten. "I wish I had thought of that. I'm ready when you are."

He swallowed and glanced at the slip of paper on the table, then up at Jane. Maybe this fantasy was about to come true.

Then he noticed that instead of snickers from the other patrons around the restaurant, they were nodding, laughing, putting their napkins on unfinished meals, talking to each other about how wonderful it would be to dance naked in the street.

Steven sat there, stunned. The entire restaurant was getting ready to follow him out the front door.

He picked up the little piece of paper with the fortune, stared at it, one word coming clearly to focus. ". . . many . . ."

Which meant not all. He glanced around at all the excited people getting ready to follow him.

There were two people out of the thirty or so who weren't getting ready to do anything. They were just sitting, looking stunned at what was being suggested around them. One was a young woman with long black hair, and the other a blond-haired jocklike man with a chiseled jaw.

Not everyone would follow his lead.

But most would.

A good lesson to learn.

He shrugged. He had to see where this would lead, but his intuition told him that it would lead anywhere he wanted it to lead.

Ten minutes later, fully clothed, he stood on the sidewalk watching as the entire customer base of the restaurant, minus two, danced naked in the street. Cars had stopped and many inhabitants of the nearby buildings were staring. Luckily, it wasn't a bad sight, considering it was a restaurant full of college students. Steven told Jane, loud enough for everyone close by to hear, to keep dancing and that he would be back.

Jane nodded and everyone kept dancing to some silent music, all stark naked. With his words, a number of pedestrians and drivers who had been watching nodded, took their clothes off, and joined in.

The two that hadn't followed him were standing in the restaurant door, staring at him.

He waved at them, then with a laugh that didn't sound anywhere near as evil as he wanted it to, he walked off down the street, thinking about what had just happened and what it meant to his future.

Fortune Cookie Tyrant had taken his second step to world domination. He was coming to understand some of his powers and he knew he was going to enjoy using them. He just didn't know what exactly to do with them just yet.

The next morning, Steven stared at the headlines in the morning paper as he sipped his morning coffee while sitting at the long counter in Larry's Diner and Deli.

NUDE PARTY BREAKS OUT IN CHINESE RESTAURANT.

The article said that no one really knew what happened, only that dancing nude in the street had sounded like fun and so they did it. Thirty-two people. Public indecency charges were pending.

Steven laughed and tossed the paper onto the counter. Being from a broken home and having been raised by his evil and uncaring aunt, Steven had very few morals. Normally, a nerd like Steven would have had few chances to push against what morals he did have. He had just assumed he would end up working some dead-end job, marry some woman who would go to fat after two kids, and die mostly broke with a bunch of grandkids arguing over his comic book collection.

But now it seemed he had a more promising future. He could run a big company, he could become a senator or even the president. Or he could just get very, very rich and live an easy life surrounded by beautiful woman.

Or maybe he could do all those things.

"Why not?" Steven said out loud.

The guy two seats away down the counter said, "I agree. Why not?"

Steven glanced at him, then around at the diner. The cook, the waitress, and the five other customers were all staring at him, waiting for him to say something, like what he might say might be important.

Creepy. Having this kind of power over everyone around him might just get old. Then Steven laughed and said out loud, "That's not going to happen."

Everyone in the restaurant nodded. "You're right," the guy said beside him. "That's not going to happen."

He glanced at the waitress. "You sure you don't mind paying for my breakfast?"

She blinked, surprised, then smiled and said, "Not a problem."

"Thanks," he said, laughing and heading for the door.

This new power was going to be a lot of fun. But first, he had a lot of planning to do.

That afternoon, Steven went back to his apartment and started to do some research on the Web. He needed to know how others had gained vast wealth and power if he was going to follow in their footsteps. He needed to know their history, and the steps they took to keep the power.

And most of all, he needed to know what they did wrong. If he was going to get as much power as he was hoping to get, he needed to know how others lost theirs.

While running computer searches on different references to power, presidents, Caesars, dictators, and other tyrants throughout history, he came across a Web site that was titled "Checklist for the Aspiring Evil Overlord."

The site was supposed to be a joke, aimed at all the bad clichés Evil Overlords had in fiction, but Steven knew better. The site was a great reference guide to stop those who wouldn't follow him. Those two in that restaurant clearly haunted him, worried him more than he wanted to let on. And the checklist was filled with rules aimed at stopping those kinds of people.

Steven printed off checklist and studied it carefully over the next few days. Most of the suggestions were things that would matter later in his climb to riches, power, and maybe even world control. He was starting to really think big.

But many of the suggestions in that list would help him on his rise to power. For example,

#28: A bullet to the head shall *never* be too good for my enemies.

Steven would always keep that firmly in mind, along with #92: I will never fail to keep in mind my strengths and my weaknesses.

Then, after posting the list on the bulletin board

in his kitchen, he took out the little slip of paper he had gotten from the fortune cookie and read it one more time.

He needed to see if what he was thinking was right, that he had somehow gotten his powers from these fortune cookies. So he headed back to the Chinese restaurant he and Jane had eaten at the night before.

The employees were amazingly happy to see him as he came through the door, considering that most of them were facing charges for dancing nude and the restaurant was being investigated for spiking the food in some manner. Even with all that, there were still twenty people eating in the place and the moment he spoke to the man behind the front counter, they all stopped and turned to listen.

"I'd love to buy a large bag of your fortune cookies," Steven said.

"Here, take ours," one man at a table close by said, offering Steven their cookies. His wife was nodding, looking like a puppy trying to please a master.

"No, thanks," Steven said, waving the man off. "You two enjoy them."

Immediately the man and woman dug into the cookies, acting as if they were having small orgasms while crunching on the cookie, paper and all.

The man behind the counter grabbed a large bag that had to have three hundred fortune cookies in it. "This good?"

"That's perfect," Steven said. "And it's very kind of you to give them to me."

"The honor is ours," the man said.

Steven laughed as he left. It was getting easier and easier to get everything for free. Whatever was happening with him, he sure loved it. He could get used to everyone waiting for him to talk. After all, that's what everyone did around those in power.

Back in his apartment, Steven opened the bag, got a glass of milk from the fridge, and cracked into the first cookie. It was the same basic fortune that Jane had gotten the night before.

"You will come into a vast sum of money."

Steven laughed. "Yeah, that's going to happen."

A moment later, before he could even wash down the cookie with a sip of milk, the phone rang. He never did get back to the fortunes that day because his evil old aunt had had a stroke and was in the hospital. He didn't much like her, but he was the only thing she had. She died before he got there, which didn't actually upset him. The last thing he would have needed was the old bag hanging on and building up hospital bills.

He spent most of the night dealing with all the details of his aunt's death, then the rest of the night at Jane's, making her do things naked that no woman outside of porn films ever really did.

He sure loved his new power.

It was the next morning, after making funeral arrangements and talking to his aunt's attorney that he came to understand what had happened. His aunt had left him everything, and the old broad had been rich. Millions rich, or so the attorney thought. It was still too early to tell just how much it might be.

Steven laughed all the way back to his apartment. Now he had his stake to get him started toward his plan of world domination. The cookie had been right again.

There was no telling what the next cookie would bring him. He could just keep opening cookies and gaining power.

Today, he would become a truly powerful being.

The bag of fortune cookies and the half-empty glass of old milk were right where he had left them. He dumped out the milk, got himself a fresh glass, then took the first cookie off the top of the bag. He cracked it open, tossed half into his mouth, then read the fortune as he ate, as excited as a kid opening a present on Christmas morning.

But this fortune didn't seem right and he had to read it twice:

"All special powers that you have been given
by fortune cookies will be forever lost."

Steven tossed the slip away like it was on fire, but it was too late. The feelings of being in control drained away from him like someone had pulled a plug in his shoe.

"No!" he screamed. "That's not a fortune!"

He slammed the rest of the uneaten cookie into the wall and grabbed another one from the bag, opening it and putting half in his mouth before reading the fortune.

It said the same thing.

And so did the next one and the next one.

He opened a hundred before giving up and sitting down on a stool in disgust.

Someone had planted the entire bag with the same fortune. But who? And why? And who would have known he was going to come back here and open all these?

A moment later the phone rang. It was his aunt's attorney again, talking some sort of gibberish about taxes and problems with the government and how there wasn't as much money as there had seemed to be earlier, maybe none at all after all the lawyer fees and hospital costs. Steven just listened in shock, said nothing, then hung up.

The money was gone as well, right along with his powers.

He stared at the kitchen counter covered in half-opened fortune cookies. He knew, without a doubt, he had lost everything, all his dreams of ruling the world.

But how? Why had someone done this to him, taken his specialness?

Then the faces of those two sitting in the Chinese restaurant came back clearly to mind. Not everyone would follow him. Someone had known what was happening, somehow, and had changed out his real cookies with these special ones.

He needed to find out who. And why.

He dumped the entire sack of cookies out on the counter. At the bottom was a note.

Dear Fortune Cookie Tyrant,

Steven stopped reading and sat down on the stool. That was a name he had only been thinking about using after he gained world domination. No one would know it now. Something wasn't right here.

Steven went back to reading the note.

You forgot rule #85. And sorry about the slow-acting and very painful poison in the cookies, but after what you did to the world over the last forty years, after all the people you killed and enslaved, we figured it was the least we could do.
Signed,
The Anti-Cookie Alliance.

Steven could feel the pain in his stomach starting to grow.

He swept all the cookies from the countertop, then doubled over in pain. He had been poisoned. He got to the phone and dialed 911, begged for them to hurry, told the operator that the poison was in the cookies, then hung up as another wave of pain hit him.

As it eased, his mind went back to the note. Rule 85? What did the note mean by that? And forty years? He was only twenty. He hadn't been alive yet for forty years.

In the distance, a siren was growing louder. Help was on the way.

Then he saw the list on his bulletin board, the list of things he would do if he became an Evil

Overlord. The list that he promised himself he would follow carefully.

With the pain in his gut causing him to stumble, he went to the board, pulled off the list, and slumped to the kitchen floor, his back against the wall. Outside his apartment, the sound of the siren stopped. He could see the flashing lights through the window.

Help would be here in a moment. He forced himself to take a deep breath to hold back the pain and flip the list to the right place.

Rule 85. Once I have securely established myself, all time travel devices in my realm shall be utterly destroyed.

"No!" Steven shouted as the pain shot through his body. "I didn't get to become an evil overlord! I didn't get to be Fortune Cookie Tyrant!"

There was a banging on the door and his name was called out.

He tried to get up, but instead fell facedown onto the tile floor.

The last words the great Fortune Cookie Tyrant muttered were, "Not fair."

DADDY'S LITTLE GIRL

Jim C. Hines

At first, I didn't recognize the land around me. Blackened ash and burned stumps covered the earth as far as I could see. Saplings and weeds proved at least a year or two had passed since the devastation, but it was a far cry from the thick wilderness I remembered.

"I think he's waking up."

I started to turn around, then froze when I spotted the ruins. Crumbled bricks lay scattered to one side of a broken, six-sided foundation. In the remains of the doorway, I could see huge iron hinges bolted to the floor. The trick entrance was only one of the traps I had designed for Tarzog the Black while he tormented me with false promises to free my wife and son. I had barely eaten or slept for almost seven years as I worked to perfect his temple to Rhynoth, the Serpent God. This was my masterpiece, broken and scattered.

I rubbed grit from my eyes, then stared at my hands. The skin was pale, pulled tight around the bones like dried leather. My nails were cracked and yellow. When I poked my palm with one finger, the indentation remained for almost a minute.

I was bare-chested, dressed in rough-spun trousers and my old sandals, though the straps had been replaced with thin ropes. I pressed a sickly yellow hand against my chest. My heart was still as stone.

I had always wondered why Tarzog's dead slaves took their resurrections so calmly. Now I understood. Whether it was a side effect of the magic or my mind's way of rebelling against what had been done to me, I felt nothing but a strange sense of detachment. Looking at my dead body, I felt like a puppeteer staring down at a particularly gruesome marionette.

"I *told* you I could do it."

The speaker was a young girl, no more than seven or eight years old. She wore a dirty blue gown and a purple half-cape with a bronze clasp in the shape of a snake. Behind her stood a slender, dark-haired woman, the sight of whom made my dead balls want to squirm up inside me and hide until she went away.

"Zariel," I said. Tarzog's necromancer looked far more ragged than I remembered. Gone were the night-black cloak of velvet, the silver claw rings decorating her left hand, and the low-cut leather vest. Her skin was rougher, her hair grayer, and she wore a simple traveling cloak lined with dirty rabbit fur. To tell the truth, she smelled rather ripe, and that was coming from a corpse.

"What happened?" I asked. My memories were blurred, full of gaps. Another side effect of being dead.

To my surprise, it was the little girl who answered. "This wasn't the *real* temple. Daddy built the real temple about half a day's walk from here, in the jungle."

I stared, trying to understand. "Why would he . . . ?"

"Prince Armand knew about Daddy's plans to summon Rhynoth. So Daddy built this place as a trap. When Armand and his men finally got to the heart of the temple, Daddy was going to collapse the whole thing on their heads. But Armand and his men showed up early. They burned Daddy in his own temple, along with anyone they found wearing his crest." She touched the bronze snake at her throat.

Was that how I had died? No, I would have remembered fire. Death had been quick, but quiet. I clutched my stomach, recalling the pain of my insides twisting into knots. I had a vague memory of stale raisin pudding, even worse than our usual fare. I remembered dropping my spoon . . . "He poisoned me!"

"Of course he did. Daddy poisoned everyone who worked on his temple. That way only he knew all the secrets."

If he had killed me . . . Tarzog was too smart to let my wife or son go after that. He wouldn't risk them coming back to avenge me. I closed my eyes and fought despair. Gradually, the rest of the girl's words penetrated my grief.

Daddy. I stared. "You're Tarzog's daughter. Genevieve."

"Jenny." She smiled and nodded so hard her blond hair fell into her face. I remembered her smaller and pudgier, a wobbly child with a miniature whip she used on trapped animals, imitating Tarzog's overseers. According to rumor, her mother was a slave girl who had abandoned the newborn baby and tried to flee. She had been caught, executed, resurrected, and gone right back to working on the temple.

"We should go," said Zariel. "This place isn't safe."

Jenny stuck out her tongue. Had anyone else done it, Zariel would have had their eyes for a necklace and their tongue for a snack. But Zariel simply turned and began walking.

"Where are we going?" I asked.

"To the other temple," Jenny said, rolling her eyes at my stupidity. "I'm going to summon Rhynoth, and then we're going to destroy Armand and his people. They all helped kill my daddy, so they can all rot in Rhynoth's belly."

I stood, barely hearing her words. I kept seeing my family, dead and forgotten beneath the rubble. No doubt by Tarzog's own hand. He was never one to delegate that sort of chore. Without thinking, I lunged forward and wrapped my withered gray fingers around Jenny's fragile throat.

The next thing I knew, I was flat on the ground, a good fifteen feet from Jenny and Zariel. Jenny folded her arms.

"I should kill you for that, but I worked hard to resurrect you. Zariel's been teaching me." She flashed a gap-toothed smile. "Do it again, and I'll make you rip out your own innards with your bare hands."

I wiped ash and dirt from my palms. Jenny's magic had shattered several ribs, and the bones ground against one another as I stood. Fortunately, death seemed to have minimized my ability to feel pain.

One thing was clear: Jenny was definitely Tarzog's daughter.

We had walked more than an hour before I worked up the nerve to speak to Zariel. This was a woman who had eviscerated children and sacrificed whole families to maintain her power. But I had to understand what was happening if I was to have any chance of stopping them.

"Why did she resurrect me?" I asked.

"You designed the first temple," Zariel said. "Tarzog followed the same plans for the real one, including all of your traps. If you get us in, Jenny and I can conserve our power for more important things."

Jenny's power. I touched my ribs. "I didn't realize she had that kind of magic."

"I'm still a beginner at death magic, but I got all of Daddy's serpent powers when he died," Jenny

said, running back to join us. "I've even got the
birthmark of Rhynoth. A snakehead, just like Daddy's, with fangs and everything. I'd show you, but
it's not in a place you're supposed to show to boys.
Not even dead boys. The prophesies of Anhak
Ghudir say only one with the mark of Rhynoth can
awaken him from his endless sleep." She tugged
Zariel's robe. "Did you remember the blood?"

Zariel sighed and drew a small, glass tube from
an inside pocket.

Jenny turned to me and made a face. "I have to
drink the heart blood of a virgin to control Rhynoth. Zaniel has to use magic to keep it from getting clotty and clumpy."

I nodded, remembering how Tarzog had scoured
the countryside for virgins in preparation. At first
he planned to drain the blood of a few babies, but
further reading ruined that plan. The spell required
an adult virgin, and those were harder to find than
you might expect. Especially once word got out
that Tarzog needed virgins. I imagine the midwives
were plenty busy the next year. "So which one of
you found a girl to—"

"No girls, silly," Jenny said, chewing a hangnail
on her thumb. "They always have lovesick boys
who try to rescue them. I had Zariel kill a priest.
They're celebrate—"

"Celibate," Zariel said, her voice pained.

"Yeah, celibate. All we had to do was find one
who had taken his vows before he got old enough
to mess around."

Zariel slapped Jenny's head, hard enough to

make her stumble. "How many times have I told you to stop biting your nails?"

I glanced around. We had left the scorched remains of Tarzog's land behind and entered the rocky wilds that surrounded Frelan Gorge. Tall pine trees cooled the air, while tangled roots fought to cling to the uneven stone. The insects were thick here, and they seemed especially attracted to my dead flesh, though none were daring enough to bite me. Instead, they orbited my body, buzzing in my ears and darting past my eyes. I began to wonder if Jenny had raised me simply to draw the bugs away from her.

"How did the prince destroy Tarzog?" I asked.

Zariel scowled. "Tarzog was a fool. As Armand's men fought their way into the temple, Tarzog ordered me to take Jenny and flee. Together, we might have destroyed them all. Instead, he stripped himself of my power and wasted precious time on his whelp."

I glanced at Jenny, half afraid to see how she would react, but she only shrugged. "Zariel's right. Daddy was stupid, so he failed. I won't." She skipped ahead, then turned around. "Do you think Rhynoth will like me?"

I didn't know how to answer, so I looked to Zariel.

"The prophecies say the god's gratitude will be like a ne'erending fountain upon the one who calls him from the earth."

"I hope he'll let me ride him," Jenny said. "I've never had a pet before. Daddy had a cat, but he burned up when Armand attacked. He was a nice cat. Daddy carried him everywhere."

I remembered the beast, a black, long-haired ball of fur and claws. He used to sneak into the dungeons and piss in the straw.

"I tried to raise him," Jenny went on, "but he bit me. So I crushed his skull and scattered his remains."

Movement to the side saved me from thinking up a response to that. Two men in the green and silver livery of Prince Armand leaped from the cover of the trees. Both had longbows drawn. One kept his arrow pointed toward Zariel, while the other aimed at me. Not that a regular arrow would do much against my dead flesh, but perhaps Armand was smart enough to outfit his men with blessed weaponry. He had fought Tarzog's dead warriors before, after all.

"Speak one word, and it shall be your last," warned the man watching Zariel.

"No!" Before anyone else could move, Jenny ran in front of Zariel and threw her arms around the old sorceress. "Please don't hurt her."

"Get away from her, kid," said the second soldier. "That's Zariel. The black-hearted bitch murdered more innocent—"

"Bitch is a bad word," Jenny said, her dark eyes wide. She held up her arms, and Zariel picked her up, smiling.

Both soldiers now aimed their bows at Zariel. "Put her down, bi—witch."

I opened my mouth to warn them. To beg them

to fire. A single shot would pierce both Jenny and Zariel. Jenny's magic might be able to destroy me, but she couldn't stop an arrow in flight.

"Stay back, zombie!" The nearest man fired, sending an arrow through my throat. Pain shot down my spine, and I flopped onto my back. Armand was indeed smart enough to prepare his men. I wondered how long it would take the power in that arrow to penetrate my dead bones, dissolving Jenny's spell. Strange to feel both terror and longing for true death.

Then both soldiers began to scream. I managed to turn my head enough to see that their bows were gone, transformed into writhing, hissing serpents. Already one had sunk its fangs into the man's forearm. As I watched, the other soldier flung the snake away and turned to flee. The snake was faster, darting forward to bite him just above the boot. He hobbled away, and the snakes slithered back toward Jenny.

"Follow him," Jenny shouted, squirming out of Zariel's grasp. The necromancer disappeared after the soldier.

Jenny walked over and wrapped her small hands around the arrow in my throat. Flesh and muscle tore as she yanked it free. She brushed her fingers over my wounds, and I could feel the skin begin to seal. By the time I sat up, the holes were closed. My ribs felt whole again, too.

"Pretty good, huh?" she asked. "I like snake magic better, though." She reached down, and one of the snakes coiled around her arm. The scales were purple, with a stripe of bright pink down the underbelly. "They're not real, though," Jenny said sadly. She wrapped her little fingers around the snake's neck and squeezed. The snake crumbled away like chunks of burned wood.

A panicked shriek told me Zariel had caught up with her own prey. Jenny's face brightened. "Make sure you cut off the heads," she yelled. She glanced at me. "Daddy always taught me to cut off their heads or burn the bodies. You have to be sure they're dead. If you just push them over a cliff or poison them and leave them to die, they always find a way to come back." She tucked a stray lock of hair back behind her ear. "It's in all the stories."

She grabbed my hand and tugged me onward. "Come on," she said. "Zariel can catch up once she finishes playing."

Hand in hand we continued through the woods, followed only by gurgling screams.

We stopped near sundown to rest and eat, though my body didn't seem to need either. Zariel used her magic to lure a pair of rabbits from the woods, then Jenny conjured tiny snakes to bite them. The snakes might have been magic, but the poison was real, and the rabbits spasmed and died before they could hop more than a few feet.

A part of me expected these two to simply rip into the rabbits with their teeth, feasting on the raw and bloody meat. Instead, Zariel swiftly and efficiently gutted the two rabbits, then impaled them on spits over a small fire.

"We have little time," Zariel said. "When Armand's men fail to return, he'll know where we are."

"Good," said Jenny. She wiped her face on the sleeve of her gown, then turned to spit out a bone.

Zariel tilted her head. "Good?"

"I summon the Serpent God. Armand and his army arrive. The god eats them." She took another bite of rabbit. Still chewing, she said, "I won't make the same mistakes my daddy did."

"You want him to find you," I said. I had designed traps for years. I knew how to recognize them.

Jenny nodded. "He killed my daddy. So I'm going to kill him, his family, and his army, and then I'm going to destroy what's left of his land."

I didn't know what bothered me more: the calm, total conviction in her voice, or the fact that when I thought about my wife and son, I knew *precisely* how she felt.

Frelan Gorge was a beautiful sight. Rather, it would have been beautiful, had I been here for any other purpose. The river far below was a ribbon of darkness, sparkling in the light of the moon. Trees and bushes covered the cliffs, transforming them into walls of lushness and life. To the north, a cloud of mist rose from the base of a small waterfall.

Jenny pointed to the fall. "That's where we're going."

"You're certain?" asked Zariel.

"I can feel it."

I followed behind, biding my time. It would have

been so easy to grab Jenny and fling her down the cliff, but I remembered how easily she had smashed me to the ground the last time I attacked her. She had dragged me from the grave, and she could send me back as quick as thought.

I frowned as I thought about that. "Why me?"

"What?" Jenny asked.

"Your father knew the traps as well or better than me. Why not resurrect him?"

"Yes, Jenny," said Zariel, a nasty edge to her voice. "Why *him*?"

Jenny looked away, and I sensed I had stumbled into an old argument. "You were nice to me. He wasn't."

"I was what?"

"When the slaves were working on the first temple. I wanted to watch them laying the foundation and mixing the blood into the mortar. I wasn't tall enough, so you lifted me onto your shoulders."

I couldn't remember. Either death had rotted the memory from my brain, or else Jenny had confused me with another worker.

Up ahead, Zariel used her magic to burn a tangle of thorn-covered vines out of the way. There was no path, so we were making our own. As I watched the vegetation smolder, it occurred to me that the burned plants would make it easy for Armand's trackers to follow.

"Besides, if Daddy were here, *he'd* want to summon the Serpent God." She wiped her nose on her sleeve. "He had his chance, and he failed. So now I get to be the God Rider."

I kept my face still and prayed she couldn't read my thoughts. I might not be able to destroy her myself, but there were plenty of traps in Tarzog's temple that should do the trick.

Thorns tore my skin as I followed them toward the falls. I could hear the water crashing, and the vegetation was thicker here, forcing Zariel to expend more of her magic. With her smaller size, Jenny seemed able to slip through the thinnest gaps like . . . well, like a serpent.

Finally, the trees thinned, and we found ourselves on a rocky shore. Water trickled over my feet, and I could see how the riverbank fell away a few steps in. So long as we stayed by the edge, we should be safe. Any farther, and the current would toss us down the falls.

"Where's the temple?" Zariel asked, glancing around. My dead eyes seemed to handle the darkness better than theirs, but even I couldn't see any sign of the temple. And Tarzog hadn't built small. His temple had been the size of a modest palace.

Jenny was kneeling near the falls, craning her head. I stepped toward her. A single push, and she would plummet to her death. Jenny glanced up, and I froze.

"I can see something behind the water," Jenny said. "A door."

"How do we get down?" Zariel asked.

"We don't." Jenny smiled at me. "Right?"

Grudgingly, I nodded. "That would be a decoy, something to delay Armand and his ilk. If Tarzog patterned this temple on the one I designed, that door is nothing but a façade. But with the water pounding down, most heroes will slip and fall to their deaths before they reach it. If not, the door at the other temple had hinges concealed on the bottom, so it would fall open to crush anyone who tried the knob. This one probably does something similar."

"Which means the back door should be back this way," Jenny said, wading upstream.

I watched a branch float over the lip of the falls, and wondered how many workers had died building Tarzog's decoy trap. "It wouldn't be in the water," I said.

They both stared at me.

"Tarzog needed men to dig and build." I pointed to the river. "The riverbed is stone, and the current is too strong."

"So where is the door?" Zariel asked.

If Tarzog had followed the same plans . . . I glanced back toward the falls. Sixty paces from the front door, and another twenty paces to the right. I hurried along the shore, then turned back into the woods, ripping through the foliage until I reached a lightning-struck tree. Half of the trunk had rotted away. Splinters of blackened wood hung down like fangs. Grubs and worse squirmed within the blackened interior.

"Go on," Jenny said. "Open it."

I nodded. It would have been too much to hope for her to go first. Reaching past the fangs, I felt about until I found a small metal lever. A quick push disarmed the trap. On the original temple, rusted nails had protruded through the doorframe. Those nails were designed to shoot down, pinning an intruder in place. An instant later, two steel blades would spring out from either side to decapitate the poor fellow. I had been quite proud of that one, actually. I doubted this tree could house such oversized blades, but I didn't want to take my chances on whatever Tarzog had substituted.

I stepped into the bug-infested rot, and my feet began to sink.

Seconds later, I was in darkness.

I brushed dirt and rotted wood from my clothes and, without thinking, grabbed the torch from the left wall. Tarzog had been left-handed, and wanted to know he could roam his temple without having to carry detailed notes about various traps. The right torch would work too, but its removal from the sconce would prime a trap eleven feet down the hall, which would spray oil down on the head of whoever passed. The oil itself wouldn't hurt anyone, but if he carried a lit torch . . .

The flint and steel hung from the sconce, good as new. I half expected the moisture in the air to have rendered the torches useless, but Tarzog hadn't skimped when it came to his temple. The black, tarry goo coating the end of the torch caught on the first spark.

I toyed with grabbing the torch that would trigger the trap, but decided against it. Even assuming dust and insects hadn't clogged the nozzles, the oil spray had only a six foot radius. There was a good chance one or both of my companions would survive.

And if truth be told, I didn't want to see Jenny burn. Tarzog had tested the trap on his tailor, who had been caught spying. I could still hear his screams, as clear as the sound of my own footsteps, and the smell would follow me to my grave. Beyond my grave, actually. Why couldn't death have taken *that* memory? I didn't think I could inflict such an end on this little girl.

Besides, there was a better way. A quicker way that would not only take Jenny and Zariel with me, but would destroy this accursed temple as well.

So I did as I had been commanded. I led them on hands and knees through the hall of gods, as the stone statues of long-forgotten deities fired poisoned darts from their eyes, mouths, and in one particularly disturbing case, from his penis. I tiptoed around the edge of the spiked pit with the crushing walls, though not without a moment of regret. I had worked hard to design the system of weights and wheels that forced the walls inward, and I would have liked to know if it still worked after so much time in the humidity of the jungle.

The plan was identical to the temple I had designed, all except that rotted tree at the entrance. I wondered if Tarzog had used a bit of necromancy to keep it decaying yet strong all these years.

"How much farther?" Jenny asked. She was chewing her thumbnail again.

I pushed open a door, ignoring the trapped knob on the right. This had been one of Tarzog's favorites. The hinges were hidden on the same side as the knob, and the door didn't even latch. Friction and a tight frame held it in place. Anyone who bumped the knob would take a poisoned needle to the hand. Actually turning the thing would trigger a spray of acid from the floor.

"We're here," I said, stepping inside.

One advantage to being dead: my body didn't react with the same throat-constricting terror I remembered from my last time in this room, back in the other temple. Or maybe my time with Jenny and Zariel had numbed me to fear. The walls bulged inward, carved to resemble barbed scales on the coils of an enormous snake. Arcane symbols spiraled around the floor and ceiling both.

"It's beautiful," Jenny said. She took my torch and ran to the closest wall to study the carvings worked into the snake's body. In one, dead warriors lay scattered before a giant serpent who had reared back with a horse and rider in its jaws.

The Serpent God was one ugly snake. Curved horns like scimitars grew in twin rows behind the eyes. In addition to the huge fangs, smaller teeth lined the jaws, each one dripping with venom.

"Look at this, Zariel," Jenny said, moving farther along the wall. "Here he's collecting his sacrifice." The snake's coils circled a pit of terrified old men, women, and children.

"Forget the pictures," Zariel snapped. "Armand's trackers are probably making their way through the jungle even now."

Jenny stuck out her tongue, then squatted down,

holding her torch close to the floor to read the symbols.

I turned my attention to the back of the room, where a thick book lay open on a raised dais. This was perhaps Tarzog's most brilliant idea. If his enemies had penetrated this far, it would mean Tarzog himself had fallen. Vindictive bastard that he was, Tarzog planted the book here to destroy those enemies.

The pages were blank, but in order to discover that, you had to set foot on that dais. Any weight of more than ten pounds would trigger a collapse of the entire temple.

I stepped soundlessly toward the book. No amount of magic or power could save them. With Jenny dead, I would be back with my wife and my children. Perhaps we would all rest a bit easier, knowing—

"Stop that," Jenny said without looking up.

My body froze in mid-step. Unable to move, I toppled forward. My wrist hit the floor first, hard enough that I could hear bone snap. I ended up on my side, staring helplessly at Jenny as she turned around.

"I'm sorry," she said. "I don't know what Daddy did to trap this room, but I can't let you get to it."

"How?" It was all I could do to force the word past my dead lips.

Jenny shrugged. "Daddy killed you. He killed your family. I knew you'd try to get me in the end. That's what I'd do."

"Clever, isn't she?" asked Zariel. Something in

her voice warned me an instant before she struck, but I couldn't have stopped her even if I wanted to. She waved her hand, and Jenny began to scream. Black fire danced over Jenny's skin. She flopped on the floor like a dying trout.

"Such a clever girl," Zariel repeated as she circled Jenny's body. "Marked by the Serpent God, heir to the power of Tarzog the Black."

Zariel snapped her fingers, and Jenny went still. She wasn't dead. She couldn't be, or else the magic keeping me in this pseudo living state would have failed. Shadowy flames continued to burn, though Jenny's clothes and skin were unharmed. Zariel's fire fed on something deeper than flesh.

"For two years I've dragged this whelp from one refuge to another," Zariel said, her voice growing louder with each word. "Two years of living like a common thief. Two years of her whining and arguing, her stubborn refusal to follow even the simplest instructions."

She turned to me, her eyes wide. For a moment, I thought she was going to destroy me, but she clasped her hands and said, "That little brat pissed her bedroll every night for six months after her father died. *Six months!*"

Zariel pulled the vial of blood from her pocket. "Well, little godling, Anhak Ghudir said you would be the one to lure Rhynoth from his rest, but the prophecies never said who would command him." She bit the stopper from the vial, spat it to one side, and swallowed the contents.

Grabbing Jenny by the hair, she dragged the motionless girl to the center of the room. Jenny's eyes were open and alert. She could see everything that was happening, just like me.

A part of me took some perverse joy at seeing her own torments turned back upon her. I might have failed, but Tarzog's line would still end.

Zariel began to chant. "She is here, great one. Descendant of your own children, heir to the powers of the first serpent." The rest was in another tongue, full of hacking, angry syllables.

At first, I didn't realize when Zariel's chanting changed to genuine coughs. Only when she staggered back a step did I realize something was wrong. One hand clawed her throat. Blood dripped from her left nostril.

The shadowy flames on Jenny's body flickered and died. Jenny's arms were shaky as she struggled to sit up. Hugging her knees to her chest, she whispered, "That hurt."

Zariel dropped to her knees. Her expression changed from panic to anger, and she raised one hand, but when she tried to speak, only a pained croak emerged.

Jenny crawled over and kicked her in the stomach.

"How?" Zariel asked, her voice hoarse.

Jenny rolled her eyes. "I swiped the blood a week ago. Daddy always told me the only henchman you could ever really trust was one who was already dead." She pulled a heavily padded tube from inside her dress. "This is the virgin blood. *You* drank a blend of four different sea snake venoms, mixed in bat blood."

She stood up, her knees still shaking slightly. With her free hand, she took the torch from Zariel, then kicked her again. The effort nearly made her fall back.

"You wanted to know why him?" Jenny whispered, pointing to me. "Because he went to stay with his family in the dungeons every night. My daddy would have let him stay in the huts with the other workers, but he refused. *He* never complained about the smell. *He* didn't tell his son to stop whining. When his boy fouled himself during the night, *he* didn't force him to sleep in his own stink!"

She ended her tirade with one last kick, then turned to me. "I used to sneak down to the dungeons to watch Daddy torture traitors. One night I saw you coming, so I followed you."

She unwrapped the vial of blood as she talked. "I'll let you die, if that's what you want. Or you can come with me." She swallowed the blood, then smiled. "I'll even let you ride the Serpent God with me. But I am going to summon Rhynoth. Armand and his men are going to die. I'm going to conquer this land, whether you come with me or not."

She glanced back at Zariel, who had stopped moving. "Who knows," she said. "Maybe you'll help me mend my evil ways." The wicked grin on her face told me how likely *that* was. "You might even get a chance to kill me."

I doubted it. Look at how efficiently she had outsmarted and disposed of Zariel. Jenny was truly her father's daughter. Even more dangerous than Tarzog the Black. After all, Tarzog had failed.

On the other hand, what purpose would my second death serve? I couldn't bring my family back. I couldn't stop Jenny. The only possible blessing I would gain from death was my own peace.

The floor began to shake as Jenny chanted the same words Zariel had. Rhynoth had awakened from his millennial slumber, and he would be here soon.

Jenny's shoulders slumped as she finished the incantation. She began to chew her thumbnail again, wincing as the nail tore free and began to bleed.

"I'll understand if you don't want to come," she said, never looking at me.

I closed my eyes and made my choice.

Prince Armand brought an army. Perhaps he knew what he was about to face. I doubted it would save him, but who knew?

All I knew was that when Jenny rode the Serpent God, her hands clinging to the horns as her half-cape flapped behind her, she didn't look like an evil sorceress. She looked like a little girl, smiling and laughing as she prepared to wipe out an entire land. And seeing that almost made me feel alive again.

GORDIE CULLIGAN VS. DR. LONGBEACH & THE HVAC OF DOOM

J. Steven York

I tell you, when I answered that ad in the back of *Popular Mechanics* long ago, I didn't know what I was getting myself into. Sure, I expected steady work, good pay, excellent benefits, and the respect and admiration of my friends and family. That goes without saying.

But I never expected the intrigue, the danger, the *adventure*!

My name is Gordie Culligan, and I'm the man from HVAC. That's **H**eating, **V**entilation and **A**ir-Conditioning to you. God, I love the smell of a fried starter-capacitor in morning!

It was a day like any other day in the Los Angeles basin, but I felt something in the air. Possibly it was the unusual number of ominous, glowing, saucer-shaped clouds moving against the wind, or the swarms of atomic robot bats flapping their way east over Burbank, or the unusual number of electric dirigibles, blue arcs of lighting crackling between their protruding electrodes, that circled over the San Diego freeway. Maybe it was just the greenish tinge to the smog. But I knew something was up.

Now sure, I know if you don't live in L.A., you'd consider any one of those things cause for alarm, but that's why you live where you live, and I live in the greatest city in the world.

Sure, it was a little startling at first, but this is L.A., baby! You live here for a while, you see things like this every day, and nothing ever, *ever* comes of it, you just start to take it for granted. Sure, there are giant robots in Tarzana and giant beetles in Griffith Park, but when you've had Conan for a governor, nothing is that strange anymore.

By now, you're probably saying, "Gordie, this is all very interesting and all, but what about the air-conditioning?" See it all ties in, and until recently, I didn't know that. You see all those crazy things, and you take it for granted that *nothing ever happens*. By you know *why* nothing ever happens?

Because of guys like me, that's why. HVAC saves the world, baby! That's what this town is about!

So anyway, it was a routine call, a 318: "unexplained noise from blower." I checked out the van and picked up Rudy, the apprentice the union had sent over. He was standing on the curb outside the break-room door, two coffee cups in his hands and a bagel bag under his arm.

He hopped in and put the cups in the holders, then pulled out a bagel for me. I looked at it skeptically through the plastic wrap.

Rudy stared at me, eyes wide, a look of concern on his squarish, freckled, face. "Sprouts and cream cheese, like you asked."

I held it back toward him. "What are those seeds on the bagel, Rudy?"

"They're seeds," he said. "All seeds look alike to me, dude."

"Your seed-blindness is probably why they kicked you out of Fresno, Rudy. Those are *sesame* seeds. I specifically asked for poppy."

He kind of cringed back toward the door of the van and looked like a whipped puppy. I immediately felt bad. They hadn't kicked Rudy out of Fresno, but that was where he was from. I think maybe he literally fell off a turnip truck. But somebody at the union must have felt sorry for him, or more likely, he had a uncle with seniority and a small wad of cash. In any case, he'd been taken in as an HVAC apprentice (service/install) junior grade with the Brotherhood of Subsystem Service Employees, and ended up with me.

Unlike a lot of guys, I don't mind an apprentice. An extra set of hands comes in useful sometimes, you can send them into those dirty ducts and crawlspaces, and they give the customer someone to yell at while you sneak off and get the job done uninterrupted. Based on our two weeks together, I'd decided that Rudy wasn't a bad kid, if a little green. That didn't keep me from riding his butt though.

I peeled back the plastic, took a bite of the bagel, turned up a Barenaked Ladies CD, and put the van into drive. Rudy seemed to relax, and I had to admit that, despite my black sense of foreboding, I was in a generally good mood too. The dispatch was to Long Beach, and that meant at least forty minutes on the freeway, which, since I was paid from the moment I left the shop, was free money.

The traffic was bad (hey, it's L.A.!) and it took closer to an hour. Fine by me. I consulted the GPS screen and we threaded our way into an industrial section. As I drove, Rudy's attention was drawn to something off in the distance. As we got nearer to the blinking red dot on the computer map, Rudy's head tilted farther and farther back. I was too busy driving to figure out what he was looking at.

Finally, he asked, "Has there always been a volcano down here?"

I blinked in surprise and looked up from the SUV in front of me long enough to see the huge, smoking crater rising above the warehouses to our right, then glanced down at the map. "Nah," I said, "can't be." But it sure looked like our air-conditioning service call was to an active volcano. "This is your lucky day," I said. "I have the feeling this is going to be some heavy-BTU machinery we're working on today."

We zigged and zagged past small factories, warehouses, refineries, and auto-wrecking yards, and the cone just kept getting bigger and bigger.

"Did you ever see that movie," said Rudy, "with Tommy Lee Jones?"

I nodded. "*Volcano,* costarring Anne Heche," I said. I'm kind of a movie buff, but then everyone in L.A. is. "Around 1997 or so. Sucked, but Tommy Lee is terrific in everything. Except *Batman Forever,* of course." I saw where he was going though. "Don't worry, kid. I've got the feeling this is a whole different scenario."

We drove up to the base of the volcano, which on closer inspection seemed to be made out of painted concrete sprayed over chicken wire. A big gas meter inside a chain-link enclosure suggested the source of the pyrotechnics at the top. I spotted a sign marked SERVICE ENTRANCE, with an arrow, and followed it around the base of the volcano to a kind of cave.

We drove inside to find a fairly standard looking loading dock with two roll-up delivery doors and a small man door to the right. I noticed a Lotus Elise, going 120 sitting still, parked incongruously in front of the loading dock. I shook my head. "Doesn't that fool know this is *Long Beach*? It's a wonder that thing isn't stripped down to the frame already." I shrugged again and parked the truck.

I sent Rudy up to the man-door on recon, and unloaded our gear from the back of the truck.

Rudy came back a minute later with a pink Post-it note in his hand. It read:

Dear AC People,
  Gone to Radio Shack for some diodes.

Gave minions the day off. Back in an hour. Please let yourself in through the crater (outside, trail to left).

   Dr. Longbeach

I glanced at the work order. Sure enough, Dr. M. D. Longbeach was the customer name.

` It looked like a long hike from the truck, so we went loaded for bear: toolbox, filter masks, a tank of R134a refrigerant (ozone friendly, if used as directed), a roll of trim-to-fit filter material, and *two* rolls of duct tape.

We quickly found the path, which was really more of a series of switchback ramps, disguised from view below by Styrofoam rocks and plastic plants. I work out three times a week, but I was still out of breath by the time we lugged all our gear to the top.

When we reached the lip of the crater we dropped our stuff and took a breather. There was a breeze off the harbor to the west. It had a taint of refinery stink, but it was at least cool. I took the time to size up what was waiting for us below, while Rudy admired the view.

"You can see the *Queen Mary* from here," he said. Then he squinted and frowned. "Dude! Is that a giant octopus climbing the smokestacks?"

"Ignore the giant octopus, kid. That's somebody else's problem. We've got a volcano with a broken AC to fix."

From this angle, looking past the ring of burners and smoke generators, it was obvious that the vol-

cano was both fake and hollow. A translucent fi-
berglass roof covered the opening, and a large
panel in the center of the roof was rolled back to
reveal a huge silo in the middle.

Rudy tore himself away from the view and
turned to look down into the open hatchway, which
was probably big enough to fly a small helicopter
through. Or launch a missile, which, judging from
the rounded nose cone visible just below, was more
likely its purpose.

Rudy's eyes widened. "Dude, is that a—"

I nodded. "Yeah, kid, it is."

"A *water heater*!"

I cringed. "No, doofus, it is *not* a water heater.
Don't you know a missile when you see one?"

"Not really."

"Nor a water heater either, I guess. You've got
a lot to learn, apprentice."

"Yeah, I guess." He stared at the missile with
growing concern. "Dude, I was happier when it was
a water heater. Should we be worried about this?"

"About what?"

"It's a *missile,* dude!"

I looked up. "Is it aimed at you? Looks like it's
aimed at the sky to me. Probably another evil plot
to destroy the moon. We had three last year in
L.A. County that I know of."

"*The moon?* Seriously? What happened?"

I shrugged. "Moon's still there, isn't it? Somebody stopped them, I guess."

"Who?"

I shrugged. "You're not an apprentice to NASA,

Rudy, you're an apprentice to BOSSE." I was careful to pronounce it "boss," the *e* is silent. Rudy kept calling the union "Bossy," and the shop stewards didn't take kindly to that.

I spotted a roof stair and a line of heavy-duty compressor units twenty yards around the crater to our right. "Come on, we've got a noisy blower to fix." We reached the stairs and I tried the knob. I'd been secretly hoping it was locked, as we'd then have to wait, with the meter running, for the customer to return. But it turned freely, and as I opened the door, I noticed that, strangely enough, the lock had been neatly melted out of the middle. "Something's not quite right here, kid. Keep an eye open."

He looked at me. "Dude, we're going into a fake volcano with a missile in the middle, and you say it's not quite right? Are you like having a Homer moment or something?"

"Homer moment?"

"You know: *D'oh!*"

I frowned at him as I headed down the stairwell. "Do not ever say 'D'oh' to your designated union journeyperson. There's almost certainly a regulation against it, and if not, I just made one up."

I turned my attention to a series of heavily insulated coolant pipes running down the wall from the compressors above. Following them would lead us to the evaporator coils and the blower. We went down three floors to find a giant octopus of another kind, a huge central air-conditioning unit from which large metal ducts snaked off in all directions.

As we stepped closer, we could hear the fan rumbling with an unhealthy, scraping noise just audible under the rumble.

I located the access hatch on the side, but found it padlocked. I held the lock in my hand and sighed. Unlike a locked roof door, this was no real excuse on this kind of system. "We'll go in through the ducts," I said.

Rudy looked surprised. "Dude?"

I nodded up toward the metal tentacles spreading out in all directions. "The ducts. Look at the size of them. We'll find a grate, climb in, and walk back to the central unit. Look at the size of those things! We'll hardly have to duck."

By now, it was becoming clear to me that we were in some kind of *lair*. Though I hadn't done much myself, mechanicals guys—HVAC, plumbing, electricians—they love lair work. Lots of mechanicals on a big scale, and price is usually no object. Where these guys get their money, I'll never know, but they aren't afraid to spend it. And for HVAC guys, a special treat: big ducts. Really big ducts. With great big registers over every secret filing cabinet, master strategy table, supercomputer, and self-destruct console.

Or so I'm told. Me, mostly I do industrial parks, big-box retail, and office buildings, so this was kind of new to me. Mostly I was going on union-picnic shop talk and secondhand info. But I couldn't let on to the apprentice. I kept my chin up and acted like I did this every day.

We walked down a stark corridor lined with

numbered doors. Maybe it was an evil lair of some kind, but except for some roof support girders and other architectural details seemingly borrowed from *Forbidden Planet* (1965, Walter Pidgeon, Anne Francis, and pre-*Naked Gun* Leslie Neilsen) it could have been a ministorage based on appearances.

Never mind that. I quickly found what I was looking for—a large, conveniently accessible air register. I hooked my fingers around the edge, and it easily popped open without the need to remove any screws. From what I'd heard around the union hall, conveniently opening registers were popular lair-specific features. I tossed my tools inside and climbed up, noticing as I did that it was far easier to see *out* through the register than *in* from the outside.

Rudy climbed in behind me, dragging the heavy tank of refrigerant, and closed the register after us.

I considered unclipping the flashlight that I carried on my belt, but it was surprisingly well lit inside the ducts. I stuck my index finger in my mouth to wet it, and held it up into the air flow. "This way," I said, heading "upstream." I noticed, as we walked, that these were top-quality ducts, heavy metal. We were able to move silently. None of that thin, galvanized sheet metal that thumps like a kid's tin drum every time you shift your weight. "Quality all the way," I said.

We followed a series of twists and turns past many other registers. Occasionally I would stop to look out into empty control rooms bristling with blinking lights, workshops equipped with menacing looking industrial robots, labs filled with colorful, bubbling beakers, and a room with the biggest damned hot tub I've ever seen (and when you're from L.A., that's saying something).

"Dude!" Rudy was really impressed with the hot tub.

Finally the rumbling of the blower started to get louder, and it felt as though we were walking into a stiff wind. Ahead, I could see the filter housing. We were quite close to the condenser coils and the blower, but we needed to get past the filter first.

I found the latches and opened the housing. As I did, a number of oddly shaped white objects clattered out onto the heavy metal floor of the duct.

Rudy bent down and picked up what looked to be a long, white bone. He grinned and waved it above his head. "Did you see that space-monkey movie?"

I frowned at him. "*Planet of the Apes* was a 'space-monkey' movie. You're thinking of *2001: A Space Odyssey*. I liked *Dr. Strangelove* better." I frowned again, and leaned closer to examine the bone, nearly getting my head conked in the process. "I think that's a human femur," I said.

Rudy went white as the bone, and dropped it like it had suddenly burned his hand. "Dude!"

I bent down and picked up the bone. The surface was bleached white and slightly pitted, but it didn't look old. "I've seen this before," I said. "Back in '99, some guy in North Hollywood tried to soup up his window AC, and accidentally turned it into a death ray."

"Dude, a death ray?"

"There are some things non-union man was not meant to meddle with."

"So, you're saying this air conditioner is a death ray?" The implications suddenly hit him, and he quickly backed away from the filter housing.

"That's not what I'm saying at all. Just that a death ray could be involved." I kneeled down and examined the other bones: scattered vertebra, a shoulder blade, several ribs, a disarticulated jaw, and a *wristwatch*. I reached down and picked it up. Rolex. Top of the line.

As I examined it, I accidentally pressed a stud on the side of the case and a needle-fine red beam shot out and heated a spot on the metal wall to incandescence before I could turn it off.

Seeing the beam, Rudy screamed like a school-girl and threw himself into a wall so hard that I thought he'd knock himself unconscious.

"Calm down," I said. "Don't you know the difference between a death ray and a laser?"

Rudy blinked in confusion. "No."

"Well, this watch has some kind of cutting laser in it. I think this is what melted the lock outside." I thought of the abandoned Lotus downstairs, and it all started to make some kind of sense. I opened the filter housing all the way, and the rest of the skeleton appeared to be there, stuck in the fuzzy filter material.

Rudy stared at the bones, panic growing in his

eyes. "Dude, there's a dead guy in the HEPA filter! We should get out of here!"

"Technically," I said, "this isn't a HEPA filter at all." I was starting to feel intrigued. "Anyway, I want to find out what happened here, and we've still got a blower to fix." I pulled out the filter frame to reveal a plenum chamber behind. Ahead, I could see the condenser coils, curled like intestines, dripping condensation.

I started to climb through the opening. I looked to see Rudy just standing there, shivering, but from fear or proximity to the condenser, I couldn't be sure. "Buck up! This is what you signed up for. Be a man!"

Rudy looked at me and nodded weakly. Slowly, he climbed through after me, still lugging the tank. We slipped past the condenser coils and I could see the huge fan spinning ahead. The scraping noise was very loud now. On the wall of the chamber to our right, I could see an electrical box with a handle on the side. I pulled it down.

There was a loud clack of relays opening, and the motor fell silent, the fan spinning down, and with it, the scraping noise quieted. The big fan slowed until the cruciform shape of the individual blades resolved out of the shimmering disk, and it slowed to a halt. I stepped up and examined one of the blades, its sharp, leading edge buried in the top of a skull.

With some effort, I pulled the skull free of the blade and held it up to Rudy. He was turning white again.

"Well," I said, "there's our noise."

"Good," said Rudy. "Dude, can we go back to the shop now?"

I looked past the fan, where a long return air duct stretched off into the distance. "Not yet," I said. "I want to know what happened here."

"Do we have to?"

"Dude," I said, "we do."

I stepped carefully past the blades of the fan and into the duct beyond. In doing so, I must have triggered some kind of motion detector. The air in front of me shimmered and glowed, forming the life-size translucent image of a short, slope-shouldered, bald man with a goatee and sci-fi looking wraparound sunglasses. The glowing image began to speak.

"Greetings, my British friend. I'm sure you think yourself quite clever, sneaking in this way, but I've prepared for *any* eventuality. You are about to become the first test subject for my—" He paused for dramatic effect, a bit too long in my opinion. *"—death ray!"*

Then he began to laugh maniacally. As he did, I saw a panel in the side of the duct begin to slide up. Something inside began to move.

I dropped my toolbox and reached back to snatch the tank from Rudy. I pulled out the filler hose and twisted the valve just as the ugly black muzzle of the death ray began to emerge from its hidden recess behind the door. Clouds of refrigerant shot out, enveloping the sinister device.

I kept the stream concentrated on the muzzle as

it locked into position and began to swivel toward us. The flow sputtered and died as the tank emptied.

The apprentice yelped in fear.

I quickly hoisted the tank over my head and slammed it down on the death ray. The super cooled metal shattered like glass.

I dropped the empty tank and turned back to Rudy, a smug smile on my lips. "You see! If you learn nothing else today, learn this: This is a central air-conditioning system. We are HVAC men! This is *our* turf, and we have advantage here. You shouldn't be afraid. Doctor what's-his-face should be afraid of us! *Fear our skills!*"

Rudy slowly drew himself up straight, the fear draining from his features.

I patted him on the shoulder. "We can do this!"

Rudy nodded. "Yeah. We can do this." Then a moment of doubt. "Uh, what is it we're doing?"

"Whatever Mr. Rolex back in the filer was looking for, it's at the end of this return duct. I say we go check it out."

More hesitation. "But—*why*?"

I gestured at the shattered death ray. "Look at this! It's an *unauthorized modification*. This Long-beach character, he's *voided his warranty,* and that's not something we take sitting down. Are you with me?"

Rudy nodded weakly. "But what if there are more death traps?"

I grinned, drunk on my own adrenaline. "Oh," I said, "there *will* be!"

I was right, too. We'd traveled maybe twenty yards when I spotted a small vent inside of the duct (looking out onto nothing) and a bunch of dead cockroaches littering the floor. "Breather masks," I said with alarm, grabbing my mask from the pouch on my belt even as I heard a hissing sound.

I slid the mask over my face, pulled the straps tight to form a seal, and then helped Rudy, who was still fumbling with his.

I had just pulled the last strap tight when the air before us shimmered. The phantom doctor grinned at an empty spot in space to my left, confirming what I'd already suspected, that the holograms were recorded. "Well, my British friend, you've cheated death once, but you won't a second time! Is it getting hard to breathe? Well, by now, you've already sucked in a fatal dose of my—" Again with the pregnant pause. "—nerve mist! Now you can spend your last moments contemplating your failure to stop my world-destroying missile from launching!" More maniacal laughter.

"Man," I said, my voice muffled by my mask, "that gets old quick." I signaled Rudy to follow me. After we'd traveled a few yards, there was a relay click somewhere behind us, and the big fan began to spin again, sucking away the clouds of poison mist.

I turned to watch them go. "Probably a good thing he gave the minions the day off," I said, "or he'd be gassing them right about now." I pulled off my mask and gave Rudy a knowing look. "Just goes to show, you shouldn't tamper with things you don't understand."

I turned and looked up the duct. It dead-ended twenty yards ahead at a single, man-size air register. That, undoubtedly, was our goal. "Destroying the world," I said, "is bad for business. We've got to stop this guy's plan, and *oh, yes,* we *are* going to bill him for the time!"

I stepped boldly forward, but as I did, I noticed yet another grating in the duct wall, from which, even over the sound of the fan, an ominous buzzing could be heard.

Hesitating not at all, I reached for the roll of filter material and slapped it over the grating, holding it in place with my outspread hands. The buzzing within grew loud and angry, and I heard the thumping of something hitting the back of the filter material, like popcorn in a popper.

There was a glow just visible at the corner of my eye, and I knew our holographic friend was back. "Well, my friend, I'm very impressed, but now taste the bitter sting of my—"

I growled. *"Oh, get the hell on with it, will ya?"*

"—mutant killer bees!"

I looked at the filter material just in front of my face, and saw many small somethings poking through. It took me a moment to realize that I was seeing hundreds of stingers poking through the material.

"Duct tape," I yelled to Rudy. "Give me duct tape! It's the only thing that can save us now!"

It was in that moment that Rudy seemed to come

into his own. All fear, all hesitation vanished from his face. He pulled a roll of duct tape free of his belt and pulled out a long strip in the same motion, ripping it off with his teeth.

He slapped the strip along the top of the filter material, then went back for more tape.

Behind the filter, the bees were buzzing, but it was Dr. Longbeach who droned on. "As you writhe in venom-induced agony, eyes swollen shut, airway tightening down until you choke, know that you've failed, and that my missile will soon disperse its cloud of self-replicating nanobots, converting the entire crust of the planet into—"

Rudy slapped more tape across the bottom of the filter. I was able to pull my hands free and reach for my own roll of tape. But I took a moment to glare at the hologram. *"Get on with it!"*

"—peanut butter! Oh, yes! All shall know the deadly, sticky-sweet touch of—"

I kept slapping tap over the filter, entombing the deadly insects. "Dr. Scholl's? Dr. Pepper? Dr. Spock?"

"—Dr. Longbeach!"

"Never would have guessed." I slapped the last strip of tape in place, and ran for the vent, Rudy hot on my heels.

I popped open the grate and stepped into a glass-walled control room overlooking the missile silo. Far below us, clouds of rocket propellant vented from its tanks, eerily like the refrigerant I'd used earlier. Above us, a fluorescent light flickered and buzzed, adding a disturbing surreality to the scene.

I looked quickly around the room. There were the usual consoles, covered with banks of unmarked, ever-flashing, and incomprehensible lights. But in the center of it all, there was one thing that I could understand, a big, red digital readout counting down toward zero.

59 . . . 58 . . . 57 . . .

And it was then, in one moment of horrible realization, I understood the gravity of our situation. Like Alice Through the Looking Glass (the 1974 TV version, with Phyllis Diller as the White Queen and Mr. T as the voice of the Jabberwock, was surreal even by the standards of Wonderland) we had stepped out of the ductwork. We were out of our element, and suddenly I felt lost.

"We've got to stop it," said Rudy.

"Tell me something I don't know."

"*Do* something!"

"Do what? I don't know anything about rocket control systems."

44 . . . 43 . . . 42 . . . 41 . . .

Rudy stepped toward the console, his hands hovering over the timer mechanism. Impulsively he reached down and pried open a panel below it, exposing a rat's nest of colored wire. He stared at it desperately. "Do something."

"I can't," I answered miserably. "I don't know how."

31 . . . 30 . . . 29 . . .

Rudy gazed at the wires. "Look, just—Just think of it as a big thermostat! A thermostat that counts seconds instead of degrees!"

I looked a him, incredulous. "That's stupid!"

"So to stop the furnace—the rocket—from going off, we need to make the temperature go down instead of up!"

"You're saying we need to reverse time?"

Rudy frowned. "That doesn't work, does it?"

"We're doomed."

23 . . . 22 . . . 21 . . .

"Look," he said, "what do they do in the movies?"

I reached for my tool belt and took out a pair of diagonal cutters. "They cut a wire. But *which* wire?" I sighed, thinking of all the countless red, digital timers I had seen in various movies. "It's usually the red wire or the blue wire."

"Unless," said Rudy, "it's the white wire or the black wire."

I groaned. He was right. The timer-readout was always standard, but the wires were always different.

15 . . . 14 . . . 13 . . .

Behind me, I heard a door creak open, but there was no time to wonder who it was.

"Just cut one," begged Rudy, "any one!"

The timer flashed. Sweat ran down into my eyes. That flickering light made my head hurt.

Cut a wire! But which one?

4 . . . 3 . . . 2 . . .

I felt someone lean over my shoulder.

A hand sheathed in a black rubber glove slipped past me, holding something.

A knife blade glittered in the flickering light.

The blade slipped into the nest of wires and smoothly plucked one out, pulling it tight and cutting it with a snap . . .

1 . . .

1 . . .

1 . . .

I sagged against the console, the diagonal cutters slipping from my cramped fingers.

Rudy jumped into the air, letting out a victory whoop. "Dudes!"

Dudes? I turned to look at our mysterious rescuer.

He stood, a titan in gray coveralls and a baseball cap. He hoisted up his tool belt, sniffed, and rubbed his bushy mustache with his index finger.

"Who," I said, "are you?"

He folded his pocketknife and slipped it back into a holster on his belt. "I'm the electrician," he said. "Somebody called about a busted fluorescent."

Dr. Longbeach appeared at the door, a black plastic Radio Shack bag clutched in his hand, and surveyed the scene. "Oh, thank God you're here. I was afraid this time I was actually going to get away with it." He shuddered. "*Peanut butter.* Eeew."

Okay, so the men from HVAC didn't save the world.

Not that time, anyway.

But we helped.

"Dude," said Rudy, looking at the electrician in admiration.

"Hey," I said to the kid, "you're *my* apprentice!" I turned to address the stranger as an equal. "You have skills, my friend, as do we. We should team up."

And that, as you've surely guessed by now, is how the Justice League of Contractors was born.

THE SINS OF THE SONS

Fiona Patton

The city of Riamo was neither so large nor so grand as the five other city-states that graced the Ardechi River. Its marble palazzos were small and compact as were its cathedral and its single monastery. Its market piazzas were neat and well laid out and its harbor sturdily constructed. It was known for the skill of its weavers and its dyers and the guilds that oversaw these industries were both prosperous and progressive. While not large enough to boast a necropolis like its great neighbor Cerchicava, it nonetheless housed five cemeteries within its ancient walls, one each for the nobility, the merchant class, the military, the Church, the trades, and the poor. Even its heretics' graveyard, built outside the western wall, was tidy, well-organized, and decently protected by a complement of city guards who took their duty seriously. The necromantic trade, so rife along the Ardechi, had never gained much of a foothold in westernmost Riamo. A fact that both the Church and the governing council were justly proud of.

Standing on the ducal Palazzo de Gagio's fine marble terrace, Luca Orcicci stared out across the river, his cold, blue eyes carefully hooded. Known as Luca Preto, a reserved foreign aristocrat with a modest fortune, he had lived in Riamo for nearly twenty years, ever since his master, Lord Montefero de Sepori, the premier Death Mage in Cerchicava, had sent him here to gain a very substantial foothold for the necromantic trade. Whatever the Church and the governing council might like to believe, far more of its citizens were damned then they would ever have imagined.

Turning his head slightly, he listened as the cream of Riamo's nobility fluttered about the palazzo's main audience hall like so many agitated geese. The Duc Johanni Gagio had been murdered in neighboring Pisario, the second largest and singlemost aggressive city-state to the east. The duc of Pisario, Cosimo Talicozzo, had immediately closed the harbors, arresting anyone even remotely suspicious while denouncing the act as loudly as possible. The public belief was that the deed had been committed by the fabled Huntsman, a mysterious crossbow-wielding assassin of consummate skill who had terrorized both Cerchicava and Pisario in the last year. But the older members of Riamo's court held to a more insidious conviction, that Talicozzo himself had been behind the murder.

It was not so long ago that Pisario had cast a covetous eye along the entire length of the Ardechi River, going so far as to wage full-out war against Cerchicava itself. Riamo could easily be next.

That no one had even whispered the suspicion that the necromantic trade might be involved struck Luca as both amusing and irritating. But such was the way in Riamo; egotistical, political squabbling with no clear understanding of the real clandestine powers that flowed beneath their lives like an underground river. It was a belief that Luca did his best to promote but lately he was beginning to wish that the complacent nobility and wealthy merchants of Riamo might, just for once, come face-to-face with reality. The tedium of security was beginning to make him restless. No doubt that was why the Huntsman had chosen Gagio in the first place. He always did have the uncanny ability to read Luca's mind.

The thought transformed his expression from one of contempt to consideration as he made his way inside. He was not fond of crowds, palazzos, or the nobility; the first clouded your thinking, the second hampered your vision and the third . . . He caught sight of Piero Bruni, his manservant, standing patiently in the wings by the great double doors and nodded his head to indicate that they would be leaving shortly. The third would betray you faster than your heart could stop beating beneath a cutter's knife. But unfortunately all were necessary evils at the moment. He would have to remember to thank the Huntsman when he finally returned home. Schooling his expression, he headed for the knot of people standing beside the ducal throne.

The Bishop of San Salvadore had a firm grip on Johanni's son, Eugene's, attention—no doubt lecturing the new duc to do nothing either rash or impolitic regarding Pisario—when Luca approached. Resisting the urge to bare his teeth at the bishop, Luca gave the young potentate a sympathetic bow before moving on with a modicum of satisfaction. Condolences having been given, he was now free to retire before the desire to see the churchman laid out on his dissection table got the better of him.

At the door, he paused a moment to speak with Dante Corsini, a long-distance trader of powerful influence in legitimate as well as illegitimate affairs. Although untainted by the necromantic trade, he was nonetheless deeply involved in all other aspects of the city's unlawful activities. The two men treated each other with a guarded respect, so when Luca gave the other man a formal nod of greeting, Dante caught up a glass of wine from a passing servant and raised it in response.

"A bad business this, Preto," he stated before the man had moved out of earshot. "Terrible for trade with Pisario."

Luca frowned at him. Most of the wealthy merchants in Riamo treated their servants as if they were blind, deaf, and mute, but generally Corsini was not so careless; such thinking had led too many men of both their acquaintances to the gallows. All of Luca's servants were members of the trade and carried binding spells so strong that their very skulls would explode if they even considered betraying him, but Corsini did not have that luxury. No matter how powerful a Court Mage he was reputed to be, only the Death Mages were capable of such precautions. The servant who had brought him his drink also carried Luca's binding spell, but Corsini could not have known that when he spoke. Outraged grief or stunned disbelief were the only safe reactions at this time and Luca said as much with a dark glance at the other man.

Corsini dismissed his concern with a wave of his hand. As he lifted the glass to his lips, Luca saw the tiny flash of a discreet, blue purity spell scatter throughout the wine and nodded inwardly. At least Corsini wasn't completely stupid. It paid to be careful, even in pedantic, law-abiding Riamo.

"I wonder if they'll linger over the funeral arrangements now that the cold weather's here," he mused, steering the conversation to a slightly less dangerous topic.

"I heard the bishop dispatched his own people to Pisario straightaway to prepare the body," Corsini answered. "And that old fart, First Minister Poggeso, sent messages out to the five cities just as swiftly. Ducal parties mean ducal security but it also means increased business opportunities." He sipped his wine thoughtfully. "I wonder if Eugene will be replacing Poggeso now," he added with a speculative expression.

Luca shrugged. "I shouldn't think he'd make any

changes until after the funeral, but if you have a candidate in mind you should bring it to his attention as soon as possible—before too many other people offer their own choices."

As one, they both glanced over to where the bishop was still monopolizing the duc's company.

"He'll be expected to take a wife now, too," Corsini noted sourly. "And you can be certain her family will be swift to exert their own influence."

"The bishop will likely come to that subject soon enough. He has a niece of marriageable age."

Corsini grunted. "So have I, but my sister married a scheming little viper and I've no intention of increasing his power base. Pity you and I didn't think to have daughters. That might have been *our* influence."

"It was an oversight, yes," Luca agreed dryly.

Corsini gave him a sly glance. "How are your sons, by the way?"

"They're well. Alesandro's finally taken over his late father's business now that the Goldsmith's Guild has accepted his membership."

"He cast the communion goblets for Santa Lucia's, did he not?"

"He did."

"He's a fine craftsman. No doubt that little shop of his will do well for him. There are plenty of opportunities in Riamo for a young man with ambition, if he knows where to look for them. His mother would be proud."

"I agree."

"And Domito?"

"In Cerchicava negotiating a new trade agreement with the Vintner's Guild."

"How old is he now?"

"Twenty-one."

"Who would credit it? Why it seems like only yesterday that you took him in. What was it, fourteen years ago?"

"Yes. His youth and vigor make me feel old."

"Bollocks. Get yourself a new wife and sire one of your own blood if you want to feel young again, or better yet, marry him off; that'll take the wind out of his sails."

Luca smiled tightly. "I understand your son, Vincent, is to be married this spring."

"To the daughter of a long-distance trader from Calegro. In point of fact, her father and I are outfitting a ship bound for the far east. It could turn a pretty profit for anyone with shares in the venture; if you're interested."

"I might be."

"Mention it to Alesandro and Domito as well. It's time they began making decisions as men. They can't hide behind their father's purse strings forever, you know."

"I'll keep it in mind."

Later, standing in the center of his workshop beneath the Palazzo della Rona, a compact riverside manor house he'd inherited from his late wife, Luca lifted a delicate glass vial containing a sliver of brain matter from Corsini's late father. The old man had died of strangulation, leaving everything to Dante. So much for not hiding behind a father's purse strings, he sneered.

Luca's own father had been terrified of the trade and had exhausted the family fortune trying to buy enough protection for the family mausoleum to keep the Death Mages at bay. A decade after his death, Luca had harvested necromantic components from every single corpse inside, including his father's. It paid to be careful in Cerchicava even more than it did in Riamo.

The crimson preserving fluid within the vial sparkled seductively in the lamplight and Luca savored the many offensive possibilities it afforded before exchanging it for a plain ceramic urn with an expression of real regret. Then, tying a leather apron about his waist, he popped the seal on the urn and poured the contents onto his dissecting table before selecting a fine bone-handled knife from the wall.

"Find out what the cargo on Corsini's new ship is and who his backers are, Piero," he said without turning. "Then make sure we have at least one sailor aboard sworn to the trade."

Hovering off to one side, the manservant bowed respectfully. "Yes, sir."

"Has there been any word from Drey?"

"No, sir. I've people waiting on the docks for him but he's well skilled at avoiding detection when he wants to."

Luca frowned. "Has there been any word to suggest that he *might* want to?"

"None as of yet. The mission was a success and word is that the Huntsman evaded all attempts to

capture him, both magical and otherwise." Piero
brows drew down. "He made an interesting choice
marking Johanni Gagio," he noted.

"A curious choice," Luca amended. "Obviously
the duc of Cerchicava was the most attractive candidate, but Drey may not have had the opportunity
to mark him properly. Gagio's death creates political ramifications a little closer to home than one of
the other ducs might have done, but nothing that
can't be dealt with." He carefully slit the piece of
human intestine on the table before staring pen-
sively down at its interior. "There's a reasoning at
work here, but whether it's the Huntsman's, Drey
Orcicci's, or Domito Preto's is still unclear; he always was a complex child." He turned, his eyes
burning a deep, dark red. "But regardless, I want
an answer, Piero. Find him before I lose patience
with the question."

"Yes, sir."

The manservant bowed and withdrew, his tone
of voice conveying his opinion of Drey's reasoning
as plainly as if he'd spoken it aloud. He'd always
believed that Drey was too *complex* to be trusted.
Trading on their years together to deflect his master's displeasure, he'd said as much when Luca
had taken the half-starved Cerchicavan orphan
into his employ and later into his family; then
again when he'd set a crossbow into his hands and
sent him out to act as the trade's clandestine en-
forcer and executioner. He was brilliant but rash,
ruthless but sentimental, too ambitious to act in
secret and too young to act independently. No

good would come of giving him so much power so soon.

Luca had told Piero to be patient, that the boy would season. He was a calculated risk that would pay high dividends in the future, and in the meantime, he wore one of the strongest binding spells possible. They were secure. Period.

This had mollified the manservant for a time. Piero had held one of the first binding spells on Luca himself in the early days of Luca's apprenticeship. At Montefero de Sepori's command, Piero had taught him everything he knew of the necromantic arts, changing him from a defrocked and condemned churchman to a highly skilled Death Mage in under seven years. When Sepori was finally taken down by the duc of Cerchicava and a young ex-cutter named Coll Svedali, Piero had escaped and fled to Riamo. Now he wore Luca's binding spell and was perhaps the only living man the Death Mage trusted, besides his son Drey.

But there were limits to both.

Eyes flashing a brilliant crimson, Luca spoke the words of a dual questing spell, then straightened with a nod as the piece of intestine turned first black and then gray before crumbling into ash. Drey was alive and Piero had not conspired to waylay him. So why hadn't he returned home?

The next day the city was abuzz with the news that the Huntsman had struck again, this time in Riamo itself. The body of Anthony Spoleto, a wool merchant and owner of several warehouses in the harbor district, had been found wedged under a dock just before dawn with the assassin's signature crossbow quarrel buried between his shoulder blades. An hour later another body, that of Ciuto Farnese, owner of one of Riamo's midsize mills, was pulled from the Ardechi River, again pierced from behind with a crossbow quarrel. By the time the Huntsman's third victim, Ferrante Ascanio, a banker for the city's Spice Merchants' Guild, was discovered stuffed into a packing crate not a hundred yards from where Ciuto had lain, the quarrel so deeply embedded in his back that it could hardly be seen, the city was in hysterics.

Bowing to the pressure of his council, the duc closed the harbors and sent his own Court Mages in to try and discern the Huntsman's identity through any trace magics on the quarrels. Despite their best efforts, they failed to discover anything about him. Rumors began to fly that he was protected by a deeper, darker magic than the Court Mages had access to and, for the first time, the word necromancy began to be heard in taverns and alehouses across the city.

His face set in a grim line, Luca sent Piero to obtain components from each corpse, and standing over the three carefully collected squares of organ meat on his table, he threw a handful of dried belladonna over them and shouted out a single word. The accompanying flash of fire told Luca all he needed to know.

"It's Drey. And he's blocking me."

Piero knew better than to ask why.

*   *   *

They received a less than satisfactory answer that afternoon. A grubby child, wearing a simple coercion spell activated by the coin in his fist that had passed through three others before coming to him, brought a message shortly before dinner. Luca read the missive silently, then handed it to Piero, who peered down at it suspiciously.

Dear Father. Negotiations in Cerchicava have become somewhat more complicated than I had anticipated but I expect to be home in time for His Grace's funeral. Your loving son, Domito. The manservant gave an unimpressed sniff. "He cocked up the duc's death somehow and now he's afraid to come home."

"Possibly." Retrieving the missive, Luca's eyes flashed red for an instant and a series of fine, scarlet lines appeared scrawled across the paper before disappearing once again.

It's nothing, I'll fix it, he read. "You're right, something's happened." Crossing to the window, he stared out at the sky, watching as the sun slowly disappeared behind the turreted roofline of the ducal palazzo. "Nothing too serious apparently and *fixable* before Johanni Gagio's funeral."

"Word is that may be as soon as three days from now. The five ducs are already on their way."

"Three days then." Luca's eyes narrowed. "He wasn't identified," he mused, "or we'd have heard."

"Every city along the Ardechi would have heard."

"Yes. The Huntsman's notorious. Every rumor,

every speculation about him, is savored like a mid-winter banquet. So he wasn't identified, and he wasn't injured—the writing would have revealed that by a darker color and a thicker line—and he wasn't captured, or he wouldn't have been able to set a cipher on his message or a coercion on his messenger."

"Or mark three Riamo merchants," Piero added.

Luca shot him a flat expression. "One puzzle at a time, if you don't mind," he spat.

"Your pardon, sir."

"He's in the city," Luca continued. "But he either can't or won't come home."

"A locate spell on the message itself should reveal where he was when he wrote it."

"Yes, and I'll leave that to you presently. He won't have lingered but it will give us a place to start looking. He'll know that and may have left another message."

"So he's going to lead us on some little treasure hunt?" Piero asked in an indignant tone.

"It seems so, and you can make your displeasure known to him later. For the moment, however, follow his trail of bread crumbs and find out what he cocked up."

"Excuse me for saying so, sir, but you could just execute a full-out locate and coercion spell on the boy himself," Piero said carefully.

"I could, and I may, but for now, you will carry out my commands."

Piero bowed at once. "Yes, Master."

*　　　*　　　*

The locate spell on the missive led to the site of
Anthony Spoleto's murder but no farther. With a
dark expression, Luca opened a small iron cask and
removed a wax-sealed ceramic jar containing the
preserved flesh of a Cerchicavan priest long dead.
The priest had been in charge of the Svedali Innocenti Foundling Home where Drey had spent the
first six years of his life. Luca had obtained the
flesh just after he'd taken the boy in and had used
it only once, when he'd given Drey the name Orcicci and taken his oaths as master and father.
Under such circumstances, the flesh would serve as
the catalyst for a powerful locate and coercion spell
that would see the Huntsman forced into Luca's
presence despite all obstacles in his path.

"Unless to do so would be to betray me to an
enemy, in which case, the dual pressure would
kill him."

Setting the jar in the middle of the dissecting
table, he closed and locked the cask once more.

"He has until the duc's funeral as requested. In
the meantime, find out everything you can about
the men he marked and what they might have had
in common."

Standing to one side, Piero bowed but said
nothing.

The next three days passed without further incident and Riamo began to breathe a little easier.
One by one, the ducs of Montecino, Rocasta, Calegro, Pisario, and Cerchicava arrived. The added security made unobtrusive movement in the city

difficult, but Piero still managed to uncover the link between Spoleto, Farnese, and Ascanio. A single name. Dante Corsini.

The morning of Johanni Gagio's funeral dawned cold and wet; the wind whipping through the tree-lined avenues of the city promised a violent winter to come. Every sconce, lamp, and candelabra in the San Salvadore Cathedral was alight when Luca took his place along the western wall in the pew reserved for foreign nobility. Drey was nowhere to be found and, eyes narrowed, Luca scanned the crowds of people, watching as the prosperous citizens of Riamo began to take their seats, most staring unabashedly at the exotic foreign dignitaries in their midst. For many, this was their first glimpse of a world outside the narrow confines of their shops and counting houses and once again Luca found himself grinding his teeth in contemptuous impatience.

Across the quire, he saw Alesandro take his solitary place in the Albergo family pew, and forcibly schooled his expression. A quiet, soft-spoken young man, Alesandro had accepted his new civic responsibilities with all the prudence and piety expected of a man of his class, but it seemed to be taking a heavy toll on him these last few months. His face was pale and his usually open countenance cloudy. As the Corsini family passed by on the way to their own pew, Dante paused to speak with him and Alesandro started uneasily. Luca's eyes narrowed.

Drey and Alesandro had been ten-year-old boys when Luca had married Vallenza Albergo, the widow of a successful goldsmith. Despite their vastly divergent upbringings the two new brothers had become inseparable companions and continued to spend time together as adults. Luca was surprised that Alesandro didn't turn to see if his brother had taken his place beside his stepfather. As the Gagio family took their seats before Johanni's ornate casket and the signal for the great double doors to be closed was given, Alesandro met Luca's gaze with a supplicant expression and Luca nodded.

The funeral was a long and dull affair dominated by the bishop who, taking advantage of a captive audience, extolled the virtues of Johanni Gagio and his administration until even the most devout eye was glazed over with boredom. When the congregation was finally released several hours later, they dispersed rapidly, heading for the city's taverns and alehouses with an obvious air of relief. Directing Piero to wait for him, Luca made his way unhurriedly across the sturdy marble bridge that linked the cathedral grounds to the tidy, well-kept merchant's cemetery to the west. Standing before the modestly decorated Albergo mausoleum as if taking a moment for a quiet prayer, he stared down at the bronze plaque that bore Vallenza's name and waited for her son to join him.

"You seem disturbed," he said without preamble.

Alesandro nodded unhappily. "It's Dom," he replied with some hesitation. "He sent me to fetch you. He's in trouble."

The tiny orphanage of San Jorge had been abandoned long before Luca had come to Riamo. The children and the priests who'd cared for them had moved to larger quarters when the last plague had swelled the orphans' numbers beyond what the small building could contain and it had never been reoccupied. Luca strode up the overgrown walkway with an air of bored disinterest while maintaining an almost painful scrutiny of every aspect of his surroundings. When Drey emerged from the open doorway, his lean face devoid of expression, Luca almost snarled at him.

"Just what do you think you're playing at?" he demanded.

"I couldn't risk returning right away, but I knew you would be getting impatient." Resetting the wards on the orphanage door, Drey leaned against the wall of the main entrance hall with a calm expression.

He explained his absence to his father in as few words as possible. The duc of Cerchicava had been his original candidate as expected but the same Coll Svedali who had aided the duc in destroying the trade in that city had intervened again, throwing a strange combined magic at Drey that had taken him completely by surprise. It had left a pale, white scar across his cheek which was only now beginning to fade. That Drey and Coll had been contemporaries at the Svedali Innocenti Foundling Home together and that Drey had encountered him at least once before without killing him made Luca's eyes darken dangerously.

"So, you allow yourself to be *marked* . . ." The Death Mage showed his teeth at Drey's response to the necromantic word, ". . . with a locate spell of unknown magic, you leave the marker *alive,* you come home, and you send for your *civilian* brother."

"I needed to get a message to you. It was the safest way."

"And how did you explain your inability to return home to him?"

"I told him I had the clap."

"And do you?" Luca echoed Drey's responding expression. "I ask only because something's obviously addled your brains. You deliberately put Alesandro at risk."

Drey's calm demeanor did not change. "Not at all. The spell is one of location only and it had already begun to fade when I sent for him."

"How can you know that? You said the spell casting was new."

"The spell casting *is* new. The components are conventional."

"There's nothing *conventional* about this threat in Cerchicava."

"Coll's only a threat to the few Death Mages remaining there and anything that weakens them strengthens us. When you're ready to step in, Coll can be removed without causing any kind of stir."

"We will set your presumptuous and naive assessment of that situation aside for the moment," Luca snarled at him. "In the meantime you will explain to me why you chose to mark the duc of Riamo."

Drey shrugged. "There was opportunity?"

"And then," Luca continued, throwing him a warning look, "decided to further destabilize the situation here by marking three Riamo merchants just to pass the time? Don't even think to deny it," he snapped when the younger man gave him a patently false wide-eyed look. "Their deaths have the Huntsman written all over them."

Drey shrugged. "The Huntsman's habits are well known. Anyone could copy them."

"Really?" Luca locked eyes with his son. "I have Farnese's corpse on my table as we speak. Do you really want me to cast an identify spell of my own brand of *conventional* magic upon it? Should the perpetrator wear my binding spell the results would be dramatic."

"I had private reasons to mark them," Drey answered a little to quickly.

"*What* reasons?"

Drey looked away. "They're not mine to tell," he said at last.

"Than whose are they?"

"Alesandro's."

"What?"

"I got into some trouble."

The other man had been waiting in the back garden for Drey to fetch him in. When Luca signaled curtly for him to explain, he ran a hand through his sandy-colored hair with a helpless gesture. "I borrowed heavily to invest in a ship bound for the far east. It was supposed to return with a cargo of gold of unsurpassed quality. When it sank, the moneylender I borrowed the original investment from called in his debt."

"Ferrante Ascanio," Drey supplied.

Luca raised one finger to silence Drey before returning his attention to Alesandro.

"I had no way to pay him back," his brother continued.

"So why didn't you come to me?" Luca asked. "Your mother's invested monies are there for you to make use of. You only had to ask."

Alesandro looked away. "I knew how conservative you were in matters of money. I didn't think you'd approve."

"And you thought I'd approve of you subjugating yourself to a moneylender instead?"

"Well, I'd hoped you wouldn't find out. I thought I could recoup my losses on the next venture, so when Vincent Corsini . . ."

"Vincent Corsini?"

"Yes. He came to see me. I told him of my difficulties and he said he knew some people who could help me. He convinced Anthony Spoleto to clear the debt with Ascanio."

"This just keeps getting better and better."

"But soon he began to make demands on the shop," Alesandro continued. "He wanted to use my cellars as storage facilities for smuggled cargos and my clientele as possible borrowers for Ascanio. When I refused, he sent Ciuto Farnese to see me. He said that Spoleto would take my shop if I didn't cooperate. That I would be ruined and the Albergo name would be disgraced. Vincent couldn't help me, so when I heard that Dom was back in the city, I went to him."

"How did you know where to find him?"

The two brothers exchanged a look before reaching into their doublets to pull out a pair of matching amulets.

Luca just shook his head. "So, what did you think Domito could do about them?"

Alesandro met his stepfather's angry gaze with an even expression. "I knew the Huntsman could kill them for me," he said bluntly.

The shocked silence in the hall was almost palatable.

"How long has he known about you?"

Luca had ordered Alesandro to go to the Palazzo della Rona and wait for them there. Once he was out of earshot, the Death Mage had taken his other son by the throat, shaking him like a dog until the rage had ebbed enough for coherent speech. When he finally released him, Drey stepped back, his usual deadpan demeanor unchanged.

"He's always known, father," he answered calmly. "Alesandro and I don't keep secrets from each other."

"Unbound?" Luca could barely get the words through his teeth they were clenched so tightly together. "You let him walk about with this kind of knowledge for anyone to discover, unbound!"

"I trust him."

"I will kill you and leave your body for lesser mages to pick out your eyeballs like carrion crows!"

"That's your right."

"Right? You don't know anything about right. Are you so witless that you can't take a lesson from your own experiences? Coll Svedali, that fellow foundling of yours that you're so unwilling to mark, left unbound by Lord Montefero de Sepori, destroyed the trade in Cerchicava with one stroke! Hundreds tortured and executed in the dungeons below their cathedral. And they have dungeons below San Salvadore too, you know. Or did you think you were so powerful you couldn't be arrested, or that Alesandro couldn't be? One night in their hands is all either of you would last. One night!"

Striding to the window, he glared out at the distant rooftops of their home barely visible in the failing light.

"Dante Corsini's behind it," Drey said to his back. "All three of the men I marked ultimately work for him."

"Yes, I know that. Be quiet a moment." Luca took a deep breath to calm himself. "There's an object lesson in this," he said finally. "A lesson about the nature of power and security; whether there's greater security in keeping your power hidden or in being so openly powerful that none would dare defy you for fear of the most terrible retaliation. Riamo is an example of the former, Cerchicava of the latter."

He turned, his eyes a dark, blood red. "You will set a binding spell on your brother at once. He's your responsibility now. Anything happens to him, anything at all, and I'll lay you out on my table. I'll not have the two of you destroying everything I've spent a lifetime building."

Drey nodded silently.

"And I," Luca continued, "will deal with our incautious long-distance trader."

Dante Corsini disappeared from his bed before dawn the next day. His body was found in Pisario a week later, stripped naked, the marks of a savage beating standing out across his face and ribs, his belly slashed open, and the organs within desecrated by the obvious signs of a necromantic collection.

The entire city of Riamo collapsed in hysterics; Eugene Gagio fled to Rocasta and the bishop declared a state of religious emergency as the citizens overwhelmed the priesthood, demanding that they strengthen the protective wards on their families' crypts and mausoleums that had been allowed to fall into disrepair from years of complacent neglect. When many of the bodies interred within were discovered to have been defiled already, the city erupted in violence. First Minister Poggeso summoned the Watch, but it was a week before order was restored.

Standing by Vallenza's plaque, Luca observed that at least the feeling of contemptuous impatience had been replaced by a stirring of curious excitement he hadn't experienced in years. It felt both powerful and refreshing after all this time.

He turned to the two young men standing behind him, matching sparks of crimson fire lighting up their eyes. "Dante said it was time you both began making decisions as men," he said, "so, here's your chance. Alesandro, you will open up trade negotiations with Vincent Corsini that strongly favor the Albergo family. Make it plain to him that he would do well to accept your business terms or he'll find himself sharing his father's fate. Be as obvious or as subtle as you wish. The days of hiding are over.

"You," he turned a jaundiced gaze on Drey. "Will find your way past the wards on the ducal mausoleum and obtain components from Johanni Gagio's body and any others you find within. You will accomplish this within the week or you will answer to Piero for it."

Turning, he caught sight of the manservant waiting for him at the cemetery gates, his expression one of barely concealed disapproval.

"I'll give you both just two pieces of advice," Luca continued. "One: listen to your lieutenants, especially when they tell you that you can't trust your own sons."

He turned to go, and Drey made an inquisitive noise.

"What?"

"The second piece of advice, father?"

"Never *have* sons in the first place."

Turning, the premier Death Mage of Riamo took his leave, already planning the next step in his conquest of the city.

LOSER TAKES ALL

Donald J. Bingle

Clint Hardaway hit the reply button before he had even finished scanning the IM from his college buddy Jason.

"Thought I might try UO."

"Ultimate Overlord? LOL. Man, you do have time on your hands. I try to limit myself to two hours a night. Let me know when you're in universe. Lots of nasties to kill. Just be sure to save some for me."

"We'll see," typed Clint. "TTFN." He clicked off the IM box without waiting for a reply, and clicked the link for Ultimate Overlord. Acknowledging Conditions of Use that he didn't bother to read, he filled out some forms, entered the number of his platinum Amex card and got ready to play. He clicked by the credits and went to the opening screen.

"Can you become the ULTIMATE OVER-LORD? The path is unclear, the rules unknown. There is no luck but the luck you make, no rewards but the rewards you earn. Everyone starts equal, but some prove themselves superior by their actions. The ultimate challenge awaits you in a universe beyond your imagining. Click here to begin your journey."

A bit hokey, to be sure, but Clint liked the approach. No tutorial of how to play and what to do. No long lists of things to do, puzzles to solve, or rules to memorize. You learned as you experienced the game, just like in life.

Of course, he knew that there were rules. Every universe has rules.

From overarching principles of cosmic import to minor fads of fashion, there were always rules that you must learn to survive, that you must master and bend to get ahead. He liked that the site said nothing about what those rules were. That would be too easy. More challenging, more interesting, to figure them out for yourself. By trial and error, by deductive reasoning, by publication, by rumor, and by stealth, you must discern cause and effect, the algorithms, formulae, and step-functions that determine success and failure, fame and fortune, life and death.

That's life, a random search for Easter eggs of hidden knowledge in a stark and unforgiving landscape.

Clint lived, had always lived, to parse out the rules and bend them to his own advantage. There was, he knew, no other way to become the Ultimate Overlord.

Even before he clicked to start the scenario, however, he made some decisions about the rules that would govern his character.

Rule No. 1. The Ultimate Overlord Is Evil. The first rule was the simplest to intuit. There's no way to become the ruler of the universe without being evil. Those who believe in goodness believe in all sorts of other warm, fuzzy, touchy-feely concepts, like kindness and consensus and democratic values and giving to those too poor to fend for themselves. This universe, he deduced, would not tolerate such suckers. No one wields ultimate power by committee; no one gains all by being nice. No one gets ahead by giving away what they have to others, whether goods or knowledge.

Besides, the good don't want to rule the world. They want the world to rule the world. They don't crave power. They crave happiness, but not for themselves. For others. For everyone. As if a limited supply of happiness could stretch so thin. As if happiness could exist if suffering did not exist for contrast.

In a world of limited resources and complex rules regarding their distribution, collection, and expenditure, knowledge, he knew, was power. He chuckled lightly to himself as he remembered his clueless high school chemistry teacher writing that in his yearbook: "Knowledge Is Power." And even then, he had known the corollary: "Power Corrupts. Absolute

Power Corrupts Absolutely." So, if you were ultimately going to be corrupted anyway, why not start out that way? It eased the path.

And let's be clear what is meant by evil. Selfish, underhanded, maniacal depravity with the sole focus of gathering power for greater and greater selfish, underhanded, maniacal depravity.

People always undersold evil. Your boss, whoever he may be, is not evil. Evil does not golf. It does not listen to management books on tape in traffic. It does not hatch diabolical plots to get a reserved parking space or rush to grab the cream-filled doughnut at a staff meeting in a conference room with comfy, adjustable chairs. It does not offer vacation time, sick days, 401(k) plans, or health insurance, no matter how crappy. It does not obsess about its receding hairline. It does not count paper clips or goof off at the water cooler.

Evil eats what it kills and sometimes eats what is still alive, even if it's not really hungry. It always wins or it destroys the game so that no one else can. It works constantly, relentlessly toward its own ends.

Your boss is not evil. You could kill your boss. You cannot destroy evil.

To win, he would need to be evil.

He had no problem with that.

Click.

Gafnar shielded his eyes and looked about the landscape. It was a barren and vile place. No water but the salty sea that had spat him onto this foreign shore. No vegetation but the blackened husks of trees burned long ago, offering no shade, no fruit, no fuel to ease his journey. The land itself was rocky and cracked by drought, a gusty wind tearing the last remnants of topsoil and blasting it into his burning eyes. Other than a few others like himself, the only creatures moving across the face of desolation were the rats. Thousands, hundreds of thousands, of ravenous rats, rampaging toward the fresh meat that had been tossed ashore by the storm and lay quivering in shock. He was that fresh meat, an offering to the rats. But Gafnar did not accept that fate; he did not even hesitate to ponder his fate. He did not wait for the horde to come to him, biting and gnawing. No, he moved toward the foul vermin and began to kill, expending every bit of strength he had left in a frenzy of death to celebrate his own life. Only later did he learn that he could eat the rats, skin their hides, loot their nests for shiny valuables. These benefits were worthwhile, but the killing was essential.

Rule No. 2. Hard Work Is Required to Become the Ultimate Overlord. Most people, he knew, played at life. They skimmed along doing the bare minimum needed to continue on their mediocre existence. They lived to joke and entertain themselves and their friends. They had no purpose, no drive. They didn't play to win. They played not to lose or, worse yet, just to enjoy the game.

Clint believed such creatures to be beneath the

rats. Competition not only fueled society, it fueled the soul. It made life interesting.

No one gives ultimate power to someone else. To do so would be to demonstrate that they didn't want it, didn't deserve it, never really had it. Power must be taken. By force, by stealth, by sleight of hand. It is not handed out by derelicts distributing coupons. It does not come as a free prize in a cereal box. It cannot be won by lottery. To obtain ultimate power, you must first have power over someone or something besides yourself. Someone gullible. Someone weak. And then you must increase that power person by person, item by item, place by place, until there is no person, item, or place that is not within your power.

Any humdrum nature video on public television will tell you the lion starts with the weakest of the herd, killing and eating those that are the easiest to bring down and devour. But the baritone narrators seldom note that, as the king of the jungle grows large and strong and hones his skills in the hunt, he may move on to faster game. He may join with others of the pride to stalk and panic an entire herd and send them rampaging over a cliff to their destruction, where they may be eaten at leisure. The lion does not join with others out of altruism or subservience, but to his own advantage. And when the drought comes, he does not hesitate to stalk and kill fiercer creatures, even man.

Most of the others that were not devoured by the rats moved quickly inland, seeking more hospitable

*environs, but not Gafnar. He feasted on the rats and
on the mayhem for as long as he could and then he
waited. And when others like him were thrown on
the shore by new storms, he quickly moved to kill
and devour them before they could get their bear-
ings, before they could begin their journey, before
the rats could devour their life force. And only then,
when he was strong and fast, did he move on to
new hunting grounds, bloody muscle in his fist, veins
in his teeth.*

**Rule No. 3. The Ultimate Overlord Has No
Friends.** "Now that you've made it off the beach,
dude, we should connect up," chirped Jason over
the wireless headset Clint was wearing as he made
his way through the game. "I'm in the hills to the
east. My avatar is called 'Alexander.' Jason. Alexander. Get it?"

Clint sneered at his computer screen, shuddering
at the banal chatter. "Sure," he lied, "My avatar is
Vrod. Keep an eye out and let me know by e-mail
when you see him. My headset is fritzing out on
me."

He knew many people associated with friends as
they made their way in the universe, but he could
not understand how a true Ultimate Overlord could
do so. An Ultimate Overlord poses as a friend to
others, but they are never his friends. He chats ami-
ably, sympathizes with their petty complaints,
drinks their wine, eats their food, and makes them
believe there is a bond of mutual affection and
trust. They are a resource to be gathered and hus-

banded and guarded from thieves in the night and then to be used or consumed or sacrificed to the enemy to gain escape or advantage. They are to be betrayed when it is to his advantage.

And if any one of them should remind him of himself, he is to be betrayed first, before he betrays. The Ultimate Overlord has no friends because all friends may become enemies.

In these more prosperous lands, men gathered together, some for defense, others for attack. Gafnar joined a roving band of attackers and learned their ways and their weaknesses. And then, when it was to his advantage, he slit their throats in the night and took their belongings and moved on.

The process repeated itself, though the betrayals varied. Some allies he killed himself; others he pitted against his enemies or left to fend for themselves when a greater force attacked.

His favorite tactic was to volunteer to act as a roving reserve for any battles. When the fighting started, he would hang back, presumably to be ready to go where most needed, but actually to assess the fighting skills and weapons of both his companions and his foes alike. If the battle went well, he would wade in just before it was over, like Russia declaring war on Japan near the end of WW II, to help finish off the adversary and share in the spoils of victory. If the battle was going poorly, he would slink away and let the attackers wear themselves down killing his erstwhile companions.

He was not stupid. He didn't tip his hand. He

always appeared to be a cooperative companion to his supposed allies. He listened to their advice and learned their ways. He imparted information that would not harm himself. He fought when he needed to fight, but only if he had the advantage.

He let others die to save their friends, to save him.

Rule No. 4. Always Loot the Bodies. Waste not, want not. That's what his mother had always told him. And she was right. So many people let so much pass them by because of social convention or morality or political correctness. Relationships, opportunities, money on the table.

He had shown he had no problem with hostile takeovers, cutthroat business dealings, holiday firings, pension fund raids. Of course you hit a person when they were down. That was when they were most defenseless. That was when they couldn't hit back. That was when hitting them meant that they would never get up again.

And then you raided their workforce, you bought up their patents for pennies in bankruptcy. If you were lucky, you could scour the paperwork from their last desperate months and find that they had done something that crossed the line of legality in their efforts to save their business; then it was an anonymous letter to the trustee or the SEC and they spent the rest of their miserable lives fighting to stay out of prison instead of hating you for your success at their expense.

When the battle was done, Gafnar would circle back and ambush the wounded and weary victor (or wait until the victor wandered off to rest and heal) and loot the bodies of the fallen. He would steal coins and gems and magic and treasure and weapons. He would thieve the boots from their feet and the half-burned torches they carried. If the loot was more than he could carry and quickly hide away in some secret spot, he would destroy what he could not steal. Better for loot to be destroyed in a pyre of flame than to let others have it after he had left.

Of course, there were exceptions. Sometimes he would leave some loot behind. Not out of kindness. Not out of fairness. But to lure his competitors to the booby-trapped body and their demise. And then he would steal from them.

And just in case someone out there was clever and evil and competitive enough to do the same, he would always firebomb from a distance any body he encountered that he had not seen fall with his own eyes. Then he would loot the crispy husk. Sure, you could lose a little treasure that way, but the most valuable items did not readily burn.

Besides, he preferred his meat cooked. Why should even that go to waste? Protein was protein.

Rule No. 5. Accept Luck; Make More. He didn't control the universe, not yet. So things were bound to happen for ill or good that he did not control. He had learned long ago to take such things in stride. He felt no guilt for benefiting from the whims of fate. Should his competitor suffer a strike or a fire or an unwarranted investigation, so much the better. Of course, a tip here or an envelope of untraceable cash there could always make your luck better. Don't talk to him of morality or fairness. An Ultimate Overlord must be evil, remember? All the circles we move in jostle one another. All universes affect one another.

Cheating is fine, as long as you don't get caught.

He clicked onto eBay and fingered his credit card.

For reasons that Gafnar could never comprehend, others that he did not know came to his aid. They intervened in his battles, they laid tribute at his feet. Some said that it was because he was favored by the gods, but he knew no reason why that should be so. Some said that it was because his reputation had preceded him into unknown realms of the universe, but it seemed unlikely to him that he had a fearsome reputation. He had always let others fight for him whenever possible, maintaining as low a profile as possible to avoid becoming a target. Sometimes he suspected these others who helped him to be sinister plotters out to befuddle and betray him. In such cases, he would slip into their yurts at night and slay them. But even when they awoke, they did not attempt to stay his lethal hand.

It was a strange world, but he could live, even prosper, with that.

Rule 6. The Ultimate Overlord Has No Family.
Family members are worse than friends. They are friends chosen not by choice, but by biology. Worse yet, they are friends with expectations. They want

goods, but offer nothing in trade. They want protection, but offer nothing toward the common defense. They wish to share in the prosperity of power without helping to create that power.

Not only are they unworthy friends, but they easily become the pawns of others. They are potential usurpers of the throne, figureheads about which others may rally the mindless masses. They peddle access, real or imagined, and increase their power from the scraps beneath your table. They create ties and obligations, or, at least, expectations. Wasn't that what the legend of King Arthur was all about? Never trust your spouse, never trust your sister, never trust your son. The classics could be so educational.

He stared at the yellow Post-it Note stuck to the side of his flat screen. "Call Mom," it nagged. Screw that.

As friendships and prosperity grew within groups in the more hospitable climes, some took blood oaths of brotherhood or created clans or mated to produce offspring, but not Gafnar. He needed no brother; he did not wish to share his wealth or power. And, so, he moved on, questing inland to the wild lands of danger, trusting not to family to protect him, but hired minions who would do his bidding for minor treasure. He did not use his minions wastefully—no resource should be squandered—but he used them to protect himself and his wealth. He took care, however, to never gather a force large enough or strong enough to threaten himself. There was no sense in paying for your own overthrow and murder. And whenever a minion began to gain power and sway the others, he was given the most dangerous assignments, until one day he never came back.

Rule No. 7. The Only Power Is Used Power. Potential energy was okay for physics class, but kinetic energy caused things to happen. It made levers move, wheels spin. It crushed objects below and inflicted pain where it hit. Any resource not expended was a resource wasted.

Clint remembered a class from college about strategic nuclear weapons and the concept of mutually assured destruction. His classmates marveled at the madness of building more weapons than were needed to destroy the earth completely. He wondered at the waste of trillions and trillions of dollars and rubles and the coopting of the best and brightest of the world's scientists to create what ended up being enormously sophisticated storage sheds for radioactive material. At some point, at some time, one nation or the other had the edge and could have obliterated its enemy forever, had it only the will to use the weapons on which it had expended a notable portion of the nation's gross national product.

Oh, a threat can be a use of power, but only if it accomplishes getting someone to do something you want them to. A threat that maintains the status quo is an empty suit.

*   *   *

Truth be told, Gafnar liked to kill. He relished it. But he didn't really like to fight. And if he could not get his temporary allies or his meaningless minions to do his fighting for him, he killed as quickly and as devastatingly as possible. He liked to blow things up. Explosions were fun. And if he didn't have a handy bomb, there was always magic or poison.

Any weapon not used was a weapon that could be used against him.

Rule No. 8. Evil Is Smart, Never Silly. Clint never hid his light under a bushel. He didn't understand the point of self-deprecating humor. He would never wear a *Star Trek* uniform to an annual meeting or strike a wacky pose for a newsmagazine cover. If you didn't appreciate his genius, then you were even more stupid than the average peasant. But he also never understood the point of telling others how smart he was. Let them figure it out too late. Let them think they had the upper hand.

At first, he had watched the chat boards for the game and their endless debates as to what an evil, all-powerful overlord would do. He would build a lair with ventilation shafts too narrow for the hero to crawl through or he would line the ventilation shaft with crushed glass or lasers or bubble wrap and on and on and on. As for Clint, he wouldn't have ventilations shafts; let the minions slowly suffocate in hot, carbon-dioxide laced air. But he didn't bother to say so on the chat boards. A real overlord would never tip his hand.

He stopped perusing the chat boards. He turned off his IM and let the e-mails gather unanswered. He had more important things to do.

Gafnar roamed an increasingly deserted landscape. His minions scattered far and wide, but reported few powerful beings. Those that were found, though, he directed subtly toward each other, goading them to battle, watching one fall, then lobbing in missiles from a distance until the other fell. He built no castle, planted no crops, designed no heraldry. Instead, he roamed the land, gathering power and expending it to eliminate his rivals.

Rule No. 9. The Ultimate Overlord Destroys All Enemies. Every petty tyrant the world has ever seen has enemies. He rails against other nations and peoples and leaders in an effort to unite his own people and wage war. But, in doing so, he increases the power of his people and the risk to himself. An Ultimate Overlord is ultimate because all his enemies have been vanquished. Anything else is an Ultimate Overlord in training, a wannabe, a pretender.

No peace is negotiated except to gain a later strategic advantage. No coexistence is tolerated except while one marshals his own forces and sends spies to poison the enemy and sow discontent among his populace. No mercy is granted, for mercy shows weakness and caring, neither of which has any place in absolute power.

What cannot be destroyed must be bought. What

cannot be bought must be destroyed. If an enemy sues for peace, agree immediately to meet, then slaughter the envoys and march on the capital at once.

What is the point of a halfhearted war? What is the logic of seeking only partial destruction? What is the mercy of prolonging the battle before the victory is achieved? Either you are willing to kill for what you want or you are not. Evil is not tentative.

Gafnar monitored closely those who, like him, gathered power and knowledge, men and materiel, magic and munitions unto themselves. He bribed with poisoned gifts, attacked without mercy, using his fiercest and most dangerous troops, and demanded tribute from all he conquered. He agreed to civilized rules of engagement, then ignored them at every opportunity. He waged total war; no respite, no surrender, no civilians. What he could not take for himself, he turned to ash.

He assumed that all his adversaries were as evil as he and punished them for their treachery, whether it existed or not. He did not hesitate to use his more powerful weapons and magics. He held nothing in reserve. He showed no honor. Victory or death were the only options. All else was for wimps.

Rule No. 10. Only an Ultimate Overlord Can End War. He always, always rolled his eyes when he heard the feminists say, "If women ruled the world, there would be no more war." For as long

as there is envy and jealousy and good things to
be had, there will be war. Someone always wants,
even if they have enough. Someone always is willing to take. Someone is always willing to try to
stop them.

Whenever he heard the idealists talk of peace,
he would recite to himself the poem he had once
heard, many years before:

> *If all men were chickens,*
> *there would still be war,*
> *because chickens are mean*
> *and fight for food.*
>
> *If all men were cowards,*
> *there would still be war,*
> *for those in fear lash out most quickly,*
> *lobbing rocks from cover.*
>
> *If all men were women,*
> *there would still be war,*
> *for a woman scorned*
> *deals destruction without mercy.*

But he knew now that an Ultimate Overlord
could end war. By gathering all goods to himself,
by eliminating all family members who would seek
to share in his goods, by destroying all enemies,
and by destroying all friends who might become
enemies (and minions who might become friends),
he would eliminate war, for there would be no one

left. All power, all goods, all places, all things would be his, forever.

The game would be won.

And when the last enemy had been destroyed and the chaos of battle still reigned on the field, Gafnar set his troops upon one another in the darkness, each targeting the other from a distance with magics and explosives. Then he poisoned the water and let loose an agent of death upon the winds to take any that might linger still. And he sat in the high tower of a captured castle and knew that he had become the Ultimate Overlord, for nothing moved upon the land.

That was when Gafnar realized that there was an endgame, that he now had a choice.

Having conquered the world, he could now become a god and create a new world in his own image. He rejected that immediately. Doing so would put at risk everything he had accomplished. Even worshipers were dangerous. Hadn't the devil once been an angel who had gotten bored?

He could commit suicide, guaranteeing that his gains would never be eroded. But what was the point of there being only one, if you just gave that away?

Or he could sit and survey his empty world and know forever that he had won.

That's what an Ultimate Overlord would do. Evil never gave in.

Clint leaned back in his desk chair, his eyes leaving the plasma panel for the first time in more hours than he could remember. How long had he played Ultimate Overlord? This session had surely stretched for days. The dark outside the windows of his high-rise penthouse confirmed that it was night and the accumulation of empty soda cans and boxes of munchies suggested that more than a day had passed. But even before this latest session, how many days, weeks, months, had he committed to the game, building a character from scratch, moving it up the ranks?

He certainly had the time. Having sold his software business at the peak of the tech bubble, he had no need to work ever again. And the thought of conquering a massively multi-player world until he was the only one standing had amused him. So he had scoured the tip sheets, bid up and purchased at online auctions any competing characters that had been offered, his aggressive bidding driving up the market and bringing more characters to the block. He had devised subroutines to handle the mundane housekeeping chores of the digital realm and generated legions of low level minions to do his bidding, finally setting them to guard the borders of the land and make sure that all new characters were destroyed before they gained power.

Months of time and mounds of meaningless money squandered to conquer a realm that existed only in virtual reality. Yet he was satisfied. Ultimate Overlord had become a massively single-player game.

It occurred to him that he might call someone to tell them of his victory, but he could think of no one to call. Clint had no friends. His work ethic in building his business had seen to that. (Even his old college buddy, Jason, no longer called. Maybe it was because Clint had seen to it that Jason's avatar, Alexander, had been destroyed. Maybe it was because Jason no longer played. Clint couldn't care less.) Clint had no enemies. He had crushed the competition long ago and now held his wealth in treasury bonds and gold bullion—items not affected by competitive forces. He had no servants. His luxury high-rise had the latest in robotic and automatic cleaning and servicing devices.

He noted with puzzlement the depth of the darkness surrounding his tower. A power failure, no doubt. Perhaps more. He noted now his computer had been operating on battery backup. The mini-fridge next to the desk was silent and the soda merely cool. The power had been out a long time. There were no lights in the distance, no cars moving on the highway, no planes in the sky.

He got up from his chair, working the stiffness out of his legs and shoulders as he moved toward the window. How long had he played Ultimate Overlord?

He had heard of hurricanes and tsunamis, back when he was still checking his e-mail to track online auctions of characters. He seemed to remember some talk or rumors of war. There was some scare story about HIV or avian flu, threats of dirty bombs and airborne agents. He vaguely remembered a flash of light and the sounds of gunfire in the distance. Or had that been in the game?

Then the power, his power, flickered and failed and he was alone in his tower. The wealthiest man on the planet. No friends. No enemies. For all he knew, the last man on earth.

He was the Ultimate Overlord. And he, too, had a choice.

He thought he knew his answer, but as the days turned to weeks turned to months turned to years, and he was eventually reduced to killing and eating rats in the darkness, he realized that he had never been an Ultimate Overlord.

He was just a lonely guy with a mouse and a flat screen monitor. He had no life, real or imagined.

He was a loser.

THE NEXT LEVEL

David Niall Wilson

The screen flashed yellow, then green, and the words "level up" appeared in a brilliant flash. Jason fell back in his seat, limp and drained. The controller dropped from his hand to land softly on the carpeted floor. So close. If one of those two things had gotten him, they would have sent him back. There was no way to save your progress in the game, you started each level from the beginning, and you made it through—or you didn't.

A door opened behind him, but Jason didn't look up.

"Congratulations." The voice floated to him from across the room.

"Thanks," Jason mumbled. He didn't feel any gratitude, but he also didn't want to piss them off. He needed to eat, and he needed to sleep. His eyes were all but closed already. He wasn't even sure he'd make it through the shower before he passed out. If he made them angry, they might make him play again, or raise the level.

"You've done well," the voice continued. "Rest."

Jason felt the belts around his chest loosen, and he rose shakily. Without looking over his shoulder, he headed for the shower and his own room. He knew there would be food and drink waiting by his bed. He also knew he didn't want to know the face of the woman behind him. He'd seen it once or twice, but it was fuzzy in his mind, and he intended to keep it that way. She was a wackobird of the first order, but she was in charge, and the last thing Jason wanted was to make it through this ordeal only to find he was in danger for knowing too much.

Behind him, he heard the game cartridge eject and the door close. He breathed deeply again and entered the small bathroom. It didn't matter who let him out of the chair, or why—only that they did.

Within ten minutes he'd showered, crammed a canned meat sandwich into his mouth, downed two sodas, and dropped across the bed, dead to the world.

General Vale paced the deck of the control room. His gaze swept the walls and stopped at each loosely covered vent. His expression was grim. His elite guard flanked the control room entrance, and a barrier manned by half a dozen others surrounded the control console. Was it enough?

Two levels below, sealed off from all points of
entry, the sorceress Makeeda, waited. He knew she
wasn't nervous; she had already seen the outcome.
She *knew* what he could only hope to be true.

Vale turned and stomped back the other way,
glancing at first one, and then another of the new
monitors they'd added to their defenses. Each of
the things Makeeda had foreseen had come true.
All of the weaknesses she had pointed out to him
were flaws he knew he should have anticipated on
his own. It drove him half mad with anger and the
desire for action. Where were they? Could she be
wrong this time?

He whirled a final time and there they were. One
of the new monitors, which showed an area just to
the left of the citadel's main gate, depicted a lone
figure stepping furtively from the cover of a stand
of trees. The intruder glanced about, gestured to
the shadows behind him, and a moment later a
group of at least twenty rebels ran across the shad-
owed space beside the citadel. There were no
guards stationed outside the walls. There were
never guards. The defenses were impenetrable. At
least that is what Vale believed.

The rebels dropped out of sight, but it didn't
matter. He knew where they were headed.

Vale gripped the captain of his guard by the
shoulder and shoved him toward the door. "Do it!
Now!" he cried.

The man rushed out of the chamber, followed by
one other. Vale spun and directed the remaining
guards into formation. He took his own place be-

hind the barrier at the main console. If all went well, there would be no need for such precautions, but he was learning that arrogance was the biggest weakness in his defenses, and he didn't have a death speech planned. He drew a long, wicked blade from the scabbard at his side and smiled.

The shaft was very dark, but Colin didn't hesitate. He'd been memorizing the layout of the ventilation system for a week. He knew how many feet stretched between one turn and the next, where the exits from the system could be located, and what the quickest route to the control center would be. He wore specially fabricated boots to minimize the sound of his passing through the hollow metal vents and his followers were similarly attired.

The outer access cover had been as easy to remove as their sources claimed it would be. He got it off and got them all out of sight and into the vents in a matter of moments. There was no alarm.

"We're in!" Felicia whispered in his ear.

He reached out and silenced her with a finger to the lips. He was as excited as she was, but they couldn't hesitate. Their entire plan depended on being quick and silent.

Felicia nodded and spun. She wedged herself into the vent, pressed her feet into the first ribbed joint, and levered herself upward. Colin followed. A few moments later they were all moving up through the floors of the citadel toward General Vale's control room.

They were nearly halfway up when the clang of

metal on metal rang out from above. Colin hissed
for them to hold their positions, and they waited
in breathless silence.

The hot oil never burned them. The impact of
heavy stones and metal, and the shock of striking
the bottom of the shaft, killed them all. Their final
screams, sharp barks of pain, fear, and confusion,
echoed from the walls of the shaft. The oil coated
the mass of broken bone and flesh and blended
with their blood. There was another, final clang
from above as the grate was closed.

Vale's men trooped out into the courtyard in
front of the citadel. They lined up in ranks around
a fenced stone circle. From the trees, rebel scouts
watched as, one by one, their fallen comrades were
dragged from the entrance to the ventilation system
and piled in the center of the circle. When they
were all in place, reaching shoulder height, General
Vale himself appeared.

The sorceress Makeeda walked at his side in se-
rene silence. She saw the pile of broken bodies,
stopped, and smiled. General Vale glanced over his
shoulder in annoyance and waited for her to join
him at a gap in the stone circle. Eventually she did
so, and he turned to the pyre.

"Bring wood," he said loudly.

Makeeda held up a hand. "There is no need,"
she said softly. She held her hands before her,
closed her eyes, and her smile broadened. The dead
rebels' clothing, soaked in oil, caught first. Flames
rippled along the length of the piled bodies and
traced outlines between them, searing flesh and

turning their uniforms to ash. The pile glowed red, smoldered and hissed, and then with a great burst of energy, was engulfed in flame.

Every man but one in those ranks flinched; most took an involuntary half step back. Only General Vale stood his ground. He watched as the flames leaped and danced, and breathed deeply as the scent of roasting flesh filled the air. Then he turned slowly and stared off through the trees in the direction from which the rebel attack had begun. He saw no one, but he glared as if nothing could block his sight. Makeeda giggled wildly and danced in circles, wreathed in the smoke of the funeral pyre.

When the last cinder of flesh had dropped to ash, and all that remained were the blackened hilts of swords and daggers and the carcasses of firearms, the general turned back toward the citadel. His men fell into ranks behind him and followed. Makeeda danced at his side, her steps nimble and seductive. She teased him with her long, dark tresses and brushed her lithe form against his back, beneath his swinging arms, even sliding once between his legs. Vale ignored her, and she never slowed his progress, blending her motion to his pace. As the last of the guards disappeared into the citadel, hoofbeats pounded away on the far side of the trees.

Jason's alarm screeched and he slapped at it in protest. His pounding had no effect; the ringing continued unabated. He opened his eyes and his dreams faded. He'd been in another place, with a woman. She'd been telling him stories and dancing.

The stark white walls of the bedroom sent the present crashing down around him and drove the last vestiges of the woman's features from his mind.

A mechanical voice spoke from the speaker in the clock radio.

"Are you ready for level ten, Jason?"

He glared at the clock, but didn't answer. He sat up, stretched, stood, and looked around for breakfast. Every day of his incarceration he'd been fed a good solid breakfast, with juice and coffee. The coffee was particularly important because once he sat down at the game console the chair would grip him and lock. He would be stuck there until he played through the level to the end, and he needed to be alert. He needed to take a leak.

The clock flashed once, then a second time. The numbers shifted, and suddenly it was a timer, counting down from ten minutes. Every morning he'd had less time to prepare and less warning. Jason dove for the bathroom, splashed cold water in his face, and relieved himself as quickly as his aching bladder would allow.

He staggered out; found two sticky cinnamon buns and half a pot of black coffee, and wolfed it down. The coffee was strong, and it bit his throat and stomach with prickly dry-rotted teeth, but he drank it anyway. There was no time to complain, and no one to hear if he did. He washed it all down with a tall glass of water from the sink, and headed quickly into the next room.

The timer on the bedside table flashed less than one minute remaining.

Jason seated himself in front of a large, flat screen monitor. The controller sat on the desk in front of him. It glowed with neon green brilliance. He picked it up and, despite his situation, he smiled. It was a good controller. For that matter, it was a good game. Played on his own terms, in his room and without so much on the line, he'd have dug it big time. Today wasn't the day to dwell on it, though. Today he had to kick butt. There were only two levels remaining, and he had to beat them both if he ever wanted to see the outside world again.

The two clamps attached to the sides of the chair rotated so that they circled his waist. He heard the *thunk* of magnets engaging, and knew he was in for the duration. Whatever it took. The screen blinked, and a woman appeared.

"Welcome to level ten. I am Makeeda."

Despite his discomfort, Jason sat a bit straighter and stared. The graphics were incredible, and the three-dimensional image facing him was beautiful. She was tall, draped in dark silk robes of many colors, slit along one side, exposing one leg. Her eyes were wide and tinted an odd lavender that fascinated him.

"The rebel attack has been thwarted, but the war is not won," she intoned. "The rebel leader, Colin, had a lover, and she is angry. The next assault will be a direct attack involving superior forces. Your mission is to thwart that attack and devise a counteroffensive using the assets allotted. If the citadel falls, you will not advance to the final level."

"Am I clear?"

As she spoke this last, Makeeda arched her back and displayed herself lewdly. Jason's mouth went dry. He nodded, and then realized how stupid it was to nod to a graphic image on a video game screen. As if catching his mistake, the woman threw her head back and laughed uproariously. As her image faded from the screen, she said.

"Begin."

"I just don't see how he can *know*," Braden growled. "Every time we make a move, he's there ahead of us, grinning. Now he's killed Colin. Maybe . . ."

"Maybe what?" Mavin asked voice cold. Her eyes flashed dangerously, and her hand dropped to the hilt of the long, thin blade she carried in the scabbard on her belt. "Maybe we should just turn around and go back to the hills and hide? Maybe Colin should just be left to blow around General Vale's courtyard, his ashes forgotten and unavenged? Maybe we should just quit?"

Braden backed away quickly, raising both hands.

"No, of course not," he said. "But what can we do? He's proven more clever in every encounter so far."

Mavin's frown deepened, but she removed her hand from her weapon. "That is strange, isn't it?" she said at last. "I've known Vale since before father's death. He was good swordsman, and a strong military man, but he was no tactician. In fact, if anything, I would have said he was too impulsive and rash to be any kind of leader at all."

"The vent access should have worked," Braden said. He smacked a fist into his palm. "We spent a year and a half getting our man into a position of trust. He served in the citadel for six months, and they were absolutely unaware of that flaw in their defense."

"Where is this man now?" Mavis asked.

"If you're thinking he betrayed us," Braden said, "forget it. He died with Colin in the vents. They didn't get word from us—they just knew. It's probably something that witch Makeeda has managed to conjure."

"Don't start any rumors," Mavis snapped. "Vale and his men are enough for us to deal with. If the men start worrying about spells and hexes, we might as well retreat now."

"They are already talking," Braden said. "Some of the men were there. They saw her light their comrades on fire with a shake of her hands. She laughed as good men's bodies burned and danced like some sort of harlot around Vale—like a victory dance. They've been talking since then, and they will keep talking until we do something to silence them."

Mavin bit her lip, and then nodded. "Assemble the officers. It's time we were a bit more direct, I think. Let's take this battle to Vale."

Braden nodded and hurried off.

Makeeda sat in a room miles away from the rebel camp. In her hand she held a small square with a glowing screen. On the screen, she saw Mavin and heard her words. Makeeda threw her head back and laughed.

The speaker crackled to life, and Jason would have leaped from his seat if he hadn't been strapped in place.

"The rebel offensive is underway," said the sultry, seductive, electronic voice. In the corner of the screen, Makeeda's face appeared. She smiled, but there was little real humor in the expression. Jason shivered at the detail in that CGI sneer. Whoever the model was for this game, he hoped never to meet her in a dark alley.

He weighed his character's assets against those of the rebel force, now registering on the enemy forces radar at the bottom of his monitor screen. He was outnumbered three to one, but he held the citadel. His defenses were operational. He had a variety of battle engines at his command, a small troop of cavalry soldiers, and about five hundred trained fighters who would do battle on foot if the need arose.

The rebels were armed, for the most part, with conventional siege weapons. They were about fifty percent mounted, but that would pose no threat to the citadel. What worried him were the two large wheeled devices located about halfway back in the ordered columns marching toward his gate. He didn't know what they were, exactly. Weapons, probably, but how to be sure? And if they were weapons, what did they do? Were they a real threat, or only meant to distract him? It was going to take more than a standard siege to take the citadel, but these rebels would know that. They had to have a plan, and he had to figure out what that plan was.

Jason flipped controls and punched buttons until the screen filled with a map of the area. The rebels appeared as green dots on the far edge of the map. Their current and possible routes to the citadel were displayed as glowing lines in varying shades of red. The brighter the color, the more likely it was that the rebels would take that route. He had one bright red line and two that were only slightly darker to either side.

He studied the terrain. The most likely route ran directly down a valley between two tall peaks. A quick calculation told him they'd have to camp on the far side of this valley. If they got caught inside at night they might not make it through, and even if they did, they'd be close enough to fear a counterattack at that point. It made sense that they would rest. A strategy formed.

He called up two of the elite guard characters and outfitted them with horses and weapons. He opened the mission menu and selected "capture." A set of icons popped up representing known members of the enemy force. The first was a strikingly beautiful woman warrior named Mavis. Jason stared into her ice-blue eyes, moved the cursor with his thumb-operated joystick, and pushed "select."

Makeeda's face appeared in the upper right hand corner of the screen. Her eyes were animated, not like a CGI-generated character at all, and when she spoke it was so real he might have been seated across a table from her.

"You have selected a capture mission. Your chosen target is Mavis, lover of Colin and current leader of the rebel alliance. Please confirm your orders."

Jason didn't hesitate. He selected confirm. He felt like the mission would accomplish one of two things. Either it would succeed, and he'd have the current rebel leader hostage, or he would send the message to the enemy that they were being watched, and that nothing they did would be a surprise. He also hoped that the party he sent out would bring word of the two unknown siege engines.

Meanwhile, he set about placing traps and barriers throughout the immediate area of the citadel itself. He made certain that the vents were still watched, and concentrated on details. He checked the timer in the lower left corner of the screen. This was a very long scenario. If his plan failed, he wasn't going to survive staying up to run through it again. He had to keep active, do everything he could think of to bolster the defenses of the citadel, and pray that his side mission wasn't a waste of time. If they could cut out the leadership of the enemy, the efficiency of the attacking forces should be crippled, at the very least. If they could use the hostage to their advantage, they might avoid major confrontation completely.

When he'd done everything he could think of to prepare, he hit the one button that gave him hope. It was marked, simply, "accelerate."

*   *   *

Locked in her room, seated in full lotus on a pile of furs and rugs so soft she sank in and blended, Makeeda stared at the small glowing square in her hand. She watched as events blurred. What had been a slow advance of rebel forces across the fields became an intricate web of quickly progressing lines of probability. She watched as one line diverged from the citadel, skirted the forest to the left of the main road, and wound around behind the rapidly approaching rebel forces.

This small force slipped in, and back out, apparently undetected, their mission a success, and moving much more rapidly than the small army with its siege engines and ground troops, wound its way back toward the citadel and General Vale.

"Excellent," she whispered.

Makeeda tucked the talisman into her robe and rose. In doing so, she missed the quick wash of colored waves across the surface. The images distorted, righted themselves, and then distorted again, but there was no one to see.

Jason panicked as the images on the screen wavered. His small force had infiltrated the rebel encampment, and somehow they'd managed to make off with the rebel leader, Mavin, but now the system seemed to have overloaded. He quickly whacked his hand against the side of the control in the universal frustrated repair tic of gamers everywhere, but it was no use. The picture wavered, cleared up, and then, with a final fizzle of static, went dead.

He sat and stared at the screen. He gripped the controller so tightly he heard a small pop, looked down, and tossed it away quickly before it could break. The straps of the chair held him fast, and he had to fight the sudden claustrophobic wave of fear that threatened to engulf him.

It took a few moments for the pounding on the door and the rasping voice crying from the other side to break through the rush of blood and too-fast pounding of his heart. There was a splintering crash, and the door burst inward.

"Police," he heard. "Don't move!"

Jason stared at the blank screen as relief flooded his sense. Then he threw his head back and began to laugh.

General Vale stared at the sorceress in disbelief. "Gone? Our contact is gone? What does that mean? Can't you break through somehow and get it back?"

Makeeda shook her head. Her expression was unreadable. Her hands were buried deep in the folds of her gown. Vale considered having her seized and searched and trying the device himself, but he knew there was no point. If she couldn't make it work, it was over.

"It does not matter," she said. "I witnessed the capture of Mavis before the connection was lost. Your men will bring her here very shortly, and well ahead of her forces. We have everything we need."

"I would have told you that the first day we spoke of this," Vale growled. "I would have been wrong, and this citadel would already be in enemy hands, ruled by that upstart Colin. I no longer trust the obvious."

"Trust me," Makeeda purred, stepping closer and sliding around him in slow circles. Her robes teased over the leather of his boots, and her hair brushed his shoulder in passing. Vale's eyes narrowed. She continued, "I am never obvious."

Makeeda curled herself in under his arm and the two of them stood there, very close, and watched the security monitors. A scout burst from the trees and not far behind him the small force Vale had sent to capture the rebel princess followed. Vale allowed himself a single ill-formed smile before unwinding Makeeda from his arm and heading down to greet his unwilling guest. Perhaps things would go well after all.

Mavis was beautiful. She was still dressed in battle gear, though her armor had been stripped from her, and her arms were bound behind her with straps of leather. Her long hair flowed down her back, and her eyes flashed fire. Vale grinned and stared at her for several minutes, making two slow, circuitous rounds to study her from all angles before speaking.

Makeeda said nothing. She stood in the corner, her lips pressed very tightly together and her brow knit in a tight frown. Every few moments she pulled the small vision cube from her pocket and shook it, but there was nothing. Not even a dim glow met her gaze. Every time Vale ran his gaze up and down the prisoner's lithe form, Makeeda shook the device in her hand harder.

"So, we finally meet," Vale said softly. "I had hoped to speak with your brother, as well, but he . . . fell on his way inside."

Mavin struggled fiercely. Her eyes blazed again, and Vale laughed.

"If I'd known how lovely you were, I'd have taken you long ago," he said, leering.

"They will take this citadel," she grated, "and they will burn you as you burned my brother. You and your little witch." Mavin spat toward Makeeda, who merely stepped back out of range. Vale only laughed.

Then he stepped closer, and though she struggled wildly, she was held as he lifted her chin, inspected her more closely, and shook his head.

"Not right for a warrior," he said dismissively, "but there are other ways you can serve."

He turned to his men.

"Take her to my chambers. Bind her to the bed. I will deal with her myself."

Makeeda started forward. Her lips parted, and then clamped shut. Vale turned to her, as if daring her to argue. Their gazes locked, and Makeeda turned away. She left the room quickly. Vale watched her go, smiled, and turned back to his men.

"Prepare the defenses. They will be here soon enough to try and retrieve their princess. We will be ready for them."

Turning, Vale strode back up the stairs to the control center. His smile was very wide.

*   *   *

When the defenses were set, and his scouts had reported, General Vale set a watch and climbed the stairs to his chambers. He'd been distracted by the moments to come since Mavis had entered the citadel, and he could wait no longer.

He entered his chambers, dropped his sword and weapons on a table in the outer room, and stepped to the doorway of his bedroom. The lights were dim, but he made out Mavis' form, bound hand and foot atop the furs, and he smiled.

He stepped closer and seated himself on the edge of the bed. Her rough gear had been cut or stripped away. She wore only a swath of silk about her middle. She stared at him defiantly, but he saw the fear that hovered just beneath the thin veneer of her courage, and licked his lips. It would be a memorable night—a small battle before finally winning the war.

"I have waited for this a long time," he said, turning and pressing his hand into the mattress on the far side of her body, staring down at her in dark hunger.

"So have I," she whispered. With a cry, Mavin lunged. Her left hand, which had appeared to be bound tightly to the headboard, hurtled forward. The sharp blade of a long, thin dagger dug into his chest and she dragged it down, crying out with each rending drag of knife through his flesh.

Vale drew back, bellowing in pain and anger, but the dagger had found its mark. He held out a hand to her, gasped, and then stared dumbly as blood poured between his lips with his breath.

"No," he croaked. "This is impossible. I'm . . . invincible."

Mavin watched him, and then turned her gaze to the curtained window just beyond him on the far wall. Makeeda stepped from behind the curtains. Her eyes glittered, and she watched impassively as her lord fell to his knees, tried to speak, failed . . . and died.

Mavin watched her warily, but Makeeda paid no attention to the bound prisoner. She pulled the talisman from her robes and stared at it. The images had not returned, but it had regained its glow. There were two words, floating in the center of the screen, bouncing from one wall to the other as if trying to escape.

She read fiery script out loud, and without warning, the sorceress began to laugh.

"Game Over."

She tossed the cube into the pooled blood on Vale's chest and turned, striding quickly from the room and disappearing into the shadows.

ADVISERS AT NAPTIME

Kristine Kathryn Rusch

It was time for Carol's nap. They always forgot her nap. Mommy says every kid needs a nap. Carol used to hate naps, but now she's *tired*. All she wanted was her blankie, her cuddly dog, and her squishy pillow.

And Mommy. They never let Mommy into the playroom with her.

They said Mommy sat outside, but once they left the door unlocked and Carol got out. She was in a cold hallway that looked like a giant tube or something. No chairs, icky white lights, and a hard gray floor.

No Mommy, no guards, no one to hear if she cried.

She stamped her foot and screamed. Everybody came running. Mommy said they were watching a TV screen with Carol on it in that room up there—

and then she pointed at this tiny window, way up at the end of the hall—and Carol got mad.

"You lied," she said, pointing her finger at Mommy in that way Mommy said was rude and mean. "You promised. You'd be right here. You said!"

Mommy got all flustered. Her cheeks got kinda pink when she was flustered and she messed with her hair, twirling it even though she yelled at Carol for doing the same thing.

"I meant," Mommy said in that voice she gets when she's upset, "I'd be able to see you all the time."

"You said—"

"I know what I said, honey." Mommy looked at one of the guards—they're these big guys with square faces and these weird helmets you could see through. They also had big guns on their sides, latched down so nobody can grab them away—and then she looked back at Carol. "I meant I'd be able to see you. I'm sorry I said it wrong."

Carol wiped at her face. It was wet. She was crying and she didn't know it. She *hated* that. She hated this place. It wasn't fun like Mommy said it would be. It was a thinky place filled with grown-ups who didn't get it.

Mommy said she'd be playing games all day, and she did, kinda, but by herself. She sat in front of this computer and punched numbers.

Once this scary guy came in. He wore bright reds, and he kinda looked like a clown. He bent down like grown-ups do, and talked to her like she was really stupid.

He said, "Carol, my dear, I'm so glad you're going to help me with my little project. We'll have fun."

Only she never saw him again.

Which was good, because she didn't like him. He was fake cheery. She *hated* fake cheery. If he was gonna be icky, he should just be icky instead of pretending to be all happy and stuff. But she didn't tell him that. She didn't tell him a lot of stuff because she didn't like him. And she never saw him again. Just his mittens.

Mommy said every important person had mittens. Everybody who worked for him could be called a mitten, which meant Carol was one, even though she didn't look like a mitten. She finally figured it was some kinda code word—everybody here liked code words—for workers.

She thought it was a stupid one—Mommy would say, *be careful of Lord Kafir and his mittens*—and Carol would have to try not to laugh. How can people be afraid of big fake-cheery guys with mittens? 'Specially when they had big red shoes and shiny red pants like those clowns at that circus Uncle Reeve took her to.

Carol had a lot of uncles. Mommy used to bring them over a lot. Then she met Lord Kafir, and the uncles didn't come to the house any more. Lord Kafir promised Mommy a lot of money if Carol would play games at the Castle with him.

Mommy asked if this was a Neverland Ranch kinda thing and Lord Kafir's mittens—the ones who'd come to the house—looked surprised. Those mittens didn't wear helmets. They wore suits like real grown-ups and they had sunglasses and guns like Carol had seen on TV.

They wouldn't let her touch the guns (she *hated* it when grown-ups wouldn't let her touch stuff) but they promised she'd be playing with "weapons" all the time.

Mommy had to explain that weapons were like guns and stuff, only cooler.

So here's what Carol thought then: she thought she'd be going to a real castle, like that one they show on the Disney Channel—maybe a blue one, maybe a pink one, with Tinkerbell flying around it, and lots of sparkly lights. She thought she get to wear a pretty dress like Cinderella, and dance with giant mice who were really nice, or meet a handsome beast like Belle did.

All the girls who go to castles get to wear pretty dresses with sparkly shoes, and they got to grow their hair really long (Mommy keeps Carol's hair short because "it's easier") and got to dance what Mommy called a walls, and they lived happily ever after.

But that's not what happened. The Castle wasn't a castle. It's this big building all gray and dark that's built into a mountain. The door let you in and said stuff like *checking, checking, all clear* before you got to go through another door.

Then there was the mittens. The ones outside the mountain door wore suits and sunglasses. The ones inside actually had the helmets and weird-looking guns and big boots. They scared Mommy—the mit-

tens did, not the boots—and she almost left right
then. But the assistant, Ms. Hanaday, joined them
and talked to Mommy and reminded her about all
the money she'd get for just three months of Carol's time (Carol didn't like that), and Mommy
grabbed Carol's hand really tight and led her right
into the castle hall mountain like it was okay.

Carol dug her feet in. She was wearing her pretti-
est shoes—all black and shiny (but no heels.
Mommy says little girls can't wear heels)—and they
scraped on that gray floor, leaving black marks.
Mommy yelled at her, and Carol hunched even
harder, because the place smelled bad, like doctors
or that school she went to for three days, and
Mommy said the smell was just air-conditioning,
but they had air-conditioning at home and it didn't
smell like this. At home, it smelled like the Jones'
dog when he got wet. Here it smelled cold and
metal and—wrong.

Carol hated it, but Mommy didn't care. She said,
"Just three months," then took Carol to this room
with all the stuff where she was supposed to play
with Lord Kafir, and that's when Mommy said
she'd be right outside.

So Mommy lied—and Carol hated liars.

And now all she wanted was a nap, and nobody
was listening because Mommy was a liar and nobody was in that room. Carol was gonna scream
and pound things if they didn't let her nap really
soon. She wanted her blankie. She wanted her
bed.

She wanted to be let out of this room.

She didn't care how many cookies they gave her for getting stuff right. She *hated* it here.

"Hate it," she said, pounding on the keyboard of the computer they had in here. "Hate it, hate it, hate it."

Each time she said "hate," her fist hit the keyboard. It jumped and made a squoogy sound. She kinda liked that sound. It was better than the stupid baby music they played in here or the dumb TV shows that she'd never seen before.

She wanted her movies. She wanted her big screen. She wanted her blankie and her bed.

She wanted a nap.

She pounded again, and Mommy opened the door.

"Honey, you're supposed to be looking at the pretty pictures."

She was leaning in and her cheeks was pink. If her hands wasn't grabbing the door, they'd be twirling her hair, and she might even be chewing on it.

"I don't like the pictures," Carol said.

"Honey—"

"I wanna go home."

"Tonight, honey."

"Now," Carol said.

"Honey, we're here to work for Lord Kafir."

"Don't like him." Carol crossed her arms.

"You're not supposed to like him."

"He's s'posed to play with me."

"No, honey, you're supposed to play with his toys."

"A computer's not a toy." Carol was just repeating what Mommy had told her over and over.

"No, dear, but the programs are. You're supposed to look at them and—"

"The bad guy always wins," Carol said. She *hated* it here. She wanted to see Simba or Belle or her friends on the TV. Or maybe go back to that kindergarten that Mommy hated because they said Carol was average. She didn't know what average was 'cept Mommy didn't like it. Mommy made it sound bad.

Until that day when she was looking at the want ads like she did *(Honey, don't mess with the paper. Mommy needs to read the want ads)* and then she looked up at Carol with that goofy frowny look and whispered, "Average five-year-old . . ."

"What?" Mommy asked.

"In the games," Carol said. "The bad guy always wins."

Mommy slid into the room and closed the door. "The bad guy's supposed to win, honey."

"No, he's not!" Carol shouted. "He gets blowed up or his parrot leaves him or the other lions eat him or he gets runned over by a big truck or his spaceship crashes. The good guys win."

Mommy shushed her and made up-and-down quiet motions with her hands. "Lord Kafir's a good guy."

"I'm not talkin 'bout him!" Carol was still shouting. Shouting felt good when you couldn't have a nap. "On the computer. The bad guys always win. It's a stupid game. I *hate* that game."

"Maybe you could do the numbers for a while, then, honey."

"The numbers, you hit the right button and they make stupid words. Nobody thinks I know letters but I do." Carol learned her ABCs a long time ago. "What's D-E-A-T-H-R-A-Y?"

"Candy," Mommy said. Her voice sounded funny.

Carol frowned. That didn't sound right.

"What's I-R-A-Q?"

Mommy grabbed her hair and twirled it. "Chocolate."

"What's W-H-I-T-E-H-O-U-S-E?" Carol asked.

"That's in there?" Mommy's face got all red.

"What's W-O-R-L-D-D-O-M-I-N-A-T-I-O-N?" Carol asked.

"D . . . D . . . O . . ." Mommy was frowning now too. "Oh. Oh!"

"See?" Carol said. "Stupid words. I hate stupid words and dumb numbers. And games where the bad guy wins. I want to go home, Mommy."

"Um, sure," Mommy said. She looked at the door, then at Carol. "Later. We'll go later."

"Now," Carol said.

Mommy shook her head. "Carol, honey, you know we can't leave until five."

"I wanna nap!" Carol shouted, then felt her own cheeks get hot. She never asked for a nap before. "And a cookie. And my cuddly dog and my pillow. I wanna go away. I hate it here, Mommy. I hate it."

"We have to keep coming, honey. We promised."

"No." Carol said and swung her chair around so she was looking at the computer.

It was blinking bright red. It never did that before.

"Mommy, look." Carol pointed at the big red word.

Mommy looked behind her like she thought somebody might come in the room. "Honey, I'm not supposed to see this—"

"What's that say?"

Mommy looked. Then Mommy grabbed Carol real tight, and ran for the door. She got it open, but all those mittens with guns and helmets were outside, with guns pointed.

Mommy stopped. "Please let us go. Please."

"I'm sorry, ma'am," the man with the biggest gun said. "You have to wait for Ms. Hanaday."

"We can't wait for Ms. Hanaday," Mommy said. "My daughter punched the computer. Now it's counting down to a self-destruct."

Carol squirmed. She watched *Star Trek*. She knew what a self-destruct was. "We gots to go," she whispered.

Mommy just squeezed her tighter.

"We gots to go!" Carol shouted.

Mommy nodded.

The guards kept their guns on them.

"A self-destruct?" one of them whispered.

Another guard elbowed him. "She's the average five-year-old. She finds the holes before we implement the program."

"Huh?" the first guard asked.

"Y'know, how they always say that the plan's so bad an average five-year-old could figure out how to get around it? She's the average—"

"Enough!" Mommy said. "I don't care if it is fake. I'm not going to take that risk."

Carol squirmed. She wanted to kick, but Mommy hated it when she kicked. Sometimes Carol got in trouble for kicking Mommy. Not always. Sometimes Mommy forgot to yell at her. But right now, Mommy was stressed. She'd yell.

"I'm sorry, ma'am," the first guard said. "We can't let you go until Ms. Hanaday gets here."

"And she is!" a lady's voice said from far away. Carol peered around Mommy, and sure enough, there was that Ms. Hanaday, in her high heels and her black suit and wearing her glasses halfway down her nose even though she wasn't as old as Mommy was.

"I wanna go," Carol whispered.

"I know, honey," Mommy said, but she wasn't listening. She was just talking like she did when Carol was bugging her. But she did set Carol down, only she kept ahold of Carol's hand so Carol couldn't run away.

Ms. Hanaday was holding a bag. Her heels made clicky noises on the hard gray floor. It was colder out here than it was in that room. Carol shivered. She wanted a jacket. She wanted her blankie. She wanted a nap.

"I wanna go home," she said again.

One of the guards looked at her real nice-like. He was somebody's daddy, she just knew it. Maybe if she acted just a little cuter . . .

"What have we got here?" Ms. Hanaday said as she got close. She reached into the bag, and crouched at the same time. She whipped out a giant chocolate chip cookie, the kind Mommy said had to last at least three meals.

Carol reached for it, but Mommy grabbed her hand.

"We would like to leave now," Mommy said.

"May I remind you, Ms. Rogers, that you signed a three-month contract? It's only been three weeks."

"Still. My daughter isn't happy, and I'm not real comfortable here. No child should have to work all day."

"It's not designed as work, ma'am. It's play."

"Is not," Carol muttered, wanting that cookie. She stared at it. Maybe if she stared hard enough, it would float over to her. She seen that in movies too.

"Did you hear her?" Mommy asked. "She doesn't think it's play."

"Wanna nap," Carol told Ms. Hanaday.

Really want that cookie, but Mommy still had ahold of her hand. Too tight. Mommy's hand was cold and kinda sweaty.

Ms. Hanaday was frowning at her.

"I don't like it here," Carol said louder this time, in case Ms. Hanady didn't hear so good. "Wanna go."

"The day's not over yet," Ms. Hanaday said.

"Delores!" Lord Kafir shouted from down the hall. Carol knew it was him because he had the funny accent Mommy called Brid Ish. Some people from England had it. Most of them got to be bad guys in movies.

Carol shivered again.

Ms. Hanaday stood up. Lord Kafir was hurrying

down the hall. His shoes didn't make that clicky sound. They were kinda quiet, maybe because they weren't official grown-up shoes.

"Is it true?" he asked Ms. Hanaday like there wasn't Mommy and Carol and all those guys with the big guns. "Did she break the code?"

"I'm afraid so," Ms. Hanaday said. She was holding the cookie so hard part of it broke. She had to move really fast to catch it before it fell to the ground.

Now the cookie was Carol-size. Carol looked at Mommy, but Mommy wasn't looking at her.

"This is the five-year-old, right?" Lord Kafir pushed past Ms. Hanaday, knocking the cookie again. She had to grab real fast and still parts of it fell on the floor. Wasted. Carol wanted to get them, but Mommy wouldn't let her go.

"Yes, sir. This is Carol. You've met her."

"That's right." He crouched.

Carol made a face at him. She hated people who forgot her.

"You look pretty smart," he said.

"I'm tired," she said.

"Are you smart?" he asked.

"Of course I am, dummy," Carol said.

"Carol!" Mommy breathed. "We don't talk to grown-ups like that."

He wasn't a grown-up. He was a mean man in bright red clothes. He was glaring at her like she'd done something wrong.

"I think you're pretty smart," he said like that was bad.

"Her teachers said she was average," Mommy said.

"We tested her IQ three times. She always came out in the normal range." Ms. Hanaday sounded kinda scared.

"You know that children often give unreliable IQ tests." Lord Kafir pushed up and looked at the other grown-ups. "I don't think she's average."

"Mr. . . . Lord . . . Sir," Mommy said. "She's—"

"The other five-year-olds couldn't beat that self-destruct," he said.

"They barely got a chance, sir." Ms. Hanaday was dripping cookie crumbs. "She got it earlier than the others—"

"Because she solved the earlier puzzles sooner. She's good at code words and passwords and secret plans. She shouldn't be this good if she's average."

"She watches a lot of television," Mommy said.

"Can I have that cookie?" Carol asked.

Everybody looked at her.

"Please?" she asked in her best company voice.

"Oh, for heaven's sake," Mommy said, but Ms. Hanaday handed her all the parts of the cookie.

Carol chomped. The cookie wasn't as good as it looked. Maybe because it got all sweaty and gooey in Ms. Hanaday's hand.

"I swear, sir," Ms. Hanaday said. "She's average."

"I'm tired of five-year-olds," he said. "It's time to implement the plan."

"Sir! We can't do that! It's not ready!" Ms. Hanaday said.

"Get it ready," he said.

"But the five-year-old—"

"Isn't average," he said.

Ms. Hanaday looked at Mommy like Mommy had gone into the living room without permission. It was like that code grown-ups had. Lord Kafir understood, even if Carol didn't.

"Have you seen anything?" Lord Kafir asked Mommy.

"No," Mommy said. She was lying. Carol looked at her in shock. Mommy was a horrible liar. She lied all the time. Carol just didn't know it before.

"She saw the red lights," Carol said. She didn't want Mommy to get in trouble with Lord Kafir. "It scared her."

"Red scares a lot of people," he said, smoothing his ugly clothes. Was that why he wore them? To scare people?

The guards looked at each other, like they didn't like any of this.

Ms. Hanaday shook her head.

"Pay the lady her three weeks and get them out of here," Lord Kafir said to her. "And wash your hands. You're a mess."

"Yes, sir," Ms. Hanaday said, but Lord Kafir was already hurrying down the hall.

The guards had lowered their weapons.

Ms. Hanaday ran a hand through her hair, making a streak of chocolate on the side of her face. It looked a little like poo.

Carol tried not to giggle.

"You know that this is all just war games," Ms. Hanaday said.

"Sure," Mommy said.

"Pretend stuff," Ms. Hanaday said.

"Yeah," Mommy said.

"None of it means anything," Ms. Hanaday said.

"I know," Mommy said.

"I'll get your check," Ms. Hanaday said, "and meet you at the door."

"Okay," Mommy said.

Ms. Hanaday hurried off after Lord Kafir. The guards just stared after her.

"I don't like this," one said to the other.

Mommy picked Carol up like she was a baby. "We're going, honey."

Carol swallowed the last of the cookie. Cookies were yucky without milk. "Okay," she said.

Mommy hurried down the hall, a different way than everybody else went. It only took a few minutes to get to the door.

Ms. Hanaday was already there, holding a long piece of paper. It had to be a check. Mommy snatched it, then said thanks in a kinda rude voice, and then hurried out the door.

Nobody stopped them. In the movies, somebody would've stopped them. 'Specially the way Mommy was breathing, like she was all scared and stuff.

Carol wasn't scared. Carol was glad to be outside where the sun was bright and the air smelled really good. She stretched. She wanted down. She wanted to run, but Mommy held tight all the way to the car.

They backed up and headed out of the parking lot, driving really, really fast.

"If you want a nap," Mommy said, "close your eyes."

"Where're we going?" Carol asked.

"Far away," Mommy said.

"Can we get my blankie?"

"Maybe," Mommy said. That meant no. Carol sighed. She hated no. But not as much as she hated that place.

"What's far away?" Carol asked.

"Good guys," Mommy said.

Carol smiled. This was how it was supposed to go. She leaned back in her chair and closed her eyes. But she couldn't sleep. Mommy was driving really bad. Fast like in the movies. Tires squealing. Going around corners on two wheels, stuff like that.

Mommy'd been watching Carol play too many games.

Carol opened her eyes. They were on a road outta town. Carol'd never been outta town before. This was kinda cool.

"Mommy?"

"Hmm?" Mommy said in that don't-bother-me voice.

"Am I average?"

"I hope so, honey," Mommy said. "In fact, I'm praying that you are."

"Because average kids beat the game?" Carol asked.

"And that means it's easy," Mommy said.

It didn't seem easy. It was just dumb. But Carol didn't say that. She closed her eyes again. She didn't care about numbers and weird letters and computers. Or bad guys like Lord Kafir. They could be scary, but they always lost in the end.

At least she got part of what she wanted. She got a cookie. She got outta there.

And now—*finally*—she was gonna take a nap.

A WOMAN'S WORK . . .

Tanya Huff

.

It was obvious that the man outside the city wall was a Hero. His plain but serviceable armor—armor that had obviously seen several campaigns—did nothing to hide the breadth of his shoulders, the narrowness of his hips, or the long and muscular length of his legs. His hair gleamed gold under the edges of his helmet and even from her viewing platform on the top of the wall, Queen Arrabel could tell his eyes were a clear sky blue with the direct, unwavering gaze of an honorable man.

Over his left arm, he wore a simple unadorned shield, designed to deflect blows, not to support his ego by announcing his family ties to the world. In his right hand, he carried a sword. It looked like a hand-and-a-half, double-edged broadsword although he was so mighty a warrior he made it seem small. She could just make out a heavy gold ring on the second finger of his right hand. It was the only jewelry he wore.

"Prince Danyel!" He called, his voice clear and carrying. "Come out and face me. Let you and I settle the animosity between our two peoples! There is no need for war; we will fight man to man! He who wins our conflict will decide all!"

The queen raised her own voice enough to be heard by her people standing along the wall. "A gold coin to the archer who puts one in his eye."

For an instant there was the sound like buzz of a hundred wasps.

Then a sound like a sudden hard rain on a slate roof.

Then silence.

Leaning a little past the battlement to get a better line of sight, the queen smiled. "Nice grouping, archers. Well done. Wallace!"

"Majesty!" Her personal aide leaped forward.

"Go down and check the fletching on those arrows—it looks like we have at least three winners." Her archers were her pride and joy, even though she knew she shouldn't have favorites among her extensive armies. "Take a wizard with you to make sure he hasn't been magically booby-trapped, then strip the body. Bring the armor and the ring to me, have the body cremated."

"And his horse, Majesty?"

The beautiful black stallion standing just to the right of the gate stared up at her with intelligent eyes.

"Archers!"

"Mother! I wanted that horse!"

Arrabel sighed, turning to her son as the stallion whirled to escape and crashed dead to the ground, looking remarkably like a horse-shaped pincushion. "Horses don't have intelligent eyes, Danyel. Nor are they able to determine who, in a group of people standing on top of a wall twenty feet over their heads, is in charge."

Danyel frowned, dark brows almost meeting over his nose. "So the Hero knew I'd win and take his horse and the horse was to kill me later. The horse was enchanted and the Hero was a sacrifice."

"I suspect the horse was no more than a backup plan. Heroes never think they're going to lose."

"I could have taken him." At nearly twenty he was too old to pout but his tone was distinctly sulky.

She patted his arm as she passed. "Of course you could have. Captain Jurin."

Almost overcome by adoration, clearly astounded that the queen knew his name, the captain stepped forward and saluted. "Majesty!"

"Send out a couple of patrols to make sure this Hero didn't leave one of those annoying sidekicks skulking about in the bushes."

"Yes, Majesty."

On the way back to the palace, she smiled and waved and noted how pleased everyone her son's age and younger was to see her. The free schooling she provided for her subjects until the age of twelve was paying off—it was so much easier to teach children how to think than it was to change their minds as adults. A strong apprenticeship program helped too. Idle hands found time for mischief and nothing straightened out a young troublemaker faster than twelve hours of hauling stone. City walls didn't build themselves, after all.

It pleased her too to see so many babies around. Young men who tried to get out of the responsibilities of fatherhood were sent to the mines and their very fair wages were paid entirely to the mother of their child. Fatherhood seemed a good deal in comparison. And the sort of man that might succeed at rebellion soon thought better of it when he became responsible for the care and feeding of six or seven screaming children—said children guaranteed schooling and employment should the status quo be maintained.

"Mother."

One child had certainly done his best to sap her energy.

"Mother!"

"What is it, Danyel?"

"There's a girl standing on your statue."

"That's nice, dear." Arrabel blew a kiss to a strapping young man and smiled to see him blush. "Which statue?"

"The one with your hand on the head of the beggar brat. Mother, you'd better pay attention to this!"

Sighing, she turned and glanced toward the statue in question. "Don't point, Danyel. It's common."

He dropped his arm with a sullen clank of vanbrace against breastplate. "Well, do you see her?"

It was hard to miss her. "Andrew, stop the coach." As the six archers in her escort moved into new defensive positions, the queen shifted over to stare out Danyel's window.

The girl had a head of flaming red hair and stood with one booted foot on the beggar child's stone head and the other tucked into the queen's bent elbow. Gesturing dramatically, she pitched her voice to carry over the ambient noise of the streets and shrieked that the queen cared nothing for her subjects.

"That would go farther if she wasn't standing in front of the hospital you had built," Danyel muttered.

The people loved the hospital. Arrabel loved it more. With all healers working for the crown at salaries too good to walk away from, the crown controlled who got healed and how.

"The queen has turned you into mindless drones in her glittering hive!"

People who might not have noticed the girl noticed the queen and the crowds began to quiet, half their attention on the flamboyant redhead and half on the royal coach.

"The queen has taken away your freedoms!" The last word fell into a nearly perfect silence and the girl's eyes widened as she stared over the heads of the crowd and realized who was in her audience.

"Like their freedom to starve?" Arrabel asked. "Do go on with what you were saying," she added, adjusting her paisley shawl more securely around her shoulders. "But I'm afraid I can't stay to listen, I have a country to run."

The crowd roared its approval as she gestured for her driver to go on. Had they not been well aware of her opinion on wasting food, she felt sure the girl would have been wearing a variety of produce in short order.

"It's weird how those types keep showing up," Danyel snorted, settling back into the velvet upholstery. "Each of them more ridiculous than the last. No one even listens to them anymore."

"I'm glad to hear that." She already knew it.

"Still . . ." He scratched under the edge of his vanbrace until he caught sight of her expression then he stopped. "This one seemed to really believe what she was saying."

"Did she? I didn't notice." Mirroring her son's position, minus the scratching, Arrabel made a mental note to have Wallace arrange a "tour of the provinces" for the young actress when she showed up at the palace to be paid. If even Danyel had noticed a certain conviction in her performance, the girl had become a liability. The last thing Arrabel wanted was for the people to start thinking.

Wallace was waiting for her in her private receiving room, the Hero's armor and ring on the table.

"The wizards have checked it thoroughly, Your Majesty. It's nothing more than the well-made armor it appears."

"And the ring?"

"Also free of magical taint." He picked it up and handed it to her with a slight bow. "It bears the eagle crest of Mecada."

It was heavy and so pure a gold she could almost mark it with her thumbnail. "A gift to the Hero from King Giorge?"

"It seems likely, Majesty."

"He's really beginning to annoy me. This is what, the third attempt at myself or my son this month? Send this to the mint," she continued tossing the ring back to her adviser before he could respond. "It'll just cover what I paid those three archers to kill him."

It was only chance that a fortnight later the queen was inspecting new recruits in the outer courtyard near enough to the palace gate to hear a voice raised in protest.

"Oh come on, mate, what I get for this here load's gonna feed my family this coming cold. You're not after burning up the food in my family's mouths are you?"

In the courtyard, Arrabel smiled at the twenty young men and women who had just been congratulated on having passed the stringent physical and mental tests required to wear the Queen's Tabard, reminded them to write their mothers weekly, and then dismissed them into the care of her Captain of Recruits. He was a genius with young people. Once he got their training well under way, they'd protect her with their lives. By the time he finished, even death wouldn't stop them.

Moving quickly, her escort falling into place around her, she arrived at the gate in time to hear a second protest.

"But I'm from all the way out in New Bella! How would I have heard that Her Majesty wants all hay delivered in tight bales?"

"Are you suggesting that my word has not reached New Bella?" she asked in turn, stepping out of the shadows. "Because if that's the case, I can repeat it more emphatically."

Very early on in her rule, she'd discovered that nothing spoke with quite so much emphasis as a troop of light cavalry armed primarily with torches and accelerant.

The carter paled as the pair of gate guards clanged to attention. "I'm sure I was the only one who didn't hear, Majesty!"

"Good. Unharness your . . ." She raised a brow at the animal, which rolled its eyes so that the whites showed all the way around and fought the reins trying to shy away from her.

"Mule, Majesty."

"Is it? Well, get it away from the cart, I'd hate for it to be injured."

To his credit, the carter had the mule away from the cart in record time.

"Burn it."

One of the gate guards dropped a lit torch into the hay, which burst into flames and ejected a medium-size nondescript man who leaped toward her, smoldering slightly. The six arrows that suddenly pounded into his torso knocked him back into the fire.

"Mercy, Majesty!" The carter dropped to his knees at her feet and laced rough, work-reddened fingers together. "He threatened my family, said he'd slit their throats in the dark if I didn't help him."

The queen sighed, ignoring the screaming as the wounded assassin burned. "How could he slit their throats if he was hiding in the back of your cart?"

"Majesty?"

"Once you took him away from your family, he couldn't slit their throats and all you had to do was drive up to anyone in a Queen's Tabard and tell them what you had hidden in the hay. Since you didn't do that, I can only assume one of two situations apply. The first is that you were delivering him of your own free will. The second is that you are too stupid to live." Twitching her skirts aside, she raised her hand. "Since the end result is the same for either," she told the body as it fell, bristling with arrows. "It's not particularly relevant which applies. Now then . . ." She turned to the gate guards. ". . . this is exactly why we don't allow carts filled with loose hay into the city. Do you understand?"

"Yes, Majesty!"

"I'm pleased to hear that. We'll let this incident stand as an object lesson . . ." The assassin had finally stopped screaming, ". . . but I'm disappointed in both of you—a rule is a rule and although you didn't allow the cart through the palace gate, you did let the carter argue. That might have given the assassin time to slip inside and then how would you have felt?"

"Terrible, Majesty," admitted the guard on the left.

"Terrible," agreed the guard on the right, his eyes watering a little from the smoke.

"I certainly hope so. If you want to make it up to me, you can find out who let this cart into the city because I'm *very* disappointed in them. Wallace!"

"Majesty!" Her aide stepped over a bit of burning wheel.

"I don't imagine there's enough left of the body to identify but check his weapons. Let me know as soon as you have something. Oh, and Wallace?" Arrabel paused, her escort pausing in perfect formation with her. "See that the mule is given a good home. Something about it reminds me of my late husband."

"His knives are Mecadain, Majesty." Wallace laid all four blades in a row on the table. "As were what was left of his boots."

There was no point in asking if he were sure. He wouldn't have told her if he wasn't. "King Giorge again."

"Yes, Majesty."

"I was planning to invade Mecada next spring."

"I think that's why he was trying to remove you, Majesty."

"Yes, well, you'd think that someone who didn't want me to invade would put a little more effort into making friends and a little less effort into annoying me." The queen walked around the table slowly, her heels rapping out a piqued beat against the parquet floor. She stared down at the knives and shook her head. "When I look at these, I'm *very* annoyed." A slight, almost inaudible sound drew her attention to her aide. "Oh, not at you, Wallace. At King Giorge. Tell General Palatat that I'd like to see him and his senior staff. And then find me a few bards who wouldn't mind a new wardrobe and an all expense paid trip to Mecada."

"A new wardrobe, Majesty?"

"I think we should let the people of Mecada know what their king has gotten them into and the bards will be able to reach more people if they're not so obviously mine."

Arrabel was the sole patron of the Bardic College. It was amazing how many bards preferred to sing warm and well-fed, permitted to travel freely about the land wearing the queen's colors. Of course, there were always a few who insisted on suffering for art's sake—so Arrabel saw to it that they did.

The queen accompanied her army into Mecada, turned a captured border town into a well fortified command center, and stayed there.

"You won't be riding at the front of your army, Mother?"

"No, Danyel. When the ruler rides at the front of the army, she only gets in the way."

"And there is also the great danger you would be in, Majesty!"

She glanced across the war room at Captain Jurin standing amid a group of staff officers and sighed. "Thank you for considering that, Captain."

He blushed.

"I'm not afraid," Danyel declared.

Arrabel settled her shawl more securely around her shoulders and stared at her son for a long moment. He squared his shoulders and raised his chin. "I'm sure you aren't," she said at last. "Chose then whether you stay here or ride into battle."

"I will ride into battle!"

She sighed again. "You're beginning to remind me so much of your father. You'll be treated as nothing more than a junior officer, say . . ." Her eyes fell on Captain Jurin, ". . . a captain. Wallace."

"Majesty?"

"Have a captain's uniform made for my son."

"Yes, Majesty."

Danyel stared at her, appalled "But—"

"Billy goats butt, dear. You'll obey your commanders because their orders come from General Palatat—"

"But, Mother, I'm a prince!"

"—and General Palatat," Arrabel continued mildly, "speaks for me." She took his silence for assent and smiled. "Don't grind your teeth, dear. Of course you'll keep the lines of communication open between the battle and this command center," she told the general. "But I trust you and your staff to do their job." Which went without saying really because they wouldn't have their jobs if she didn't.

Queen Arrabel's army had the advantage of numbers, training, and motivation. King Giorge's people, invaded only because they were next on the list, had only the moral high ground.

* * *

"Free bread and beer, Mother?" Danyel, back in full royal regalia, rubbed at a smudge on his vanbrace as he rode beside his mother through the conquered capital.

"It doesn't take much to make the people like you, dear. It's worth making a bit of an effort."

"But you just conquered them."

"Most people don't care who's in charge just as long as someone is."

"And the people who do care?"

"Are easy enough to replace." Arrabel stared out at the city—many of its buildings damaged by her siege engines during the final battle—and began working out the amount of stone it would take to rebuild it. And, of course, there were schools to be built. Some of the more recalcitrant nobility could start hauling blocks in as soon as possible.

She let Danyel emerge first at the palace, waiting until her escort was in place before she stepped out of the carriage. She wore her usual neat clothing over sensible shoes and was well aware that next to her more flamboyant son she looked like a sparrow next to a peacock.

People tended not to shoot at sparrows.

"Mother, why didn't you wear your crown?" Danyel asked her as they stepped carefully over the shattered remains of the palace gate.

"Everyone who needs to know who I am, knows." Tucking a strand of hair behind her ear, she stopped in the outer courtyard and glanced over at a group of Mecadian soldiers—prisoners now—huddled next to the smoking ruin of what had probably been a stable.

"Wallace."

"Majesty?"

"Make sure they let their mothers know they survived."

"Yes, Majesty. And the ones who didn't survive?"

"Well, they'll hardly be able to write home now, will they?"

General Palatat met them outside King Giorge's throne room in front of the enormous brass-bound doors. "The door's been spelled, Majesty, we can't break it down. But they're still in there—King Giorge, Queen Fleya, both princes, both princesses."

"Personal guards?"

"They died out here, Majesty, covering the royal family's retreat."

"All of them?" She glanced over at the liveried bodies piled out of the way. "My, that was short-sighted."

"Yes, Majesty. One of the princesses has been talking through the keyhole. She says her brothers want to negotiate a surrender but they'll only speak to you. Royal to royal as it were."

"They could speak to me," Danyel muttered.

His mother ignored him. "Do you think the princes will negotiate in good faith?"

"They are considered to be honorable men," the general told her. "They will do what they feel is right regardless of the consequences."

"They take after their father then." The queen

stared at the door to the throne room. The smart thing for King Giorge to have done would have been to get his family out of the country when it became obvious he'd lost—which would have been about half an hour after the first battle had been joined. Arrabel assumed he'd refused to leave his people or some such nonsense. "Well, tell them I'm here."

At the general's signal, one of the Queen's Tabards banged on the door with a spear butt.

"Is she there?" Interestingly, the girl sounded more annoyed than distressed.

"I am."

"There's a secret exit at the end of the hall, by a statue of my father. Do you see it?"

"The statue?" There were ankles on a plinth and rather a lot of rubble. A bit of the rubble seemed to be wearing a stone crown. "No but I can see where it was."

"My brothers will come out, stripped to their breeches so you can see they're weaponless. You approach them alone and they'll give you our father's terms of surrender."

"I'm to approach alone?" A raised hand cut off the general's protest. "At two to one odds?"

"We know you have archers with you. You always have archers with you!"

"True enough. Very well, given that I have archers, I will meet you at the end of the hall." She sighed and smoothed a wrinkle out of her skirt. "Wallace?"

"Yes, Majesty?"

"Am I getting predictable?

"Only in the best of all possible ways, Majesty."

Arrabel glanced over at him and when he bowed, she smiled but before she could compliment his answer, a section of the wall at the end of the hall slid back and a half-naked young man emerged. And then a second.

Both princes were in their mid-twenties, not quite two years apart in age, and, given that very little was left to the imagination, in obviously fine condition. Muscles rippled everywhere muscles could ripple. One wore his golden hair loose, the other tied his darker hair back, but except for that they could have been twins. That she had an appreciation for handsome men was no secret so she suspected Giorge had sent out his sons because he expected they'd get better terms.

"Mother, I could take them."

"Not now dear, Mother's going to go negotiate." She walked purposefully forward and stopped a body length and an equal distance from both princes. "Well?"

The blond cocked his head, gray eyes narrowed. "You don't look like I imagined."

"Is there any reason I should?"

Before he could respond, the brunet charged at her, screaming.

At least one, maybe two of the arrows passed so close she felt the breeze. As the prince hit the floor, she rolled her eyes. "That was stupid."

"No," the other prince snarled. "That was a sacrifice. Your archers cannot save you now; my brother's death has disarmed them. For what you have done to my people, I will kill you with my bare hands and yes, I expect to die just after but . . ." He stopped and stared in astonishment at the half dozen arrows suddenly protruding from his chest, one of them adorned with a small piece of fabric. "But . . ."

"My archers can reload, aim, and fire in under seven seconds," Arrabel told him as he dropped heavily to his knees. "Never pause to gloat, dear," she added, patting his cheek as he sagged back.

"Mother! Are you all right?"

"Of course I am."

"But what if he'd grabbed you and used you as a shield?" Danyel grabbed her arm to illustrate and a long, thin knife slid out from under her neat, lace-trimmed cuff, scoring a line along the enamel on his vanbrace.

"Then I'd have dealt with it myself," she said, pulling free of his slackened grip. "Although I'm just as glad I didn't have to." The knife disappeared. "I'm quite fond of this dress and I'd hate to have gotten blood all over it. And speaking of this dress . . ." she turned to face her archers, brandishing the hole in her full skirt. "Who took the shot that went through here?"

A very pale young man stumbled forward and dropped to one knee. He was shaking so hard it sounded as though he was tapping his bow against the floor.

"Conner Burd isn't it? Your mother runs a small dairy on the outside of the capital."

The young archer managed part of a nod.

"Let that be a lesson to you all, if my life is in danger, don't worry about my clothing and don't feel you're redundant just because another five arrows are heading for the target. Those arrows could miss. Good shot, Conner. General Palatat."

"Majesty!"

"Stop trying to break through the door and go through the wall."

"Majesty?"

"No one ever thinks to have a wizard spell more than the door. Get a few strapping young men up here with sledgehammers and go through the wall." Her tone suggested she'd better not have to repeat herself a third time.

The queen was not the first to step through the breach in the wall. The queen was the sixteenth to enter, after fourteen soldiers, General Palatat, and her son. The first soldier through the breech took a tapestry pole to the back of the head.

The throne room was empty except for the royal family. King Giorge sat slumped in his throne, head on his chest. Queen Fleya sat at his feet, sobbing. One of the princesses, her hair a mass of tangled mahogany curls and showing just a little too much cleavage for the situation, stood snarling by her father's side, the tapestry pole having been taken away from her with only minor damage. The other princess, blond hair neatly tied back, arms folded over her sensible cardigan, stood just behind her sister, frowning slightly.

"You can't touch him now," Queen Fleya cried

as Arrabel approached the throne. "He's gone beyond your control!"

Arrabel cocked her head and studied the king,
his lips and eyelids were a pale blue-green. "Took
poison, has he?"

Eyes red with weeping, Fleya's lip curled. "He
knew he could expect no mercy!"

"It's hardly practical to leave live enemies behind
me now, is it?" she answered switching her attention to the queen. "I wonder what he thought I'd
do with you."

"You will force me into exile with my daughters
and the body of my dead husband and we will live
out our lives torn from the country we love." She
wiped her eyes and straightened her shoulders.
"It's what is done."

"Really? The upholstery on the throne—it's ex-
pensive is it?"

Fleya looked up at the embroidered gold velvet
under her husband and back at Arrabel, confused.
"Yes but—"

"Hard to keep clean?"

"I expect so but—"

"General Palatat."

"Majesty."

"There's no reason to make things more difficult
than we have to for the staff. Have King Giorge's
body dragged down to the floor then behead him."

The queen and the dark-haired princess screamed
out versions of, "You can't!"

The second princess said nothing at all.

When Giorge's head came off enough blood gushed

from the stump of his neck to partially obscure an impressive mosaic map of the kingdom set into the throne-room floor. Released by the soldier who held her, Queen Fleya ran to her husband's side.

Danyel said, "But Mother, he was already dead."

"Dead men don't bleed like that, Danyel." Arrabel stepped back as the blood spread. "The poison only feigned death. After the three of them reached exile it would wear off and Giorge would rise from his supposed grave to seek vengeance."

"But how did you know?"

"It's what I would have done, dear. Wallace."

"Majesty?"

"Make sure he's cremated."

"Noooooooooooooo!" Fleya's wailed protest drew everyone's attention. Sitting on the floor, her silk skirts soaking up the king's blood, she held his headless body clasped tight in her arms. "You will not take him from me! I will not go into exile without my Giorge!"

Arrabel sighed. "Of course you won't." She raised her hand. Because of the late king's body, four of the arrows went into Fleya's upper torso, the other two went one into each eye. "All right, who risked the eye shots?" When two of the archers admitted as much, she smiled at them and pointed a teasing finger. "There's no need to show off, I know how good you are. Now then . . ." Lifting her skirts, she walked around the growing puddle. "This is taking far too long. You." The same finger pointed at the dark-haired princess, held struggling between two Tabards. "You'll marry my son, giving his claim to rule this kingdom validity."

"Never!"

She raised a hand. "I expected as much," she sighed as the body hit the floor and pointed at the second princess. "*You'll* marry my son and give his claim to rule this kingdom validity."

The girl stared into Arrabel face for a moment then shrugged. "All right."

"Don't shrug, dear. It's common." A slight frown as recognition dawned. "That was your voice at the door."

"Yes."

"The poison was your plan."

"Yes."

"And your brothers' attempt?"

"My plan."

"Really? What's your name?"

"Mailynne."

"How old are you, Mailynne?"

"Seventeen."

"I imagine you have some ideas about how the kingdom should be run."

Mailynne's gray eyes narrowed. "Yes."

"Good."

"Mother, I don't want to be married." Danyel reached to grab her arm, noticed the gouge on his vanbrace and thought better of it.

Arrabel and Mailynne turned together. "That's not really relevant, dear."

"But . . ." He paused, mouth open. "Wait. I'm to rule this kingdom?"

"Under my guidance."

"But you'll be at home?"

"Yes."

Dark brows drew in. "And I'll be here?"

"Yes."

"Oh." His smile showed perfect teeth and an enchanting dimple. "Well, that's different then."

His mother placed her hand in the center of the princess' back and gently pushed her forward. The girl was wearing some kind of harness under her sweater that probably held at least one weapon. "You will rule Mecada with Mailynne at your side."

"As you say, Mother." Danyel bent and kissed the princess' hand. "I want an enormous wedding," he announced when he straightened.

"Don't be ridiculous, dear. You don't bankrupt a county that's recently lost a war just so you can have a party. Wallace."

"Majesty?"

"We'll need someplace central with good security but high visibility."

"And somewhere we can release a hundred white doves!"

"Doves aren't really relevant right now, Danyel."

"The surviving nobility that served my father should be there," Mailynne suggested as her future husband pouted.

Arrabel turned a maternal smile on the girl. "That's not really relevant either, dear."

The wedding was short but beautiful. As a wedding present, Arrabel left a regiment of the

Queen's Tabards in Mecada to help keep the peace. Her new daughter-in-law narrowed her eyes but accepted the gift graciously.

Because there was correspondence to go over, Wallace rode with her in the carriage on the way home.

"Wallace?"

"Yes, Majesty?"

"How long do you figure Danyel will last?"

"Majesty?"

"I expect she'll keep him around until she has an heir. And I expect that will happen as soon as possible."

"But Majesty . . ."

"As much as he adored me, he was becoming a distraction. Mother this and Mother that and eventually he'd distract me at a bad time. This girl was a good choice, Wallace, I won't live forever and I'd like to think—on that very distant day—that I was leaving my people in good hands. Hands that wouldn't undo all the work I've done."

"She does remind me a little of you, Majesty."

"Yes." Arrabel picked up the wrapped slice of wedding cake from the seat beside her and tossed it out the window. "She does, doesn't she?"

TO SIT IN DARKNESS HERE, HATCHING VAIN EMPIRES

Steven A. Roman

I poisoned my niece today.

Just turned six, and still wondering why her mother—my younger sister, Sienna—never comes to see her anymore. Desperately seeking assurance from me that it's not because Mommy stopped loving her; that it wasn't something she did wrong that made Mommy go away.

It's heartrending to watch a child try to come to terms with something they may never understand, try to find the logic in an illogical situation. They'll work on the problem, attempt to examine it from every angle, rack their brains trying to recall the precise moment, the one event, when everything in their young life started to come apart. And finally, when no answer presents itself, they reach the only conclusion their young minds can comprehend: Something bad happened, and it was all their fault.

What, exactly, that "bad thing" might be they can't put into words because, really, they don't know themselves. But experience has taught them that adults can be rude and angry and abusive; that adults don't always have a logical reason to be mad at someone; that adults can often take out their frustrations on their children. And if an adult, especially a parent, stops talking to you, stops coming to see you, then you must have done something so unbelievably terrible that they never want to see you again.

But now she won't have to trouble herself with such thoughts. Gillian is, as the old saying goes, in a far better place than this . . . although considering the state of the world today, that really isn't saying much. Heaven, hell, purgatory, the void—*any* place would be better than here. All I sought to do was end her suffering (well, hers *and* mine). And if I were the type who believed in God, I might be able to console myself with the image of a mother and her daughter reunited for eternity in the afterlife.

No, her mother hadn't stopped loving her; of that I have no doubts. And I had no trouble in telling her she wasn't the one responsible for Mommy's absence because she had done nothing to anger my sister. What proved difficult for me was in trying to explain the real reason for the disturbing lack of motherly attention. Gillian was meant to visit me for a weekend; after a year, I'd run out of excuses for why Sienna had never come back to pick up her daughter.

Yes, I suppose I could have just told her the

truth, but I never did. I never could. Perhaps it was out of some ridiculous notion that I was protecting her in some way—from what, exactly, I haven't a clue. Or maybe it was sheer cowardice that stilled my tongue—fear of how negatively she might have reacted were I to tell her everything. (Although why I should have been bothered by the thought of a child directing her hatred at me, when I'd spent a lifetime accumulating enemies who wanted me dead, still escapes me. No doubt it had something to do with our familial connection.) The bottom line was that I'd never been able to work up the nerve to tell her what really happened: that her kindly uncle Josiah was the one who made Sienna go away . . . along with the rest of the earth's population.

I mean, how do you explain to a child that you murdered an entire world, even if it was by accident?

There was still a hint of December in the April winds that afternoon when everything went so horribly wrong: the sort of temperate breeze that made it too chilly for T-shirts, yet too warm for winter coats. That didn't keep the multitudes indoors for long, however—with the first sign in weeks that winter had finally started to relax its five-month grip on the city, the lunchtime streets of Amicus were fairly overflowing with humanity. Secretaries and bike messengers, businessmen in shirtsleeves and mothers with their infants, the first ice cream truck of the year parked at the curb in front of the park—was there any better proof that spring was fast approaching? And the beautiful young women passing by in short skirts and tight jeans, their blouses filled to bursting . . . my God, they were everywhere, it seemed. Like sleek-limbed gazelles prancing across the veldt, eyed hungrily by the young cubs sprawled on the grass.

Truly, it was the sort of day when, as a far better poet than I once put it, "a young man's fancy turns to thoughts of love." But all *I* could think of was, *It's almost a pity they're all going to die . . .*

Now, when I rose from bed the day before, formulating a plan that might result in the deaths of dozens, perhaps hundreds, of innocent men, women, and children wasn't the first thing that entered my mind—such fanciful notions never were. In fact, I rarely started my mornings contemplating murder on such a grand scale. It wasn't something you could just rush into; rather, it was a mindset you gradually eased into during the course of the day. Burned toast, having to shower with cold water because the heater was on the fritz, reviewing profit-and-loss financial statements based on the last failed attempt to subjugate humanity— of such minor annoyances were plans for widespread anarchy born. It really wasn't until early afternoon that I'd built up a good head of steam to begin my plotting, and then only after I'd checked the papers and cable news channels to see what mayhem had been wrought in the world while I was getting a good night's sleep. I hated devising a truly masterful scheme only to discover that some third-rate dictator from a postage-stamp-size European country no one had ever heard of had the very same idea . . . especially when *he* was able to carry it out for a third of the cost I'd budgeted for mine.

It made me feel . . . inadequate.

But whenever I slipped into such periods of ennui, Elsinore, my beloved paramour and second-in-command, was there to bolster my spirits. "Of *course* he was able to do it on the cheap, my love," she would tell me, "and that is why his plan was doomed to fail from the start. Remember: 'You have to spend money to make money.' And if he wasn't willing to invest in top-of-the-line battle armor for his legions, or purchase a *real* thermonuclear device instead of just an empty casing for show, then how could he possibly have expected to control a major city?"

As the Righteous Brothers—the musical group, not that trio of do-gooding idiots with the fake Spanish accents—once put it, she was my hope, my inspiration. Elsinore had seen me through the good times and the bad, the highs and the lows, the victories and the lengthy prison sentences. And not once had she ever complained—not during that (I now admit) crazed period when I insisted she wear pink thigh-high boots, hot pants, and sheer blouses, and not that time I ordered her to shoot my former second-in-command for betraying me to the authorities. No greater love had a woman ever shown for a man then when she executed her own father while he begged for mercy.

Dear, sweet, raven-haired Elsinore. I miss her so, these days—the touch of her skin, the sweet taste of her lips. How I wish it hadn't been necessary to strangle her as she drifted off to sleep, but after a year in this underground hell, what little stale, recycled oxygen remains is a precious commodity. And yet, I'll always have that last night of passion to remind me of the love we shared. That, and the terrified look in her dimming eyes as she desperately clawed at her pillows, only to realize I'd already removed the gun she kept under them. Sometimes, late at night, I can still feel her lying beside me in bed, her warm body quivering against mine as the garotte tightened around her slender throat; can still hear the almost sensuous whisper of her death rattle as she struggled to draw that one final breath past the cord that had closed off her windpipe.

But I'm getting ahead of myself.

Once I was satisfied that my latest idea hadn't been duplicated, I sat down with my trusted advisers to discuss how best to implement it. Krayle normally handled the tactical aspects of the operation, hiring any dimwitted, strapped-for-cash "muscle" needed to replace those lost in the last debacle, then working with me on agent positioning, contingency plans, and escape routes—one never knew when a hasty retreat might have been required. In this case, however, I was working with a much smaller canvas: the operation only required a single synthadroid placed in the heart of the city. Smythe was in charge of intelligence gathering, using my global network of undercover agents, computer hackers, and surveillance satellites to provide me with all I needed to know about the chosen target area: traffic flow, law enforcement presence, average number of city dwellers on the streets at a certain hour, etc. Alessi ran accounting, making sure we never went over budget, even when it came to some of the more . . . esoteric items I often required. (You couldn't just go down to Costco and pick up a cold fusion reactor, after all.) I must say, he was quite pleased with this small-scale project—at least at the start. And Gillian . . .

Gillian was no different from other children her age. Happy and playful, inquisitive and devilishly clever, sweet as a gumdrop yet incredibly advanced for a child still finding enjoyment in endless repeat viewings of *Snow White* and *Shrek* on DVD (I *still* have trouble getting that damn Monkees song out of my head at times). No doubt that heightened intellect came from the genetic material on my side of the family—that boorish lout Sienna married could barely hold a conversation. If my sister hadn't been so mawkishly devoted to Bernie, I'd have annulled the marriage years ago—with the aid of a gun. My sister deserved better than a trash collector.

Gillian was my fail-safe, my logic being that if a child could pick out the faults in my plan, then so could any of my enemies (even the dullards who failed their advanced algebra classes back in high school). On more than one occasion had Gillian spared me the indignity of a failed operation by assessing the initial plan and reaching the conclusion it was a load of "poopie."

Poopie.

From the mouths of babes, indeed.

What I came to call the "April Retribution"—although, in hindsight, "Judgment Day" might have been a far better sobriquet—passed the Gillian Test with flying colors. She even giggled when the three-dimensional computer simulation depicted just how widespread the devastation would be . . . although I equated that more to her enjoyment of video games and their colorful graphics than out of any sociopathic desire for bloodshed. Still, my spirits were buoyed by her enthusiastic reaction. Now I was certain it would prove to the citizens of Amicus that Professor Josiah Plum was a man to fear—and assure a highly intelligent little girl that not *all* of "Uncle Josie's" plans were steaming piles of excrement. That the old boy still *had* it.

In retrospect, of course, I shouldn't have been so focused on further inflating my already sizable ego. Years of experience should have taught me that, but no upstanding member in the brotherhood of villainy had ever gotten anywhere by listening to the voice of reason. And I was as guilty as the next in allowing my actions to be directed less by common sense and more by sheer arrogance. And arrogance could sometimes be such a costly—and unnecessary—distraction in my profession.

Former profession, that is.

Ah. My title. Not quite the sort of name you were expecting from a criminal mastermind of my caliber, I imagine. Professor Plum—sounds as though I've escaped from a game of *Clue* (and yes, I've heard that more times than I care to remember). Why didn't I go by a flashier name, like "General Malpractice" or "The Biochemist," is that it? Well, to quote the Bard, "What's in a name?" In my . . . former profession, noms de guerre and gaudy costumes were a dime a dozen, and Professor Plum had better things to do with his time than dig behind sofa cushions looking for spare change. And honestly, no one wearing enormous metal shoulder pads, waving around a gun the size of a missile launcher, and calling themselves "The War Machine" ever struck fear in the hearts of the average citizen. As those of my generation well knew, it was the *deeds* that made a villain, not a ridiculous code name—a fact that was unfortunately lost on our younger, fashion-challenged brothers and sisters. More importantly, it was the amount of creativity one exhibited in carrying out a criminal act that often determined the level of respect one received from one's peers. Blow up a tank or police car? Extremely commonplace, and the sort of distasteful, over-the-top showmanship most self-respecting intellectuals abandoned immediately after their first public appearance. Level a building? Dramatic, to be sure, yet lacking any real style. But cut off the satellite feed to a Super Bowl or the Academy Awards, and the world erupted in chaos. There were few as creative as I in those days, and the majority of the recidivistic community greatly respected my ingenuity. As for those members who refused to acknowledge my artistic superiority . . . well, they weren't around long enough to make the same mistake twice.

But I digress.

Krayle, Alessi, Smythe, and Elsinore all agreed with Gillian's approval of the plan, and "April Retribution" was placed on the fast track for implementation. I'd been out of the public eye for eighteen months—having faked my own death for what must have been the twenty-fifth time—and was eager to show the world not only that I'd returned from the grave (again), but that I was ready to pick up where I'd left off. Looking back, I realize I should have done a bit more planning before greenlighting the project. The exuberance of resurrection, I suppose.

Still, it wasn't as though I lacked the necessary materials to carry out the operation. I have a veritable army of synthadroids—synthetic androids, to the laity—stored on the bottommost level of this underground lair, so activating one was a simple as pressing a button. Most of my artificial henchmen lack features, because more than a decade ago I discovered that the sight of faceless warriors precision marching down a street will do more to incite panic among civilians than roving bands of thugs wearing helmets fitted with Plexiglas visors. A hundred or so of my mechanized legion, however, were constructed with features that matched my own: stunt doubles, as it were, who stood in for me when it became apparent that faking my own death was the only option left available if I wanted to ensure my escape from a particularly sticky situation. A suicidal leap from a cooling tower into the heart of a nuclear reactor; vaporized in the explosion that ripped apart my base in Antigua; chewed up by tentacled, interdimensional creatures from a parallel universe—synthadroids provided me with countless ways to cheat death and avoid capture. And not only were they relatively inexpensive to manufacture (one of the many advantages of outsourcing jobs to southeast Asia), but they were biodegradable as well. Ten minutes after their "deaths," the androids would either dissolve or turn to dust, leaving behind no trace of evidence that might have proven to my enemies that I still lived . . . although I'm fairly certain they knew, anyway. As the saying used to go in my line of work, "Just because you *saw* them die doesn't mean they're really dead."

I *did* manage to keep them guessing more times than not, however, and that was due to the lifelike actions of my stand-ins: they mimicked my physical characteristics so well that even Elsinore could be fooled into thinking she was talking to me and not a mechanical fabrication. Yet in a way she *was* talking to me, through the aid of one of my more inspired creations: the Psychelmet™. By putting on this device (which, I'm sad to say, looked not unlike an overturned colander with wires and jumper cables attached to it), I could transfer—or upload, to use the more accurate terminology—my consciousness into the synthadroid's computerized brain, and direct its actions from a distance of up to five miles. Usually, that meant I was nowhere in the immediate vicinity of whatever final confrontation was about to take place with my opponent, but through my body double I could still experience the pleasure of beating some costumed cretin to a bloody pulp without actually having to be there. And when the odds eventually turned in my enemy's favor, as so often they did . . . well, all I needed to do was withdraw my consciousness from the android at the last possible second, and let the hero (or heroine) dispose of my now-lifeless doppelganger in some typically dramatic fashion—unwittingly, of course.

So I had the means to deliver my message of retribution to the world. Now all that was needed was a way to ensure it would be heard . . . and understood. But I'd already settled on a solution to that minor intellectual challenge an hour before I convened with my lieutenants.

A decade ago, a series of experiments I was conducting with wormhole technology resulted in the weakening of the vibratory barriers that separate this world from its counterpart in a neighboring dimension: a parallel Earth. It exists temporally out of sync with mine, just seconds apart—a hairsbreadth in distance on a cosmic scale. As the years passed and I was able to stabilize the wormhole to permit travel through the barriers, I learned there were other Earths, in other dimensions—an almost infinite number of them, in fact. And on none of the parallel worlds to which I made excursions did I find a single superpowered man or woman. To say I was shocked would be accurate; to say I was delighted by this revelation would be an understatement. That's not to say there are *no* dimensions brimming over with costumed lunatics; I'm almost certain there must be, somewhere. It's just that I saw no evidence of spandex-wearing simpletons on the Earths *I* visited.

On one such alternate—not the one inhabited by the tentacled monstrosities that devoured my synthadroid stand-in, thankfully—I learned of a powerful explosive invented by my counterpart, an acclaimed scientist praised for his humanitarian work and idolized by the world at large.

I killed him, naturally. Put a large caliber bullet through that much-loved brain of his, and stabbed him in both eyes.

As I may have mentioned before, feelings of inadequacy tend to bother me a great deal.

My late dimensional brother christened his explosive "hellfire" because of the intense heat and flames produced when the mixture was detonated—in poetic terms, it provided a brief glimpse into what "hell on Earth" might be like on a small scale. Or so he believed. As it turned out, he'd never actually put his wondrous discovery to use, although he *had* submitted a patent for "Plum's Controlled" something (it looked like "Detonation"—his handwriting was atrocious) "Compound." According to his notes, he wasn't certain of what might happen if the mixture were set off or even whether the explosion could really be controlled, but had no intention of finding out. Like Alfred Nobel, who was condemned for *his* invention, dynamite (and who then used the vast fortune he amassed from

sales of the explosive to establish the prizes he
named after himself, so the world might think better of him—the fool), Other-Plum was concerned
more with his legacy than with demonstrating to
his scientific peers that his was the greatest
intellect.

And you wonder why I killed him.

Unlike my altiverse twin, I wasn't the sort who
trifled in making busywork for myself that no one
would ever see. And if he was too timid to make
use of Plum's Explosive Compound, I wasn't.
Based on his notes—some words of which I had to
guess at, that bad handwriting of his again—and
my computer simulations, it appeared that a two-
pound charge of this "hellfire" was sufficient for
the task I'd set.

The charge was shaped and fitted into the chest
of the Plum synthadroid. All that remained was for
me to make my dramatic reappearance.

I chose a bench at the southeast corner of Cor-
man Park as the location from which to stage my
comeback, situated as it was at a large intersection
close to the financial district. The spot was also
directly across the street from the criminal courts
building, home to the multitude of prosecutors and
judges I had come to know—and despise—so well
over the decades.

An unmarked white van, driven by one of my
underlings, delivered the android to the target.
Then I slipped on the Psychelmet™, slipped into the
robot's mind, and stepped out to greet my ador-
ing public.

The panic that ensued was glorious and, unfortunately, as short-lived as it had ever been. Because within two minutes of my appearance, the Devil chose to confront me, as he had so many times in the past.

DevilHawk, I mean, not Lucifer . . . although an appearance by the Prince of Lies would have been a welcomed change after enduring so many encounters with the heroically-garbed pissant who play-acted at being him.

I never understood the Hawk—his motives, that is. Why a grown man would choose to dress in gaudy red spandex and black leather, glue a tiny pair of horns to his temples, and parade around in public beating up people could probably be better explained by a mental health care professional. *I'd* always been too preoccupied with killing him to give it any real consideration.

He swooped down from the noonday sky on red glider wings that were attached to his gauntlets, and landed a few feet away. Keeping his distance, naturally.

"Hey, Prof," he said casually, knowing full well how much I hated being called that. "Finally decided it was time to crawl out from under your rock?"

I eyed him closely. "You don't seem surprised by my return, Hawk."

He shrugged. "Nah. I figured you were still out there, somewhere, waiting for the right moment before you dragged your sorry ass out of whatever hidey-hole you'd slithered into." I could tell he was lying, though—I always could. He'd literally jumped for joy when he thought I'd fallen into that reactor core. Seeing me again (even if it wasn't the *real* me) was troubling him deeply; it was obvious by the way he kept nervously shifting his weight from one foot to the other.

I directed the android's servomotors to twist the corners of its mouth into an approximation of a smile. "Yes, well, now that I've 'slithered' back out, I have just one question for you."

He tensed, no doubt expecting me to attack. "And what's that?"

"Are you familiar with the Book of Revelations?" I asked.

DevilHawk started, then shook his head in disbelief. "Huh. Never figured you as the type to get religion, Prof." He flashed that insufferably condescending grin of his. "You gonna start quoting Scripture now?"

"Just a verse or two," I replied. I cleared my mechanical throat. " 'And when he opened the fourth seal, I heard the voice of the fourth beast say, Come and see. And I looked, and behold a pale horse; and his name that sat on him was Death. *And Hell followed with him.*' "

As planned, that was the moment when my— or, rather, the synthadroid's—chest began beeping. Counting down.

The Hawk's eyes widened. His jaw slackened. It was such a delicious moment when he finally realized that he'd been conversing with a machine. That he'd been denied another opportunity to pound my head down around my ankles. And that my stand-in was about to explode.

I immediately pulled out of the computer brain and returned to my body. I'd had the last word; now I could observe what came next from the safety of my lair. Overnight, Smythe had dispatched a squad of technicians to install hidden cameras throughout the area, so I could enjoy the festivities. All I had to do now was sit back and watch.

The Hawk leapt forward, grabbed hold of the android's shirt, and tore it open. No doubt he expected to find a timer under there, one that would give him some idea of how much time remained before the blast. Time enough, I suppose, for him to find a way to defuse the bomb.

There was no timer, however; I'd stopped using those years ago. Perhaps if DevilHawk had paid for a subscription to *Scientific American* instead of *Maxim,* he would have been able to keep up with the recent changes in mad scientist technology, instead of focusing all his attention on the cup size of the latest cosmetically-sculpted supermodel. I, on the other hand, learned of and quickly invested in some of the more popular trends in terrorist equipment, such as biological weapons, laser-guided missiles . . . and voice-activated switches. In this case, quoting from Revelations was the trigger; the bomb was set to detonate five seconds later. Long enough for me to savor the horrified look in the costumed hero's eyes as he saw the end coming.

The explosion was . . . spectacular. Like Vesuvius

unleashing its molten fury or the gates of hell being thrown wide open. Every one of my hidden cameras were vaporized in a split-second; a minute later, my lair was struck by an intense shockwave— even three miles down—that knocked out the generators and plunged us into darkness. By the time we were able to get some of the systems back online and the monitors restored, I was left with only the views provided by my spy satellites to see what was taking place in Amicus.

And what a sight it was. The flames roared high above the spot where the city should have been, extending upward into the atmosphere as though the devil himself was reaching up with a giant hand to pluck the stars from the sky. And when I focused the cameras on the ground, I saw no evidence that Amicus still existed—every building, every tree, every person had been consumed.

"Oh, my God . . ." I heard Elsinore whisper behind me. I, on the other hand, was at a loss for words.

It was a much larger explosion than I'd expected. And it didn't stop.

Suddenly, the sky itself was aflame, and the fire began spreading, moving outward from Amicus in all directions. And as the conflagration began its apocalyptic race around the planet, I recalled a declassified U.S. government document I'd once come across in my studies: a report filed by Arthur Compton, one of the scientists working on the Manhattan Project in the early days of atomic bomb research. In it, he mentioned that a fellow scientist, Edward Teller, had expressed some concerns about the first test explosion—that the possibility existed they might wind up igniting the atmosphere through the fusion reaction of nitrogen nuclei. He was proved wrong, of course. Atomic bombs were incapable of setting fire to the atmosphere.

Hellfire, however, could. And did.

And as the world burned, I came to understand just why Other-Plum had steered away from testing his compound. He knew—feared—this might happen.

I came to another chilling realization at that moment, for my subconscious had never stopped trying to decipher the crudely scrawled word I'd seen on my twin's patent application for Plum's Controlled Compound. It had finally worked through the puzzle; now I had my answer.

It wasn't "Detonation." It was "Deflagration"— the continuous process by which combustion spreads via thermal conductivity, as when something hot, like an uncontrollable flame, heats and then ignites something cold.

Like the atmosphere.

That was a little over a year ago. The flame front circled the globe in a matter of hours, burning brightly until the lack of oxygen finally extinguished it. By then, every human and animal, bird and insect, flower and tree had either died from asphyxiation or been incinerated—save for those men and women (and one child) who were gathered in this underground facility. And even that situation would change, over time.

The first three months were especially trying. As the realization that they would never see their loved ones again, never be able to set foot on the surface for the rest of their lives, finally sank in among my followers, problems arose. Some committed suicide; others slowly went mad. The majority, however, decided to turn their anger on me. Elsinore did her best to keep the rabble in line; eviscerating the most vocal among them seemed the best deterrent, though they never stayed quiet for long. By the time things finally settled down, I was reduced to thirty underlings from a staff of more than one hundred.

Well, it certainly helped to make the emergency rations last longer. But it did nothing really to resolve a far greater crisis: what to do for breathable air when the oxygen supply ran out seven months later.

Thankfully, most of the surviving noncombatants were technicians, not soldiers, which meant we could focus on carrying out my solution to the predicament: abandon the lair and travel to another Earth via the dimensional portal. Unfortunately, a number of the gate's power cells had been damaged by the explosion's shockwave, and repairing the system would require cannibalizing other equipment that had been damaged just as badly. It would also take more time to accomplish the work than we had available air in the oxygen reserves . . . unless the ranks were thinned even further.

I put that consideration on hold until the repairs were well underway. What little chance we had of departing the necropolis this Earth had become served as a great motivator for my staff, and I was not about to deny them that hope, especially when it meant the difference between escape and another potential uprising. Still, I knew cuts would be necessary at some point, given the dwindling amount of supplies on hand—there was no getting away from it. Yet I couldn't just start . . . firing the techs. I needed their expertise. That left upper management, and I knew I would have to personally oversee those terminations.

Alessi was the first to be "let go." In this brave, dead world I'd created, accountants were superfluous when budgetary concerns had to be cast aside in favor of basic survival needs. I'm sure he would have approved of my cost-saving decision—if I hadn't slit his throat first. Krayle and Smythe followed him two months later. With no martial campaigns to map out, or intelligence to gather, I thought it best to downsize those departments on a permanent basis.

I have no doubt Elsinore could see her demise coming, might even have considered some ways in which to prevent it. And yet, her love for me was so great, so utterly blinding, that she could never bring herself to raise a hand against me, and apparently believed that I felt the same toward her.

Pitiful, really. You'd think a woman ordered to slay her own father would know better than to trust her life to the same man who'd *given* her that order . . . but no. At least she died knowing that her noble sacrifice would allow me to go on living a few days longer.

By the time the air grew heavy with the stench of the decaying bodies scattered throughout the facility, the repairs had been completed and the gateway reactivated. In six hours, it would be at full power, and then this blackened husk of a world would be just a distant memory. So with everything up and running, and my technicians' services no longer required, I now had an opportunity to make the final staff cuts. But I didn't bother with guns or explosives to do the job.

Instead, I held a birthday party.

Gillian, my now emotionally traumatized niece, had actually turned six a month earlier, but with my top priority being the restoration of the portal, her special day hadn't been properly celebrated. I promised to make it up to her then, and Josiah Plum always kept his word . . . in some form or another.

I found a stale angel food cake and a can of chocolate frosting in the back of my private pantry, then made a stop at my laboratory, where I added an extra ingredient to the frosting: a hint of one of my faster-acting poisons. Just to give it a little kick. Then it was off to the party in the main control room, where I found the remaining staffers had hung a large handmade banner that read HAPPY BIRTHDAY GILLIAN.

Charming.

The party was an overwhelming success, and the

cake quickly devoured by one and all—except for me. I complained of a minor toothache. No sweets for me, thank you, so Gillian happily gorged herself on my slice, in addition to her own.

It didn't take long for the poison to run its course. Gillian, having consumed the greatest amount, slipped away quickly . . . although I hadn't expected her passing to be quite as disturbingly violent as it turned out. No doubt an allergic reaction to the drug. It was something to keep in mind for future reference . . .

The others died among a chorus of screams, whimpers, and vituperative utterances—directed at me, of course. Eventually, though, the bothersome noises trailed away, and the only sounds that could be heard in the control room were my labored breathing . . . and the hum of the dimensional portal.

And now I stand at the gateway, ready to cross over to a new world. There is nothing left here for me to come back to, so I've programmed the facility's generators to overload minutes after my departure. One final, explosive gift for the dead planet I once called home. Yet I feel no sense of melancholy, no desire to choke back any tears, for a *new* home awaits on the far side of the portal, and I am eager to place my mark upon it.

The mark of its conqueror.

And should the inhabitants—whether costumed or not—foolishly decide to oppose me, then perhaps I will introduce them to the amazing, literally earth-shattering qualities of a special formula I like to call Professor Josiah Plum's Controlled *Detonation* Compound (Patent Pending).

I'll get it right next time.

In the end, I always do.

STRONGER THAN FATE

John Helfers

Deep within his Ebon Citadel, ensconced firmly if not altogether comfortably, on the Throne of Black Blades, Khazerai the Undying drummed his thin, ring-bedecked fingers on the cold arm of his chair, and wondered where it had all gone wrong.

How could it have come to this, when everything else has happened according to plan? he wondered. Granted, his rise to total dominion over the entire continent of Cauldera had not been without its setbacks, but overall things had worked out exactly as he had expected.

First, he had deposed the weak and ineffective ruler of the small kingdom of Yulen after quickly working his way up the royal chain of command to become the king's personal adviser. A nip of poison in each of his twin sons' drinking goblets to emotionally cripple the old man, and a series of successively larger glasses of wine before bedtime had ensured the old fool's complete ignorance as Khazerai had slowly replaced the guards and staff with men loyal to him. When the coup happened in one swift stroke, the people were actually hailing him as their savior, which he was, he supposed, of a sort.

Next came the annexation of the surrounding lands, during which his agents sowed unrest among the peasants by promising them their own land in return for harsh but not totally crushing taxes to fund the monarchy, leading to an uprising when he invaded each country with his small but well-trained force. Soon Yulen was four times its original size, and its army was anything but small.

Khazerai then had his men trained and equipped with the best weapons and equipment that could be made or bought, and declared brutal war against the rest of the kingdoms. Often this announcement was initially met with derision, as several of the other lands had been unwilling to believe that Yulen, previously known only for producing exceptionally fine chicken eggs, was now on the warpath. Several swift victories ensued, with Khazerai's trained men overwhelming the ill-prepared, unwieldy enemy armies in a series of swift tactical strikes.

Others thought themselves safe behind the ramparts of the Duchy of Tolera, which was twice the size of Yulen in both holdings and its military. But Khazerai's spies had also brought that kingdom down from within, whispering to each of the three sons that he should be in charge when their father passed on. When the duke suddenly expired from an overdose of a sleeping draught in his nightly wine, each of the sons, thinking that both of the others had moved to kill their father and claim the throne, declared war on his siblings, dividing up the armies and navies and battling each other. All of which left the kingdom's borders wide open. With such an invitation, how could Khazerai refuse?

Once again, the ruler of the Yulen Empire was hailed as a savior both behind and in front of the scenes. His men had brokered treaties with each of the three armies in turn, then destroyed each prince when the time was right; one vanquished on the battlefield, one assassination, and the third one by mob reprisal after it was learned about his (completely false, mind you) unnatural attraction to farm animals. Each prince's death had been blamed on one of the other two, and Khazerai had gladly stepped in to stop the princes' reign of battle and bloodshed, and replace it with a more moderate reign of fear and secrecy.

With Tolera's rich farmland, ore-laden mountains, and healthy population under his control, the rest of the continent only needed to be mopped up, either by a show of diplomacy—usually by parking half of his army at a soon-to-be-subjugated land's border while sending the other half around to flank. While his army was out consolidating his rule, Khazerai did not fear reprisal at home either. As soon as he had taken power in Yulen all those years ago, every able-bodied man and woman had been required to serve a two-year term in the military and spend one weekend a month and three weeks a year fulfilling their duties, making them more than able to fend off an invading army until he could return. But who would even dare try such a thing? *No one, that's who,* he thought.

The churches? Hardly. As soon as Khazerai took over a kingdom he banned all religion, stating a policy of "Humans first, everyone else after." Once he exposed the prelates, bishops, and priests of the local churches as "the hypocritical, greedy swine that they are, the fat, bloated ticks on the backside of the populace, sucking the hard-working men and women—you people—dry, and what do they give you in return? Nothing in this world, that's for certain." The commoners had eaten it up. And since the all deities in the pantheon of Cauldera were dependent on the unwavering faith of the masses to grant them their powers—well, in his infamous speech to ten thousand Tolerans, Khazerai had said, "Those who giveth can also taketh away." The gods' influence had disappeared almost overnight.

Regardless, with Khazerai standing in front of his seemingly endless Yulen legions and requesting to "parley," swift acquiescence soon followed. And so, a mere quarter century after he had taken over the small country of Yulen, Khazerai now ruled the entire continent.

And it had all been so easy, he thought. *Too easy?* No, there had been a fair share of difficulty along the way. The attempted coup in the early days of his reign by a trusted lieutenant leading a small contingent of soldiers still loyal to the old Yulen king. They had been dispatched immediately and announced as traitors to the new regime, which they were. He could count half a dozen assassination attempts by other rulers, which had always ensured that their land moved up to the number one position on his "next to be conquered" list. There had been spies in his own camp to root out, laughably underplanned and underequipped treason plots to uncover, tributes to collect, the usual business of running an all-powerful empire.

And yet it could all come tumbling down around my head if I do not stop what is happening, he thought. Now Khazerai heard the clamor of swords on steel outside the citadel as his troops engaged the invading enemy. The two immediate options were fight or flight, and yet he sat on his throne for a few more seconds, pondering the inexorable chain of events that had led to this.

It had all started about a year ago, when his lieutenant had come to him with a report on what the dictator had thought was a minor matter. "My Eminence, there has been a disturbance on the outskirts of the Western Marches. A family was in arrears for taxes, and the local magistrate had them executed and their pig farm confiscated as an example to the others of your far-reaching will. However, the youngest son of the assistant pig tender survived, and has vowed revenge on both you and the empire."

"The orphaned son of an assistant pig tender is coming after me?" Khazerai was hard-pressed to contain his mirth. "Post a ten khaz reward for his head, and send the local patrols out with orders to kill him on sight."

"It will be done, My Exaltedness."

And Khazerai had thought that would be the end of the matter. However, a few weeks later, as he had been deciding whether to expand his empire to the east, where the Torlingan horsemen roamed the grassy plains, or to the west over the mountains, long rumored to be a land of untold wealth and strange, foreign races, his lieutenant strode up and bowed low before the Throne of Black Blades.

"Most Powerful One, I have news from the Western Marches."

"Whatever about? Is the mud harvest especially good this year?" Khazerai asked, having long forgotten about the son of the assistant pig tender.

"Remember that orphaned boy who swore revenge against you?"

Khazerai looked up from his maps. "Orphan, orphan—something about swine, wasn't it? What about him?"

"He has eluded or ambushed several patrols, claiming that they are a tool of the Evil Empire—"

Which they are, but calling my realm evil is a bit much, Khazerai thought.

"—and people in the area are already talking about him as a leader of the small group of rebels in the mountains there."

Well, that won't do at all, Khazerai thought. "Increase the bounty to fifty khaz and send a troop of my Night Guards down there to eliminate this local pestilence. Also, if he really wants to come after me, I expect he'll need some weapons training. Instruct your men to find all of the weapons masters and either hire them or remove them."

Khazerai was about to turn back to his maps when a thought struck him. "You know, not that I don't trust our men's abilities, but I do believe in being thorough. Hire a squad of Ladian assassins and send them there as well. Do not let either group know of the other's mission. We'll see who gets him first."

"Immediately, Exalted One."

With that Khazerai turned his mind back to more pressing matters. Two of his overbarons had been squabbling for weeks over a border dispute, and he decided to tour both holdings, to see for himself what the best way to handle the matter would be. During his month-long tour, he discovered malfeasance on both sides and promptly arrested both men and had them put to death, installing easily controlled puppet rulers in each one's place.

But that had taken up an inordinate amount of his time, and he had scarcely returned to the gates of the Ebon Citadel when his lieutenant ran up, sweaty and disheveled.

"Forgive me, My Master, but this pig tender's son—"

"Who?"

"The one who swore revenge on you a few months back when the local guards killed his family for nonpayment of taxes."

"Ah, yes, been killed, has he?"

"No, I'm afraid not. In fact, there are several fiefdoms that are fomenting open revolt against the empire. They are led by this youth, who claims to have brought back the power of the gods to Cauldera."

"What? What about the Night Guards that were sent over to kill him?"

"Lured into a trap in the mountains and crushed under an avalanche."

"And the Ladians?"

"Um, well, that's partially how he's claiming to have brought the gods back, My Majesty. Apparently, while they were able to poison him, friends of his managed to find the leaves of the rare deusex plant, make the even rarer antidote, and save his life. He claims that during the time he was suffering from the poison's effects, he spoke to the gods, and was charged with bringing their might back to your lands, and also eradicating the quote blight of evil unquote that hangs over Cauldera."

"How melodramatic. Well, if it's a fight he wants, then let's give it to him. Assemble the Third, Fourth, and Fifth Dark Brigades and send them to the Western Marches. Scour the land and destroy this boy and anyone that stands with him. Do not take any prisoners, do not bring him back alive. Just kill him. Handle this yourself." For a moment, Khazerai was seized by the mad impulse to add, "and you know the penalty for failure," but with an effort, he restrained himself. However, in the back of his mind, he wondered *where did that come from*? Of course his soldiers knew the penalty for failure; demotion and, if they really screwed up, corporal punishment. He wouldn't just kill them on a whim because they couldn't complete one assignment. Good lieutenants were always hard to find, and killing the ones he had out of pique wouldn't help morale at all. *Perhaps this pig tender's boy is bothering me more than I'd like to admit. However, I'm sure that this will be the end of the matter.*

Unfortunately, that was not the case. Although Khazerai's lieutenant did return with the charred remains of what he swore was the body of the rebel leader, along with a fairly stirring account of how the Dark Brigades had flushed the rebels out, encircled them, and burned almost all of them alive, reports over the next few months kept popping up about sightings of the leader of the rebels, the populace's new messiah. Khazerai speculated that either the peasants were trying to keep his memory alive as a martyr, or the tenacious little bastard had somehow escaped the trap, and was running around sowing discontent throughout his empire. Neither option was acceptable to him, and so the chase was on.

"Dispatch a Shade Legion to every location where this assistant pig tender's son has been sighted and track him down. I want his head—nothing else—delivered to me within the next month."

But even that hadn't worked. Oh, his legions had done their job well, wreaking fear and terror throughout the populace wherever they marched, but the assistant pig tender's son, through some arcane legerdemain, managed to escape several dire predicaments, such as:—

—When his legions had trapped the youth in a network of caves and then flooded the entire complex, drowning several dozen miners and their families.

—Another time when his Twilight Riders had harried him to the cliffs overlooking the Teglan Sea and one of them had even wounded him with a lucky shot from a crossbow (earning him an increase in rank; Khazerai always believed in promoting from within) and sent him plunging two hundred feet into the churning waters.

—And the time when one of his most trusted vassals had actually captured the youth alive and thrown him in jail. Apparently this lord had not gotten the "kill on sight" memo, for by the time a messenger had been sent informing Khazerai of the capture (he hadn't even finished reading the message before sending a three-word message back—*Kill him immediately*), the boy had escaped, getting the vassal killed in the confusion.

And on it went, with the assistant pig keeper's son escaping mortal situation after situation, sometimes sacrificing a trusted companion, but always popping up after Khazerai was sure he had been killed. And always along the way, he gathered followers to his cause like bees to honey.

Like vultures to a dead carcass, if I have my way, Khazerai thought. He couldn't believe the boy's luck, and a small part of him wondered if indeed this one was protected by the gods. Shaking his head, he dismissed the thought—the gods were no more, Khazerai himself had seen to that.

So then, what to do with this boy? Whatever he was going to do, it had better be quick, as Khazerai now heard the clang of sword on shield and the shouts of the victorious, and the screams of the dying right outside his main chamber. *And I'm sure he's there, leading the way, just like in the legends . . .*

The thought gave Khazerai pause, just as he was also resisting an insane urge to go out there and to see if he could lend a hand. Direct confrontation had never been his style, he always preferred using the more subtle arts to achieve his goals and, failing that, following up with the army. *But it would appear that my army is in the process of being routed, which doesn't leave many options.* Flight wasn't an option, for even if he could make it out of the Ebon Citadel, his face was known throughout the empire, for in a moment of supreme egotism several years ago he had ordered his own face placed on all the coins—well, that, and to stop the rampant counterfeiting that had been happening. Regardless, he wouldn't be able to go as far as the next county without being caught. Surrender? Not likely, as they no doubt would tear him limb from limb before he could even reach trial, assuming that they would even bother with such a formality, and not just try to burn him alive.

Khazerai tried to concentrate, as something about the legends of the people was niggling at his mind, something about the stories of the heroes who, no matter what the odds were against them, always managed to defeat evil at the end. Impossible odds, odds like—

—Exactly like what has been stacked against this boy from the very beginning, he thought. *And he has come through all of it not without difficulty, but he has vanquished everything in his path to destroy me.*

The thought rocked Khazerai. Could it be true, could they somehow be caught up in a cycle that was larger than the both of them, the endless struggle of good versus evil? Could there be a force beyond men, beyond the gods, beyond even his incredible comprehension, that somehow ensured that evil was defeated in every confrontation, no matter how long it took?

If this is true, that would certainly explain my odd impulses lately, he thought. But if that was the case here, how would he manage to salvage victory from what looked like certain defeat?

Before he could even begin to contemplate the answer to that question, the huge double doors burst open, and his trusted lieutenant backed into the room, valiantly fending off what could only be the assistant pig keeper's son, now clad in gleaming chain mail and swinging a shining sword like a man possessed. The fighting pair was followed by several other men from both sides, all cursing and hacking at each other with crimson-streaked blades. Khazerai stood up as the approaching battle spilled toward him.

Although Khazerai's lieutenant was a most capable warrior, he had also suffered several other wounds during the fighting, and was now hard pressed to defend against the crusader's relentless assault. As Khazerai watched, the young man slashed his henchman across the wrist, disarming him, then beat down his shield with hammering blows, driving him to the ground. The lieutenant's shield arm buckled, and his battered armor fell to the side, exposing his chest and head. The young warrior raised his sword to finish him off, and when his sword was just about to come down, Khazerai spoke.

"Don't kill him, if you please. After all, it's me you really want."

At the sound of his voice, the young man started and looked up. When that happened, Khazerai's lieutenant managed to draw a small blade from the back of his shield and glanced up at his liege's face, waiting for the command to strike.

Khazerai shook his head just enough to negate his man's intended action. He felt it more strongly now; the sense that theirs was a battle that had raged for centuries, millennia even, since before the dawn of time itself. He knew how this would play out, indeed, how it must play out for the cycle to continue. And strangely, he was content with this. *After all, I had a good run,* he thought. *Perhaps it is time to pass the torch on.*

What? Absolutely not! another part of his mind said. *This is not how it will all end, accepting this fate like a mewling lamb to the slaughter.*

But how am I to defeat him then? Khazerai thought. *Everything is on his side, the army, the gods, momentum—*

And in a trice Khazerai had the answer. He nodded to the young man, who was breathing hard with his exertions as he stood there in his armor the likes of which this world had not seen for hundreds of years. Seeing the glint of wildness in his enemy's eye, he chose his next words carefully. "You have defeated my army, and destroyed all that have come against you. Now you have me at your mercy." He spread his arms, palms up, out in a show of submission. "Congratulations, you have won."

"Not yet I haven't," the young man snarled, raising his sword again. "Not until your foul stain is erased from this world!"

Before anyone could move, the young man bounded up the steps to the dais of the Throne of Black Blades and stabbed Khazerai in the chest, right through the heart. "With the Sword of Laighmon, granted to me by the gods themselves, I strike you down. And before you die, know that Ardon, son of Laot the pig tender, was the one that destroyed you."

Even through his pain, Khazerai couldn't help smiling at the boy's theatrics. "So . . . be . . . it."

The youth pulled his sword out, and with dazzling speed, whirled and beheaded Khazerai in one smooth, powerful stroke. The despot's head bounced down the steps to land facing the young warrior, his eyes open in sightless accusation. The headless body fell back into the chair, the jet of blood from the neck already subsiding.

The young warrior turned to the assembled soldiers before him. "People of the Yulen Empire, your suffering is at an end. Your cruel overlord is no more, and today heralds a new dawn of peace and tranquility—"

He might have gone on like that for hours if Khazerai's body hadn't risen from the chair behind him, grabbed the young man's sword out of his hand, and lopped off his golden-haired head in one stroke. As the young man's cranium bounced to the ground, Khazerai's body kicked the shaking torso off the dais and strode to where his head lay. Everyone watched, aghast, as the body dropped the sword of the gods, picked up its head and set it on top of his neck again. As the men in the room stared, the flesh of Khazerai's neck knitted together, drawing the wound closed until there was just a thin red line marking the injury, and in a few seconds, that was gone as well. The hideous·gash on his chest had already closed up as well, leaving no trace that he had ever been cut at all. The men all knelt down on the floor, first his own, then the soldiers of the former enemy army, each one prostrating themselves before him.

He walked over to his lieutenant and motioned him up with one hand, then addressed the rest of the men in the room. "Go forth and let the rest of your people know that your leader is dead, and if they lay down their arms right now, I will be merciful. However, this is not negotiable, and they have, oh, about five minutes to decide. Now get out of here."

The vanquished men wasted no time in scrambling out of the throne room, Khazerai's intense gaze following them the entire way. Swiveling his head back and forth, he tested the muscles in his neck, feeling them stretch and pop as he moved. He rubbed his jaw, which throbbed when he touched it. *That's going to bruise nicely*, he thought. Picking up the once shining sword, he wasn't surprised to see that it was just an ordinary weapon, with no magic about it at all. Dropping it, he glanced over at the quivering body of the young warrior, blood now staining his once-gleaming armor a blackish-red, and shook his head.

"What part of 'Khazerai the Undying' didn't you understand?"

ART THERAPY

Nina Kiriki Hoffman

My best friend Rusty and I used to hide out in an abandoned refrigeration unit in the middle of the junky vacant lot next door to our compartment building. We were in the lot when the fridge was dumped. We turned it sideways, then used our own locks to secure it outside and in, and covered it with so much noxious junk nobody else ever went near it, though there were lots of people in the vicinity who were looking for hideouts.

The fridge must have been used in an industrial kitchen; it had room enough for the carcasses of several butchered animals, and its perpetual internal light source still worked most of the time, even with the door shut. Aside from a few holes we punched through the superinsulation so we could breathe, it was soundproof. So what if it smelled like really old blood? It was bigger than both our sleeping niches put together.

It was inside that old fridge we swore our undying loyalty to each other and pledged to support whoever rose to power first, as long as the other was second in command. We swore with blood oaths.

Rusty knew *all* my secrets. If I had been following Ruthless Master protocols, I would have had him killed early in my career.

Now that I have achieved ultimate enough power to run things the way I like them, I am known as Darkblood, Incarnation of Exquisite Evil. Only Rusty ever calls me Spiff, and only when no one else can hear us.

In my current power hierarchy, Rusty is known as my trusted lieutenant, Shrike the Impaler, Purveyor of Irresistible Torture.

Rusty and I have been indispensable to each other in a series of country- and world-conquering power plays. We have ruled six countries and two planets, and would have settled into comfortable despotism several countries ago if only heroes weren't so thick on the ground.

I really thought Ruritraya was going to be our retirement community. It had plenty of mineral wealth to exploit, a sturdy population of underlings and peasants with decent work ethics, a nice coastline, constant small-scale wars with neighboring countries to keep any native thinkers distracted, and exquisite cuisine.

We kept watch for the various standard hero approaches, but no one had challenged us in a year.

Things were going too well.

I was lulled. Despite my determination never to relax my vigilance in all directions, I was lulled.

Betrayal came from a direction I never expected.

Rusty led the intervention on me. When I get out of Rehab, I'm going to spend some quality time with his head. I don't care what happens to the rest of his body.

The rest of my top staff participated, though some of them wore masks. Masks could not hide their visages from my awful wrath. I know the name of everyone who conspired to humiliate me. At night, when I am strapped to the bed, I use the point of a loose screw to inscribe their names, one by one, into the patina. My bed stinks of fresh paint because the minions here are efficient and desire that everything remain pristine, so they paint over my list every day. I don't care that my list disappears. I am really scribing the names in my memory while I try to erase the things my inferiors said to me.

The things they said to me!

"We caught you being nice to a random dog."

"Your personal assistant used sarcasm on you, and you didn't have him flogged."

"You smiled in public, and it wasn't the smile that sends small children screaming into the night."

"You're letting the intervention proceed without ordering us all killed immediately," said Rusty. "Boss, you're losing your edge. Trust me. You need help."

*　　*　　*

Refocusing Personality Rehabilitation takes place in a satellite orbiting an unnamed planet that is not on most star or node charts. I knew about Rehab because of jokes people told at supervillain reunions. I laughed, same as everybody else, about those weak-willed idiots who came here.

I never even noticed Rusty putting a jump node to Rehab in our palace, another indication that the intervention was probably timely; I was slipping.

Most of the patients here have no living family. Family is what drove us to be evil dictators and ruthless overlords in the first place. We would have been better off without them in the beginning of our lives, and most of us rectified that situation by the time we hit our teens.

Nevertheless, there is a portion of our treatment called Family Therapy, a.k.a. "Group," where those nearest to us participate in group sessions. This is when I see Rusty every week.

My roommate Bob, the Purveyor of Ultimate Misery, has four trusted lieutenants who come to Group, and a wife. She is not one of those trophy wives you marry just to ruin her life, foil the aims of her Hero, whoever that might be, and because you get off on humiliating her. Bob's wife is dumpy, and she knits. Her major vice seems to be a love of large, inappropriately flashy jewelry. She wears a new and clashing assortment every week, which demonstrates that Bob has been overly generous in the past.

This is what's good about Bob's wife, Rose: she never says anything in group. Her sole virtue, as

far as I can see. And yet, Bob envies me Rusty.
That's what he told me at breakfast, just before we
headed in to another of those nightmare extended
torture sessions called Group. "I wish someone
cared about me the way Rusty cares about you,"
Bob said.

I don't think Bob has much of a future in this
business, revealing a weakness like that to someone
he doesn't know well.

Or maybe he knows me too well. Because of all
the things Rusty says during Group.

There are so many people I'm going to have to
kill when I get out of here. For a while I'm going
to have to risk looking like a Hero. I know their
respective worlds will be happier places with these
Multifarious Crushers of the Many Flavors of Joy
removed, but I have to kill them anyway.

If I were orchestrating Rehab, it would have a
whole different outcome. Anyone sent to this place
would immediately be rendered into fertilizer and
sprinkled somewhere they could make people sick.
Obviously we are all failures in our chosen fields,
both because we are vulnerable to something as
lame as an intervention, and because someone felt
they could subject us to such a thing in the first
place. Failures deserve no mercy.

I'm not sure how I would spin the whole thing to
the media, which I would absolutely control. Probably I would use one of the lesser euphemisms. I like
"aneurysm." I enjoy words with *y* in the middle.

I have big plans for someone in denial about his
own shortcomings.

Just now I'm in art therapy, supposedly drawing pictures of large-scale destruction to reinvigorate my imagination with possible future triumphs. I never drew anything before, but I find I enjoy art therapy, even though I demonstrate no real skill. Mostly I like it because I'm using it to mask a couple of other activities.

The art therapy dictator is staring at me, but I don't think she can read this particular code, which I'm writing in red, part of a large picture of a village in flames.

My mind has been fragmented while I stay here; I can't concentrate with my usual focus and finesse. I suspect some sort of drugs in our water or food, though what the aim is, I don't know. Somehow it helps me think to use art therapy this way. I'm the only one who will ever know what I write here, and I will burn this picture as soon as I finish it.

The art dictator just came by and castigated me for not creating a picture with more scope. Why did I decide to destroy a mere village instead of a major city, or even a planet? Such thinking demonstrates how reduced my ambitions and abilities are. I'm behaving in a self-limiting fashion, she said.

I told her the scene I'm painting is not just any village. It is the village where I was humiliated as a small child, and I set it on fire when I left town. I am using it to build up my anger at my past so I can reinvigorate my tyrannical tendencies.

She believes this fabrication, which demonstrates how incompetent she is. If she had read my file, she would know that Rusty and I grew up in the megalopolis called Tourist Trap on the planet Sanitation.

She allowed as to how painting the destruction of a village where I was tortured might be a legitimate use of my art therapy time, and moved on to harass Alan, Supreme Leader of the Dark Legions of Destruction. He was painting giant flowers. I, too, considered his project an exercise in lameness, until he told Supervisor Susie he was imagining flesh-eating flowers with concealed teeth, his favorite tactic for use in subduing inferiors: lull them with a false and pleasing surface, and when they least expected it, leap out with teeth and chew them in half.

This place is full of useless, time-wasting activities, like meditations in the blood chapel to attract a new and more ruthless personal god. I think gods mix everything up and get in the way when you least need their help. Sometimes they switch sides in the middle of the battle. Once I had a personal relationship with Krrgoth the Blood Reaver, and the Hero I was opposing, who professed to honor life in all its forms, even the lowliest, grubbiest churls, sacrificed six beautiful virgins (where he found them in that particular kingdom I don't know; lord knows I had scoured the hills for them before he got there, and used up all the ones I could find) to Krrgoth in one big bloodletting gorefest, and the damned god helped the Hero overthrow me.

That Hero went on to be a worse tyrant than I ever was. The peasants used to whisper my name

(Darkblood, not Spiff) longingly years after I had left. Some even hung tapestries of me in their living rooms—tapestries that could be reversed to show the image of a popular clown figure if any government troops dropped by for inspection.

Rusty told me about the aftermath of my overthrow. He survived the coup in the palace and hung around looking enough like a halfwit that the Hero recruited him as an informer. This is one of our tactics in the event of revolutions. Whoever isn't in power does their best to undermine the other's successor, as long as it is no risk to life and limb. This Hero needed no help in driving the populace to accomplish his downfall. One of my more satisfying aftermaths, I must say, and much of its success due to the machinations of Rusty.

Rusty! My rage at him resulted in me smearing several plumes of flame. I can't think straight enough to encode for a few minutes. How could he speak of Ellen in Group this morning?

After art therapy I am scheduled to visit the cryptic chapel. They're going to have a prognosticator there who will select an appropriate god to get me out of my slump.

I hate fortune-tellers. Too many of them have given me false tales, accused me of having a kind heart. They sang a different tune when I applied red-hot irons to various portions of their anatomies.

I ended up having to torture them all. Except that one woman, Blind Mariah, who saw all too clearly. She accurately predicted the entrance of a particular Hero, and told me how to foil him. For that, I let her go. I thought about sending an assassin after her, but in the end decided against it. A good seer is hard to find, and I might need her again.

She left me with several uncomfortable utterances. I remember a portion of her prophecy that made no sense at the time, but now that I think of it, it probably predicted my sojourn in this place. "Down the darkest well," she said, "one can see daylight stars."

I wish I had my crystal pear. I acquired it on a short stop on Lymaztla, where they specialize in hidden dangers. At home, I affected the quirk of always having the pear in my left hand, and sometimes tossing it. I found it soothing, in truth, though it started as a calculated affectation. At the pear's heart is a toxic vapor for which I have taken the antidote. I could shatter it on the edge of the table here during a meal and kill half the evil dictators in Rehab, and most of the Rehab staff. A lovely prospect.

Group this morning was more distressing than usual. Rusty has totally betrayed me, I fear, a slow and fiendish betrayal I would have thought beyond him: each secret he tells in Group makes me that much more vulnerable to an assortment of other evil people, including the staff at this institution. This morning he revealed that I had cried when the Hero killed my consort Ellen, several kingdoms ago.

This sounds like a more egregious weakness than it was. Everyone who knew Ellen, my Peerless Enchantress of the Darker and More Secret Passions, cried after her death. Possibly all of them had been intimate with her before she hooked up with me. That would explain their copious tears; she was the best lover I ever knew. Even the damned Hero who killed her cried (she had seduced him, at my behest; things were going well before he figured out she was still loyal to me and was telling me everything he revealed to her during their intimate moments).

He was one of those self-hating heroes who believe chastity is a gift to his prudish god, and to violate his vow of singularity was a mortal sin; he punished Ellen because he could not punish himself enough. I did it for him after he killed her. Once the bones are carefully broken, there is not much a Hero can do to evade repeated blows from a meat tenderizing hammer, spread out over several hours, applied with a precision that does not allow him to die with any speed.

At the time, Rusty told me anybody would cry at a loss like mine. Or ours, I suppose. Ellen was generous with her favors. In Group, fifteen years later, when he told everyone about it, it sounded much more pathetic than it had been.

He is weakening me an increment at a time. At first I did not understand. I thought he had my welfare at heart; it's the only reason I agreed to give up my defenses and come here. Anything worth doing is worth overdoing. I thought this place would strengthen my skills—that's what Rusty told me—but I see now it isn't so. This place is a prison. I am certain now that all the news Rusty relays to me about Ruritraya in my absence is false. He has told them I am dead, and stepped forward to steal my country. Perhaps he presented himself to them in the guise of a Hero. We know how they operate. He could easily act the part.

"Here's another piece of paper, Darkblood," said the art dictator. "You should start over. You've messed up your current picture." She pointed to the flames I smeared when rage overcame me.

"I'm not creating something for a gallery, Susie," I snarled. "Smears are part of any great campaign."

"You should know better than to continue a project with obvious flaws," she said.

"Those are not flaws. It's art," I said, but I took the extra piece of paper.

The art dictator. This is the zenith, the acme she has reached with her tyrannical disposition. She's a failed despot, except in this tiny, unimportant sphere. I know there's a lesson here, but I'm not in the mood to learn it.

The only thing that keeps Susie alive is that stun-shield she wears. I am fortunate I saw Ziggy attack her before I decided to try. He lay twitching on the floor for the rest of the session. I was dismayed but unsurprised to discover all the staff wear these shields.

Yesterday afternoon I had my regular reinfliction of childhood damage session. When I first entered Rehab, the staff had the psych computer run a deep hypnotic regression on me, for diagnostic and forensic purposes, they said. The computer knows everything that's ever happened to me, so it, along with every staff member and probably all the outside aides, will have to die when I put my escape plans in motion.

At first I thought the reinfliction sessions were the most effective part of the treatment. Reliving my father's denigration, beatings, and coldness, my mother's inappropriate desires, my two brothers' deaths at our parents' hands—yes, I remembered again why I became a supervillain. I was ready to leave Rehab after my first session. I had a wide array of ideas on how to lock down Ruritraya.

But they didn't let me leave after that first session. Instead I have to endure all their other programs: art therapy, family group, twelve step group, inflating your esteem group, seminars on improved tactics for basic activities such as blackmail, stealing, politicking, manipulation, nefarious weapons updates, and conscience crushing. There is also physical therapy to beef up our bodies so we can be more imposing. PT and art therapy are the only places where they release the restraints on our arms and legs; otherwise I'm sure we'd all kill each other. If I'm going to escape, it's got to be during PT or art therapy.

I have a reinfliction session weekly, and I'm becoming numbed and tired of the whole thing. Sure, my experience was difficult at the time, and I've used those memories to justify all sorts of behavior since, but anything, even one's personal tragedy, can lose its power if one sees it endlessly repeated.

I'm so over it now that I spend the session contemplating ways I could reprogram the reinfliction computer to make it more amusing. First, I need to download its information about everyone else's reinfliction sessions so I can blackmail them into being a cadre of useful helpers in my escape. After that, I contemplate what I'll have the computer to do to the staff here, each program tailored to the appropriate person. My scenario for Susie the art dictator changes daily.

She just returned to the table. "You're being too meticulous and cerebral," she told me. "Forget those tiny brush strokes. I gave you a giant piece of paper for a reason, Dark. You're supposed to think large. Open up. Envision world war." She tried to snatch this drawing out from under my fingers. I unleashed a fraction of my inner berserker, though I made no attempt to actually touch her. I rose to my feet, planted my hands flat on my paper, let my rage kindle into fire, and growled at her. Softly. Knowing that flames danced in my eyes—a surgical enhancement I arranged for three dictatorships ago, one I've never regretted.

She paled and backed away, stammering, "That's—that's all right. It's your project." She glanced around to make sure my guard was aware of my threat posture. His stun gun was aimed in my direction. I was glad this was only a fraction of my berserker. If I let the whole out, I would be stunned and twitching on the floor by now.

One more growl with less grit in it, and I settled back in my chair, loaded my skinny brush with red paint. Back to what I increasingly realize is more of a mental ramble than therapy, but oh well, it's for an audience of one.

Rusty has probably discovered my stash of cocoa-coffee candy by now. I wonder if he's sleeping in my all-comforts bed, whether he knows where the massage button is. Maybe he just rings the bell to call Layla up for a skin-to-skin session. She probably likes him better than she ever did me; it's hard to tell whether the women appreciate me for myself or for my power. Most of the time I don't care, but something about Rehab breaks through my indifference and makes me wonder. I'm going to need another form of Rehab when I escape this one. I want to go to a planet where it's legal to hunt humans, and have some of them dress up as the people I most resent so I can shoot them with zero consequences.

Today is not the day I'll put my escape plan into action. Alan the Supreme Leader is the only other patient (or client, as they call us) in the room with me; they only let two of us into art therapy at once, since this is a restraint-free activity, and few creatures are more dangerous than frustrated supervillains. I've created a small coalition of the unwilling in Rehab, but Alan isn't a member. I only recruited people who know the secret hand language of the Tillia Undersea People (now extinct), which narrowed my pool of potential partners to one woman and an animal. I need to act when Bituba, Scourge of the Unworthy, is in art therapy with me. Staff cycles these things randomly, though, and she and I haven't been paired in more than a week.

What meaningful work can I do in today's session, below the radar of Commander Susie?

This morning I asked Rusty, right before Group and his betrayal about Ellen, how anybody got out of Rehab. "The staff get together and discuss each case," he said. "If they've seen real progress, they can decide to release you. What's the matter with you, Spiff? Why is it taking you so long to return to your real self? Aren't you getting the help you need? What can I do to help?"

"Maybe I just need more downtime," I told him.

What if he goes even farther back in our history? What if he talks about what happened in the fridge when his older brother discovered how we used it? The computer in reinfliction must know about that incident, though it hasn't used it in the matrix of memories it assaults me with each week. It's a key to both Rusty's and my subsequent characters, how we dealt with that two days of terror and entrapment, the heat and fear when Big Bro plugged our airholes. I was the one who scraped a finger raw getting two of the airholes open again, and Rusty was the one who collapsed into whimpers about twelve hours into our ordeal when the perpetual light failed. I acted, and he panicked.

That's the way I remember it, anyway.

I've drawn enough flames on this picture for now. A thought struck me I don't want to think about. I'm going to ask the guard to burn the picture, and tell Officer Susie I'm ready to quit.

Superirritant Susie is suspicious about Bituba's last gesture to me. As well she should be.

Today I'm painting a cityscape under a pall of

reddish smog. My skills aren't up to this project, but Susie tells us skill level is irrelevant; all that matters is flow. She's angry at me again because I took one of the brushes and cut most of the hair off it so I can paint with narrower lines. What's therapeutic about sloppiness?

It's not as easy to work code into blocky city buildings. Flames gave me flow, if that's what it was. I feel more driven to be precise in this format.

Precisely, Bituba has just signaled that she's ready when I am.

I'm not ready yet.

Yesterday the prognosticator at the blood chapel gave me a new god, Arisia the Mediator. What kind of a terrible name is that for a god? Would anyone feel threatened when you invoke a god like that? No one I'd care to intimidate.

The prognosticator asked me if I wanted to dedicate myself to this new god and said it would help me in the future if I did so. I don't say yes to everything here in Rehab; I think ready acquiescence would indicate I can never rise to my full level of evil again. I wanted to refuse this ridiculous charge, but with my plans so close to fruition, I didn't want to give anybody an excuse to overmonitor my actions, so I said, "What the hell," and let them open a vein to spill my blood into a dish at Arisia's statue's feet. She is one of those gods with lots of arms and only two legs. Could be fun in the sack.

I read from the script the prognosticator handed me. "I, Darkblood, hereby dedicate myself to the worship of Arisia and invite the god to feast on my essence, binding her to my will in accordance with our covenant. Arisia, be thou my shield and sword, my victory song, my blood transfusion in times of want. In return I give you my own blood promise; I will sacrifice in your name."

I give lip service to a lot of gods, but since Krrgoth burned me so badly, I don't give a lot of credence to any of them. I didn't know what Arisia was promising me, and I didn't care. All I cared about was getting through another useless time-wasting activity in Rehab.

I was surprised by a strange feeling after I finished my oath to the goddess, a kind of shudder all through me as though I had planted myself and was growing roots.

Last night I had a series of dreams. I dreamed each kingdom and planet Rusty and I had conquered, watching us from some distant point as we arrived, insinuated, manipulated, blackmailed, bought our way into power and moved up, up, and on, rising on stairs built of those we had destroyed and betrayed. In my dreams I smiled at the evidence of our finesse, how neatly we out-thought our opponents, how deliciously we set plans into motion, watching as each consequence followed each action.

I remembered the Heroes, too, the many who had failed against us (and the punishments we meted out to them) and the few who had succeeded.

From a distance I studied Ruritraya, my retirement country. I saw that I had not trodden down the populace enough. Systems Rusty and I had developed and refined across the years, plans I could script in my sleep—I hadn't initiated half of them. We had an ideal structure of power, and the one I built on Ruritraya was missing several pillars and could unbalance at any moment. The only wonder was that no Heroes had yet arisen to challenge us.

Rusty was right. My heart wasn't in the job. I had let him down.

"This is what you have bought with your blood," whispered the goddess's voice through the edge of my dream. "Now you must decide which way to go."

Arisia has to be the least fun goddess I've ever dedicated myself to. Another flaw in this stupid Rehab system. Why don't they choose from the dark pantheon? What's with these gray, nuanced gods?

I have my list of people who must die so I can continue to enjoy my evil, debauched, and luxurious lifestyle. I've devised an appropriate death for each of them. I have my plans and backup plans for escape. I know exactly who to promote to support me when I get back to my palace in Ruritraya, and who to incarcerate, and which dogs to kick. I have a map of my immediate future. Why is the goddess messing with my head?

"You're focusing too much on the details," Bossy Susie just said. "What about the big picture? There's no balance."

I snarled at her and let my eyes scare her again, but I didn't stand up this time and intimidate her physically. I wanted until she turned to Bituba, and then I actually looked at my picture.

Odd how text and art can war. When I let my eyes unfocus so I can see the image I've been drawing instead of the words I've been writing, I see that Susie is right. I sketched some outlines to engage most of the paper, dusted in rancid smog here and there, and then hunkered down and wrote the outlines of a few buildings over in the corner, leaving the wider space without definition. Just now I'm coding in a fountain in the city's central square. I like the ease of writing water.

Bituba just glanced at the chronometer and then at me. We only have ten minutes left in this session, and after that, who knows when we'll be together again? I wish I'd never had all those stupid dreams.

I'm going to signal her now.

Everything fell into place, just as I planned it. Bituba and I overpowered our guards, tied up Susie with her own stretchy body stocking, stuffed her mouth with wadded up sketches, and made our way to Rehab's Node Central, overpowering guards and security measures as we went. We collected our third conspirator, the station ferret, part of companion animal therapy (they apparently didn't realize that he had been genetically enhanced for intelligence and opposable thumbs; he was instrumental in spying out a blueprint of the station and getting us the guard schedules, also in telling us where the necessary supplies were) and jumped many nodes in rapid succession. Bituba had stashed

emergency identity-making supplies on one of the
worlds where she'd been overthrown. She had a
secret node to a deep dungeon there; she'd guessed
that the Hero who succeeded her would never use
it. So we kitted up, changed all our identifying
marks, and jumped some more.

Bituba wanted to go back to the country she'd
been ruling before her mother-in-law did the intervention on her. She was ready to chop off enough
heads that she could regain her old power. I'm not
sure that's a good idea, myself. Once a populace
has seen you taken down, they often won't stand
for your rising again.

I have lost some of my fire. All those murders I
know I need to do? Can't work up the energy for
them. Just now I'm sitting on the balcony of a luxury
resort in some winter mountains on an innocuous
tourist world, with this piece of paper and a set of
colored pens in front of me. The ferret's a warm coil
of furry weasel on my lap. He has a certain musky
smell I don't care for, but I owe him a lot, so I'll
learn to like it. Bituba and I had a custody battle
for him; we decided to share, so we have to keep
each other apprised of where we are. This is the
kind of weak spot I would never have counte-
nanced in my previous incarnation. Anyone who
learns about this could bring about both our
downfalls.

The picture I'm drawing, even though I no longer
need to code my words because I can burn this
document myself, is of a forest. Trees lend themselves to code. This is a coniferous needle-bearing

forest, so I have the luxury of writing words in sweeps of branching green. For the bark I am reserving the names of all the people I would kill if I were my old self. The list is long enough to make for tall trees.

I plunged into the galactic newstream last night and sought out information about the current state of Ruritraya. Shrike the Impaler is running the country as a regent for Darkblood. A series of political cartoons lampooning some of Rusty's more ridiculous mannerisms made me nostalgic. One caricature captured his nose by exaggeration in a way that was somehow more true than a photograph.

Just now my pen moved on the page and drew a picture of Rusty the way he looked when he was ten T.S. There were no words in this picture, and it doesn't fit into my forest; his head floats in a space where I haven't penned needlesprays. Now I am writing around his face, as if I could enfold it in foliage, make him part of my forest of confusion and revenge.

The ferret churrs and drops from my lap. He has spotted a vole on the edge of the balcony and wants to pursue it.

I am here in this distant place, where the maid service is invisible, the food is good, and the bed is comfortable, with enough money from Bituba's stash to support me for a lifetime, a new face, eyes, fingertips, and footprints, and blurs on a few of my genes where they won't interfere with life support. Only the ferret connects me to anyone else. Only my drawing connects me to who I was in Rehab.

Yesterday, though, the waiter who brought my room service tray saw a sketch I'd done, my recollection of Bituba before she changed her skin color and the shape of her nose. He asked if he could have it.

I couldn't see what appeal a picture like that would have for a creature shaped like a squared lump, with a few stumpy limbs, a featureless nodule for a head, and a bowtie. I was flattered, though. Then I thought twice. Perhaps he was the kind of creature who leaked things to whatever passes for media here, and he recognized Bituba. Can't let any of that out. Plus, I'd coded on her face, and I can't believe I'm the only one left who remembers Pitcairn pothooks. I drew a portrait of the waiter instead and gave it to him. He seemed just as pleased, if I interpret the flushes of color across his flesh correctly.

Here where it's safe to wonder, I think about Ruritraya, and wonder if a Hero will knock Rusty off his regent's throne before I go back there.

Maybe I'll draw him a postcard. First I have to finish my forest.

Tad Williams

THE WAR OF THE FLOWERS

0-7564-0181-X

To Order Call: 1-800-788-6262

TAD WILLIAMS

Memory, Sorrow & Thorn

THE DRAGONBONE CHAIR
0-88677-384-9

STONE OF FAREWELL
0-88677-480-2

TO GREEN ANGEL TOWER (Part One)
0-88677-598-1

TO GREEN ANGEL TOWER (Part Two)
0-88677-606-6

To Order Call: 1-800-788-6262

DAW 42